PENGUIN BOOKS

826

MAIGRET TRAVELS SOUTH

GEORGES SIMENON

D1513070

Georges Simenon

MAIGRET TRAVELS SOUTH

TRANSLATED FROM THE FRENCH
BY GEOFFREY SAINSBURY

PENGUIN BOOKS

Penguin Books Ltd, Harmondsworth, Middlesex
AUSTRALIA: Penguin Books Pty Ltd, 762 Whitehorse Road,
Mitcham, Victoria

—

First published 1940
Published in Penguin Books 1952
Reprinted 1961, 1963

—

Made and printed in Great Britain
by C. Nicholls & Company Ltd
Set in Monotype Garamond

This book is sold subject to the condition
that it shall not, by way of trade, be lent,
re-sold, hired out, or otherwise disposed
of without the publisher's consent,
in any form of binding or cover
other than that in which
it is published

CONTENTS

—

CHAPTER I

The Dead Man and His Womenfolk

IT began with a holiday feeling. When Maigret got out of the train at Antibes, half the station was bathed in a glare of sunlight through which the people moved like shadows. Shadows in straw hats and white trousers, with tennis-rackets in their hands. Spring had come with a burst, and the air hummed with the heat. On the other side of the platform were cactuses and palm trees, and farther off a strip of blue sea.

Someone dashed up to him.

'Inspector Maigret, I think? I recognized you at once from a photograph in the papers. My name's Boutigues. I've been handling the case. . . .'

Boutigues! What a name! Maigret could hardly take it seriously. The young detective had already relieved Maigret of his luggage and was leading him towards the exit. He wore a pearl-grey suit, and boots with half-cloth uppers, and had a red carnation in his buttonhole.

'Is this your first visit to Antibes?'

Maigret mopped his forehead and tried to keep pace with his guide, who threaded his way nimbly through the crowd of passengers. A minute later they were climbing into a cab. Not a taxi, but a good old-fashioned *fiacre* with a cream-coloured awning fringed with little tassels.

A long-forgotten sensation – the dandling of the springs, the crack of the driver's whip, the dull sound of the horse's hoofs on the hot soft asphalt.

'We'll have a drink first. . . . Oh, yes! After a journey like that. . . . Driver! Stop at the *Café Glacier*, will you?'

It was only a few steps farther on.

'In the Place Macé,' the detective explained. 'The centre of Antibes.'

A charming square with a garden in the middle, cream- or orange-coloured awnings at every house. Under one of them, on the terrace of the café, the two men sat down and sipped their *anis*. Opposite was a shop-window full of bathing-costumes, beach-pyjamas, and so on; on their left a window full of cameras; and some beautiful cars were drawn up by the kerb.

Yes, it was more like a holiday than . . .

'Would you rather see the prisoners first? Or perhaps the house where he was killed?'

'The house,' answered Maigret, hardly more conscious of what he was saying than if Boutigues had asked him: 'How are you?'

*

The holiday feeling continued. Maigret was smoking a cigar Boutigues had offered him. The horse trotted along the road by the seashore. To the right were villas hidden amongst the pine trees, to the left some rocks and then the expanse of blue sea, uninterrupted save by two or three white sails.

'I may as well tell you where we are. We've left Antibes behind us, and from now on it's the Cap d'Antibes. Nothing but villas, most of them pretty grand. . . .'

Maigret was ready to agree to anything that was said. His head seemed to be full of sunshine. His companion's carnation made him blink.

'Boutigues, did you say?'

'Yes, that's it. I come from Nice – a *Niçois*, or rather a *Nicéen*. . . .'

In other words, the real thing! A *Niçois* to his finger-tips, to the marrow of his bones.

'There you are! Just lean over this way a bit . . . You see that white house? . . . That's it.'

Maigret wasn't putting it on: he simply couldn't take it seriously, couldn't bring himself to believe that he was on a job, that he was there because somebody had been killed.

True, his instructions had been somewhat unusual:

'A fellow called Brown has been murdered at the Cap d'Antibes. The papers are taking it up. It's a case that needs tactful handling.'

Quite so.

During the war Brown had worked for the French intelligence service – the *Deuxième Bureau* . . .

Quite so! All the more so!!

So here he was with his head full of sunshine, having travelled six hundred miles to be tactful. The cab stopped. Boutigues took a key from his pocket, opened the gate, and led the way up the gravel path.

'This is one of the poorest villas at the Cap.'

All the same, it wasn't so bad. The air was heavy with the sweet smell of the mimosas. Small orange trees still bore a few oranges. Some queer-shaped flowers that Maigret had never seen before . . .

'The place over the way belongs to a Maharajah . . . He's probably there by now. Farther along on the left is a famous writer – *Académie française*. And beyond him is a ballet-dancer who lives with an English lord.'

It was all very well, but what Maigret wanted more than anything was to sit down on the seat in front of the house and have a nap. After all, he'd been travelling all the previous night . . .

'I'd better say a word about the household first.'

Boutigues had opened the door and they were standing in a cool lounge hall whose windows looked out over the sea.

'Brown's been living here for at least ten years.'

'What was he?'

'Nothing. He must have had private means. Just lived here with two women. "Brown and his two women": that's how people spoke of them.'

'He always had two?'

'Only one was his mistress: Gina Martini. The other one's her mother.'

'Has Gina been arrested?'

'They both have . . . There was no servant.'

The house had certainly not been kept any too well. There were admittedly a few beautiful things in it, a few pieces of good furniture, and here and there something that had had its moment of splendour. But it was all dirty, and the good things and the rubbish were jumbled together without discrimination. Too many carpets, table-cloths, and hangings; too many dust-collectors.

'Now, here are the facts . . . There's a garage in the garden where Brown used to keep his shabby old car. He used it chiefly for shopping in Antibes . . .'

'Yes,' said Maigret as he watched a man with a split reed fishing in the clear water for the sea-urchins that lay on the bottom.

'For three days, however, the car was left standing night and day in front of the house. People noticed, but nobody bothered. It was nobody's business to . . . And it wasn't till Monday evening . . .'

'Just a moment: it's Thursday now, isn't it? . . . Right. Go on.'

'On Monday evening a butcher was driving back to Antibes in his van, when he saw the car start . . . You'll see his statement . . . He was coming up behind it . . . First of all he thought Brown must be drunk, as the car started kangarooing forward. Then it went along steadily for a moment, but at the first bend it crashed into the rock by the roadside . . .

'The butcher drove up and stopped, but before he reached it, two women got out of the car and started running towards the town . . .'

'Were they carrying anything?'

'Three suitcases . . . It was getting dark. The butcher didn't know quite what to do. In the end he simply drove past the women and reported what he'd seen to the first policeman he found – the one in the Place Macé. Word was sent out, and a watch was kept. Before long they were spotted making for the station at Golfe-Juan. That's a couple of miles from here in the other direction – over towards Cannes.'

'Had they still got their suitcases?'

'They'd discarded one on the way. It was found yesterday amongst some tamarisks . . . They were obviously hard put to it to explain their conduct. First of all they said they were hurrying off to see a sick relation at Lyons. But the chap that caught them was shrewd enough to ask them to open their luggage. And what should he find but a packet of bearer bonds and some hundred-pound notes!

'It was a fine evening, with lots of people about. Quite a large crowd collected and escorted the two women, first to the *commissariat de police* and then to the local prison, where they were locked up for the night . . .'

'The house was searched?'

'First thing next morning. At first they found nothing. The two women pretended they didn't know what had become of Brown. Finally a gardener, who had poked his nose in, pointed out a place where the earth had recently been dug up. And a couple of inches deep they found Brown's body, fully dressed.'

'What did they say to that?'

'They changed their tune at once. What they said now was that three days before their flight, Brown had driven up to the house. They were surprised that he didn't put the car away at once. Gina looked out of the window and saw him staggering up the garden path. Thinking him drunk, she started scolding . . . Then he fell full length on the doorstep . . .'

'Dead, of course.'

'As dead as could be. When we examined the body we found he'd been stabbed between the shoulder-blades.'

'And they kept him in the house three days without saying a word about it?'

'Exactly. And they can't give any plausible reason for it. All they can find to say is that Brown hated everything to do with the police. In the end they buried him and took to their heels, taking with them the money and the bearer bonds and all the valuables they could carry. You can understand the car's standing three days on the road. Gina could hardly drive at all. She'd had a few lessons, but wasn't up to backing the car into the garage . . .'

The two men had moved on into the drawing-room.

'Wasn't there any blood in the car?'

'Not a sign. But then they swear they washed it off.'

'Is that all?'

'Yes. Except that they're furiously indignant and demand to be released. They've been moved to Antibes now.'

The cab-horse neighed. Maigret had had about enough of his cigar, and would have liked to throw it away.

'Have some whisky while you're here,' said Boutigues as his eye lighted on a liqueur cabinet.

No. Somehow it was all wrong. Boutigues' story fell flat. For the life of him Maigret could not summon any interest. All because of the sunshine, and the oranges and mimosas, and that fisherman who was still plunging his reed into the clear water, aiming at the sea-urchins a fathom and a half below.

'Can you leave the keys with me?'

'Certainly, now that you're taking the case over.'

Maigret swallowed down his glass of whisky, looked idly at the record that was on the gramophone, and fiddled with the knobs of the wireless set, which at once responded:

'. . . Wheat. Forward delivery. November . . .'

At the same moment he caught sight of a photograph standing just beside the wireless set. He picked it up to study it.

'Is that him?'

'Yes . . . Though I never saw him alive myself . . .'

Maigret switched off the wireless with a touch of impatience. Something had clicked inside him. Interest? More than that!

A confused sensation, and as a matter of fact rather a disagreeable one. So far Brown had been merely Brown, an unknown stranger who had come to a bad and more or less mysterious end. What sort of a man he had been, what he had thought, felt, and suffered, were questions that had not yet arisen.

And now, suddenly, looking at the photograph, Maigret was troubled by the sensation that the person it showed him was someone he already knew, a man, however, whom he had never set eyes on – of that he felt quite sure.

A broad face that gave an impression of health – the complexion must have been ruddy. The hair was getting thin; the moustache was close-clipped; the eyes were large and clear . . .

But it wasn't the features in themselves that struck him. It was a much vaguer, more general impression. There was no doubt about it, however: there was something in Brown which resembled Maigret himself. There was the same look of almost exaggerated calmness. The same expression – at once good-natured and ironical – about the mouth. And then the line of the shoulders, which were very slightly hunched . . .

Brown-the-corpse was forgotten. Here was a man, a man who intrigued Maigret whether he liked it or not, a man he must know more of.

'Another spot of whisky, Inspector? It's not too bad . . .'

Boutigues was in jocular mood. But if Maigret had been none too responsive before, he was still less so now, as he looked about him with an absent stare. Boutigues did not know quite what to make of him.

'Shall we give the driver a glass?'

'No. We're leaving.'

'You won't go over the house?'

'Another time.'

He'd go over the place alone, and when his brainpan wasn't humming with the sunshine. On the way back he was silent, only nodding to Boutigues' remarks. The latter began to wonder what he'd done to offend him.

'You must see the Old Town . . . The prison's just beside the market . . . The early morning is really the best time for . . .'

'Which hotel?' asked the driver, turning round.

'Perhaps you'd like to be right in the centre?' Boutigues suggested.

'Leave me here. It'll do me nicely.'

They were just coming to a modest hotel – more of a *pension de famille* – half-way between Antibes and the Cap.

'Will you be coming to the prison tonight?'

'Tomorrow more likely, but I'll see.'

'Would you like me to call for you? But perhaps you'd like to go to the Casino at Juan-les-Pins. After dinner, I mean. In that case I'd be . . .'

'Thanks, but I'm too sleepy.'

He wasn't really feeling sleepy. He simply wasn't feeling bright. He was hot and sweaty. Going up to his room, which faced the sea, he turned on the water for a bath, then changed his mind and went downstairs again, his pipe between his teeth, his hands in his pockets.

As he went out he had a glimpse of the dining-room, little white tables, napkins folded fan-shape stuck into the glasses, bottles of wine and mineral water, a waitress sweeping.

'Brown had been killed by a knife-wound in the back and his "two women" had made off with the money . . .'

It had not yet really taken shape in his mind, and his eye wandered aimlessly over to where the sun was slowly sinking, and then along the whole stretch of the horizon to Nice, where the Promenade des Anglais was just visible as a white line. Finally turning his back on the sea, he stared at the still snow-covered mountain tops.

Facing the sea once more, he inwardly recited his lesson:

'Nice on the left, fifteen miles away; Cannes on the right, less than seven . . .'

It was a little world, a narrow strip between the mountains and the Mediterranean; a world of simmering sunshine, queer flowers, feverish flies; a world of mimosa scent and cars gliding on soft asphalt; a world whose centre for him was the villa where Brown had lived with his two women.

He couldn't face the half-mile walk into the town. So he went back into the hotel, the *Hôtel Bacon*, and from there rang up the prison.

'Can I speak to the *directeur*?'

'He's on his holiday.'

'His assistant, then?'

'There isn't one. There's only me.'

'All right. Now, I want you to bring me the two Martini women. I shall be at their villa . . . Say in an hour's time.'

The warder's head must have been full of sunshine too, for he forgot to ask Maigret for an official order, merely answering:

'Right . . . And you'll return them to us when you've finished . . .'

Maigret yawned and stretched himself, then refilled his pipe. Even it didn't taste the same down here!

'Brown had been killed, and the two women . . .' It was becoming a refrain.

He strolled slowly to the villa. When he came to where the car had crashed, he nearly laughed. Just the place for a beginner! It was almost inevitable. The struggle with the gears, the car jerking forwards, and then the sharp bend coming before she'd had time to recover. He could see it perfectly. The butcher overtaking them in the twilight . . . The two women trying to run with three suitcases to carry, and finally chucking the heaviest into some tamarisks by the roadside.

A limousine passed, chauffeur-driven. At the back an Indian face – no doubt the Maharajah. The blue of the sea was darkening, except towards the sunset where it became orange and finally red. Lights were switched on, looking pale in the half-light.

Maigret seemed very small in the evening vastness. Quietly he walked up to the garden gate like a man returning home. He unlocked it and left it open as he went up to the front door. The trees were full of birds. The creak of the door must have been a familiar sound to Brown.

Inside, Maigret sniffed. For every house has its own peculiar smell. What predominated in this one was some strong perfume, probably musk, though it was somewhat obscured by the cigars he and Boutigues had smoked that afternoon. He went into the drawing-room, switching on the light, and sat down between the wireless set and the gramophone. It must have been Brown's chair, as it was the one that showed most signs of wear.

'The man had been stabbed, and his two women . . .'

The light was dingy, but Maigret caught sight of a standard lamp with a huge pink silk shade. When he switched that one on too, the room began to come to life.

'During the war he had worked for the *Deuxième Bureau*.'

The fact was known, and that's why the local papers had pounced so eagerly on the case. With the public, any reference to spying was always sure to provide a thrill. Maigret had looked at some of them during the last part of his journey. Absurd headlines:

> *Une Affaire Internationale*
> *Une Seconde Affaire Kotioupoff*
> *Un Drame de l'Espionnage*

Some papers thought they could detect the hand of the Cheka, others that of the British Intelligence Service.

Maigret looked about him. Something seemed wrong with the room. Of course, that's what it was! The large uncurtained window with the blackening night outside. He got up and pulled the curtains to.

He tried to picture an ordinary evening in that room.

'Say, one of the women sitting sewing over there . . .'

There was in fact some embroidery lying on the little table close at hand.

'And the other in that corner . . .'

In the corner where a book was lying – *Les Passions de Rudolf Valentino*.

But that was as far as he could get. He'd have to wait for Gina and her mother. Listening intently, he could just hear the rippling of the sea against the rocks below. He took another look at Brown's photograph, signed by some photographer in Nice.

'A case that needs tactful handling . . .'

Quite so. In other words, find out the truth as quickly as possible so as to keep it the better hushed up. There were steps on the gravel path, and a bell in the hall rang with a low and very musical note. Opening the front door, Maigret saw two women with a man in uniform.

'Thank you, you can go. I'll take charge of the ladies. . . Come in, will you?'

They might have been his guests! He hadn't yet seen their features, but his nose had at once caught a strong whiff of musk.

'I hope they've at last realized . . .' began the mother in a croaky broken voice.

'Of course, of course. Do come in and make yourselves at home.'

They came into the lighted room. The mother's face was very wrinkled, and covered with a thick coat of make-up. Standing in the middle of the drawing-room she looked round her as though to assure herself nothing was missing.

The other, more on the defensive, looked warily at

Maigret, while adjusting the folds of her dress and assuming a smile that was meant to be winning.

'Is it true they've brought you all the way from Paris?'

'Do take off your coats ... Sit down just as you would any other evening.'

They couldn't quite take it in. They were at home, yet at the same time they weren't. They were afraid of walking into a trap.

'We're going to have a little chat, the three of us.'

'Have you found out anything?'

It was the daughter who asked the question, and her mother quickly snapped at her:

'Take care, Gina!'

Even now that the work was beginning, Maigret found it very hard to take his part seriously. The old woman was horrible to look at in spite of all her make-up ... or perhaps because of it.

As for Gina, she was a buxom girl with almost too ample a figure. In her dark silk dress, she obviously meant to be a dangerous woman, but it didn't quite come off.

And that perfume of hers! What he had smelt before was nothing to this. In no time the air in the room was reeking with musk. It was like the *loge de concierge* of a little theatre.

There was no drama, no mystery. Just a mother who did embroidery while keeping an eye on her daughter! And a daughter who read the love-story of Rudolf Valentino!

Maigret, who had resumed his place in Brown's chair, looked at them with wonderment, asking himself, and with a shade of embarrassment:

'How the devil could this creature Brown put up with those two women – and for ten years?'

Ten years! Endless days of ceaseless sunshine laden with the scent of the mimosas, and that unbroken stretch of blue sea ... And ten years of endless evenings, with the wireless as the only deliverance from the mother and her needlework and the daughter reading under the pink lamp-shade.

Unconsciously Maigret's hand felt for the photograph of the dead man who'd had the cheek to look like him!

CHAPTER II

A Talk About Brown

'WHAT did he do with himself in the evenings?'

Maigret, with his legs crossed, looked bored. He was chiefly bored with the old woman, who never stopped trying to be ladylike.

'We seldom went out ... As a rule my daughter read while I ...'

'Let's talk about Brown!'

At that she was offended, and answered curtly:

'He did nothing.'

'He used to listen to the wireless,' sighed Gina, lolling in her chair with studied nonchalance. 'The fonder one is of real music, the more one hates ...'

'Let's talk about Brown! Was his health good?'

'If only he'd listened to me,' began Madame Martini, 'he'd never have been bothered by his liver or his kidneys. ... When a man's past forty ...'

Maigret looked like a host who has to listen politely to the prize bore who laughs so much at his own story he can't get on with it. They were absurd. One was as bad as the other: the mother with her prim pretentiousness, the daughter with her luscious graces.

'You told the police he drove up just after five, walked up the garden path, and then fell on the doorstep.'

'Yes. Like a man dead-drunk,' answered Gina. 'I shouted out to him from the window that he could come into the house when he was sober again.'

'Did he often come home drunk?'

Madame Martini answered:

'If you only knew the patience we've had during the ten years we've been . . .'

'Did he often come home drunk?'

'Whenever he went off – or nearly every time . . . On one of his bouts – that's what we used to call them.'

'And these bouts were frequent?'

Maigret couldn't help smiling. He felt happier. So Brown hadn't, after all, spent every evening of those ten years face to face with these two women.

'Generally once a month.'

'How long did they last?'

'He'd be away three days, four days, or sometimes even longer . . . And when he came back, he'd be dirty and soaked with drink.'

'But you didn't stop him going off again next month?'

A silence. Madame Martini stiffened and looked sourly at the inspector.

'But surely the two of you had some influence over him?'

'We couldn't stop him going to get the money.'

'And you couldn't go with him?'

Gina stood up.

'This is all very painful, Inspector,' she said with a sigh and a gesture of lassitude. 'But I must explain the situation. . . . You see, we weren't married . . . Of course, William always treated me as his wife, even to the point of having *Maman* to live with us . . . And I was known to the people here as Madame Brown . . . Otherwise I should never have accepted . . .'

'Neither should I,' added the other.

'Still, it was never quite the same thing . . . I don't want to speak ill of William . . . But there was just one point where he made a distinction, and that was in money matters.'

'Was he rich?'

'I really don't know.'

'And you don't know where the money came from,

either? I see! That's why you let him go off every month.
To get his money.'

'I've tried to follow him – I admit it . . . But hadn't I a
right to? . . . He was on his guard, however, and I never
succeeded.'

Maigret was at his ease now. In fact, he was beginning
to find the case amusing. He was reconciled to this wag of
a Brown who could live for ten years with these two
harpies without letting them find out the size of his income.

'Did he bring back a lot each time?'

'Hardly enough to keep us going a month. During the
last week we'd have a job to make ends meet.'

It was a sore spot! Merely to think of it made them both
furious.

As soon as funds got low they would begin to watch
William anxiously for signs of an incipient bout. But they
couldn't very well say to him:

'Run along now like a good fellow and have your little
binge.'

It would hardly have been ladylike. But no doubt they
dropped what hints they could.

'And who did he give the money to?'

'To *Maman*.'

'She did the housekeeping?'

'Of course. And the cooking too. There wasn't money
enough to keep a servant on.'

Maigret tumbled to it. He could see exactly how they
managed it. Towards the end of the month they would
produce the most impossible meals, and as soon as Brown
said anything they had only to answer:

'I'm afraid it's all we can manage on the money that's
left.'

Would it take a lot of that to get him moving? Or was
he only too glad of the excuse to get away?

'When he went, what time of day would it be?'

'Any time. He'd be out in the garden or fiddling about
with the car, and suddenly we'd hear him starting it up.'

'And you tried to follow him?'

'Yes, but he shook me off. All I can tell you is that he kept the car in a garage at Cannes . . . I do know that much. . . . It would be standing there all the time he was away.'

'So he might have gone on by train to Paris, or anywhere else for that matter?'

'Perhaps.'

'Or he might have stayed all the time in Cannes?'

'Though we've never heard of anybody seeing him there.'

'And it was after one of these bouts that he was killed?'

'Yes . . . This last time he was away a whole week.'

'Did you find the money on him?'

'The same as usual: two thousand francs.'

'If you ask me,' said Madame Martini, 'I think his income was much bigger than that. Four thousand a month, or even five . . . Only he preferred to squander the rest of it by himself, leaving the merest pittance for us.'

Maigret was leaning back luxuriously in Brown's easy-chair. As questions and answers followed each other his smile grew broader and broader.

'Was he very selfish?'

'William? He was the best of men.'

'Tell me about your everyday habits. Who got up first?'

'William. More often than not he slept downstairs on the divan in the lounge, and we'd hear him moving about early. Sometimes it was hardly light . . . Again and again I've said to him . . .'

'Excuse me! Did he make the coffee?'

'Yes. Though it was always cold when we came down at ten.'

'What would he be doing then?'

'Pottering about . . . In the garden . . . Or in the garage. And sometimes he went and sat on the beach. And then the shopping . . . He'd take us in to the town. And that's another thing: I could never get him to dress properly first. He used to go in his slippers and without even brushing his hair. And anybody could see he had his night-shirt underneath his jacket.'

'A night-shirt?'

'Yes, he never wore pyjamas. And he'd be like that right in the middle of Antibes, waiting for us outside the shops.'

'He dressed before lunch?'

'Sometimes . . . sometimes not . . . He's been as long as five days without taking his night-shirt off.'

'Where did you have your meals?'

'In the kitchen. When you've no help in the house you can't afford to have crumbs in all the rooms.'

'And in the afternoon?'

The two women had a nap. And then . . . well, the day dragged on somehow . . .

'Were there many rows?'

'Hardly ever. Though I must say William had a most aggravating habit of simply ignoring you when you spoke to him.'

Maigret refrained from laughing. But he was beginning to regard Brown as quite a pal.

'And then somebody killed him . . . Could it have been as he came into the garden? . . . But you say you found blood in the car . . .'

'We've no reason not to tell the truth.'

'Of course not. And you didn't see anybody . . . So some-one killed him elsewhere, or rather wounded him. And instead of going to a doctor or to the police, he fetched up here . . . You carried the body indoors?'

'We couldn't very well leave it outside!'

'And now tell me why you kept it dark. I'm quite sure you've good reasons.'

'Yes, monsieur,' answered the old woman, bouncing up from her chair, 'very good reasons indeed, and I'd like you to know them. In any case, you'll find out all about Brown sooner or later . . . You see, he was already married, long ago in Australia . . . he was Australian himself . . . and his wife's still living. For reasons best known to herself she would never divorce him. And it's all her doing if we lived as we did instead of in the finest villa along the whole Riviera.'

'You've seen her?'

'She's never been out of Australia, but she managed all right from where she was. Schemed and wangled until she'd ruined him. For these ten years we've been looking after him and trying to make up for all he's suffered ... And thanks to us, there's a little money put aside ... But if ...'

'If Mrs Brown had heard of her husband's death, she could have seized everything, as she was still legally his wife.'

'Exactly. That's all the thanks we should have had! ... And it's not only that ... I'm not by any means penniless myself. My husband was in the Army and I draw a small pension. A lot of the things in the house are my own property, only it wouldn't have been easy to prove it. She'd have had the law on her side if she'd wanted to take the house and all that was in it and simply put us into the street ...'

'So you hesitated. For three days you were turning it over in your mind, while the body was lying there on the divan in the lounge ... Is that where it was?'

'Yes, but only for two days. After that we buried it.'

'Then you thought things over for another twenty-four hours and finally gathered up what you could and ... But where were you making for?'

'Anywhere. Brussels perhaps, or London ...'

'Had you ever driven the car before?' Maigret asked Gina.

'Never. But I once had a few lessons, and I thought perhaps I might manage it.'

Quite the heroine! But they must have been in the deuce of a stew by that time. A precipitate flight from the body that was only a couple of inches below ground ... and then trying to run with three suitcases.

Maigret had had about enough of it: the atmosphere of the house, the smell of the musk, and the rose-coloured light shed by the pink lampshade.

'You don't mind my having a look over the house?'

They had recovered their self-possession and their dignity, though they were puzzled and perhaps a little disconcerted by this inspector who took it all so calmly, who seemed, in fact, to regard the whole business as though nothing could be more natural.

'I'm afraid the place is very untidy . . . But you'll understand.'

Indeed it was untidy, except that untidiness was hardly the word. Sordidness was better. For there was something of the pigsty about it mixed with bourgeois pretentiousness and petty pride.

An old overcoat of Brown's was hanging from the hat-stand in the hall. Maigret went through the pockets, discovering a worn pair of gloves, a key, and a box of cachous.

'He used to take cachous?'

'When he'd been drinking – so that we shouldn't smell his breath . . . We were always telling him not to drink whisky. We often hid the bottle.'

Above the hat-stand was a stag's head with large antlers, to one side of it a bamboo table with a silver salver intended for visiting-cards!

'Was he wearing that coat?'

'No, his mackintosh.'

The dining-room shutters were closed. It was evidently only used as a lumber-room. You could tell Brown had been a fisherman by the lobster-pots on the floor.

Then the kitchen, where the range was never lit. All the cooking was done on a spirit-stove. On the floor beside it were fifty or sixty empty mineral-water bottles.

'You see, the water here is so full of chalk . . .'

The stair-carpet was worn, the brass stair-rods tarnished. You could have found Gina's room with your eyes shut by merely following the trail of musk! Dresses had been thrown on to the unmade bed. Gina had hurriedly gone through all her wardrobe to pick out the best.

No bathroom. Not even a *cabinet de toilette*. Maigret didn't feel like going into the mother's room.

'We went off in such a rush . . . I'm ashamed to show you the house in such a state . . .'

'I'll come and see you again.'

'Does that mean we're free?'

'That is: you won't go back to the prison . . . at all events for the moment . . . But if you try to get away . . .'

'We shouldn't dream of it!'

They accompanied him to the front door.

'A cigar, Inspector?' said Madame Martini in her most ladylike voice.

But Gina went farther. She couldn't go wrong in winning the sympathy of so influential a man.

'Take the whole box, do. William will never smoke them, poor thing.'

They were too good to be true, the pair of them! In fact, they were almost too much for Maigret. When he got outside he did not know whether to laugh or to grind his teeth. Then, looking back from the garden gate, the villa presented another aspect altogether – so restfully white against the trees and bushes. The moon was just at one corner of the roof. On the right the glittering sea, and the quivering mimosas.

With his mackintosh over his arm he walked back to his hotel, pensive but not really thinking. For it was merely a host of vague impressions that drifted through his mind, some of them so disagreeable as to be almost painful, others comic.

'What a man, that blessed William! . . .'

It was getting late. In the hotel there was nobody about except one of the maids reading a newspaper. And suddenly Maigret noticed that it wasn't his mackintosh which he had on his arm, but Brown's, a filthy thing covered with grease-spots.

In the left-hand pocket was a spanner, in the other a handful of small change, and some square brass counters marked with a number for use in one of those slot-machines that are found in the more common bars.

Maigret counted them. There were ten.

*

'Hallo! Is that you, Inspector? Boutigues speaking ... Would you like me to call for you at your hotel?'

It was nine in the morning. From six o'clock onwards, Maigret had been dozing intermittently, luxuriously, conscious of the Mediterranean spread out before his window.

'What for?'

'Don't you want to see the body?'

'Yes ... No ... This afternoon perhaps. Ring up again at lunch-time, will you?'

The first thing to do was to wake up. He was in that delicious state of morning sleepiness in which the events of the day before seem hardly real. The two women, for instance. Vague as a dream, or rather a nightmare!

They wouldn't be getting up yet awhile. And if Brown had been alive he'd have been messing about in the garage or the garden. All by himself. Unshaved and unwashed. And the coffee getting colder and colder in the kitchen.

As he dressed he caught sight of the brass counters, lying in a little heap on the mantelpiece. He had to make quite an effort to realize what they were.

'So Brown went on his periodic bout and was stabbed either just before driving home, during the drive, while going up to the house, or inside it ...'

When his right cheek was shaved clean he started muttering again.

'Brown can hardly have frequented the little bars in Antibes ... If he had, Boutigues would have told me ...'

Then hadn't Gina said that he kept the car in Cannes? A quarter of an hour later he was telephoning to the Cannes police.

'You know the things I mean ... Those slot-machines ... Can you give me a list of all the bars that have them?'

'They've all been done away with. An order was brought out a couple of months ago. They're illegal now. You won't find one left on the Riviera . . .'

Maigret went downstairs and asked where he could get a taxi.

'Where do you want to go to?'

'Cannes.'

'You don't need a taxi for that. There's a bus from the Place Macé every three minutes.'

So there was. In the morning sunshine the Place Macé was even gayer than the day before. Maigret thought of Brown there, taking his two women shopping, with his night-shirt showing at the neck.

He took the bus, and half an hour later he was in Cannes looking for the garage Gina had mentioned, and which he found near the Croisette. Everything here seemed white. Huge white hotels. White shops. White trousers and frocks. White sails on the sea. It might have been a theatrical set, a charming *décor* in blue and white.

'Is this where Mr Brown used to leave his car?'

'That's right.'

'What do you know?'

'There you are! I said it would mean trouble for us as soon as I read about it in the papers . . . But I don't know anything. I've nothing to hide . . . He'd simply bring it here one day and fetch it again a few days later.'

'Drunk?'

'That's how I knew him best.'

'And you've no idea where he was?'

'When? While the car was here? Not the slightest.'

'And you cleaned it up and kept it in order?'

'Not a bit of it. In fact, it's a whole year since he had the sump drained.'

'What did you make of him?'

The man shrugged his shoulders.

'I never bothered.'

'Rather eccentric, wasn't he?'

'There are too many eccentric people on the Riviera for one to take any notice. We're used to them by now. Yesterday, for instance, an American girl came in here. Wanted a new body on her car – something in the shape of a swan. Well, it's her business, isn't it? She pays the bill . . .'

Maigret had drawn a blank. He'd only the brass counters now to help him. By the harbour he went into a bar frequented by the sailors belonging to the yachts.

'Have you got a slot-machine?'

'They're prohibited. Two months ago . . . But they're bringing out a new kind to get round the regulations. It'll be two or three months before they're stopped too.'

'There are none left anywhere?'

The answer was neither yes nor no, but:

'What can I get you?'

Maigret asked for a vermouth. He looked at the line of yachts moored head and stern in the harbour, and then at the sailors in the bar with their yachts' names in red letters on their jerseys.

'Did you know Brown?'

'What Brown? . . . The one that's been killed? . . . He never came here.'

'Where did he go, then?'

With a vague gesture of ignorance the landlord moved over to serve some other customers. Although it was only March, everybody was perspiring. It smelt of summer.

'I once heard someone talking about him,' went on the landlord, with a bottle in his hand, 'but I can't remember who it was.'

'Never mind. What I'm after is a slot-machine.'

As a rule, Brown's women would no doubt go through his pockets when he returned from a bout, so the brass counters probably dated from the last one. This time they'd had other things to think of . . .

But it was all so vague. Really, what had he to go on? And then this blaze of sunshine made Maigret want to sit peacefully in front of a café, like other people, and watch those white sails that hardly moved across the flat sea.

Pale creamy yellow trams . . . Smart cars . . . He found himself in the main shopping street of the town, parallel to the Croisette. But what was the use of that?

'If Brown had his bouts in Cannes,' he groaned, 'it certainly wasn't here.'

He walked on and on, stopping now and again at a bar where he'd have a vermouth and a chat on slot-machines.

'It's not the first time they've been stopped – nor the last either! It only means we have to have a new sort every three or four months . . .'

'Know anything of Brown?'

'The chap that was killed?'

It was a monotonous business. Twelve o'clock had struck, and the sun's rays were beating down mercilessly into the streets. Maigret felt like going up to a policeman, like a holiday-maker, and asking:

'Where does one go to have some fun?'

If Madame Maigret had seen him, she'd have thought his eyes shone a bit too brightly. The vermouth was to blame for that.

He turned one corner, then another. And suddenly it was no longer Cannes – at least not the Cannes of the great white hotels. This was quite a different world, a world of narrow lanes and alleys with wire washing-lines stretching overhead from one side to the other.

Two bars facing each other. On the right, *Aux Vrais Marins*. On the left, *Liberty Bar*.

Maigret went into the one on the right and, standing at the zinc counter, ordered a vermouth.

'That's funny! I thought you had a slot-machine . . .'

'We *had*!'

Maigret's head was heavy and his legs felt weak.

'Some places have them still.'

'Yes. *Some* have,' said the barman acidly as he wiped

over the counter. 'There's always some that take no notice. Only that's none of our business, is it?'

He shot a glance opposite. Maigret threw some money on the counter.

'*Combien?*'

'That's it. *Deux francs vingt-cinq.*'

Maigret walked across to *Liberty Bar* and pushed open the door.

CHAPTER III

'*Liberty Bar*'

THERE was nobody in the bar, which was very small – hardly more than six feet by ten. You had to go down two steps, as it was below street level.

A narrow counter. A shelf with a dozen glasses on it. The slot-machine. Two little tables.

At the back, a glass-panelled door with a muslin curtain. Through it Maigret could just make out some heads turned towards him. But nobody got up to greet the customer. Only a woman's voice calling out:

'What are you waiting for?'

Maigret went through to the room behind, going down another step, as it was still lower than the bar, so low that the bottom of the window was flush with the paving-stones of the back yard. In the dim light he saw three people sitting at a table.

The woman who had called out went on eating, with her elbows on the table. But at the same time she looked at Maigret exactly as he was accustomed to look at others, placidly, taking in every detail.

At last, with a jerk of her chin, she directed him to a stool, sighing:

'You've taken long enough about it.'

On one side of her was a man in nautical uniform. Maigret could only see his back and his fair hair clipped short at the neck.

'Go on eating,' said the woman to him. 'There's nothing to worry about.'

Lastly, on her other side, facing Maigret, sat a girl with the pale complexion of a Southerner and large eyes that stared at him mistrustfully.

She was scantily covered by a dressing-gown. The whole of one breast was visible, but nobody seemed to take any notice.

*

'Won't you sit down? You won't mind if we go on with our lunch?'

Was she forty-five or fifty? Perhaps even more, but it was difficult to say. She was fat, smiling, and self-confident. You knew at once that she was afraid of nobody, that she had seen all there was to see, and felt all that could be felt.

The merest glance had told her what Maigret had come for. And she hadn't even moved from her seat. She cut half a dozen thick slices from a leg of mutton which caught Maigret's attention. He had rarely seen one looking so juicy and tender.

'I suppose you come from Nice or Antibes, since I've never seen you before?'

'From Paris. *Police Judiciaire.*'

'Ah!'

And this 'Ah' made it clear she understood the difference and appreciated her visitor's rank.

'So it's true, is it?'

'What?'

'That William was some kind of important person?'

Maigret could see the man side-face now. He wasn't an ordinary sailor, since he was dressed in 'fore-and-aft rig' with a peak-cap. On the latter were the arms of a yacht club; and he had a gold stripe on his arm. He seemed embarrassed at being where he was, and kept his eyes studiously on his plate.

'Who is he?'

'We call him Yan. I don't even know his proper name. He's the steward of the *Ardena*, a Swedish yacht that comes here every winter. That's right, Yan, isn't it? Steward? Monsieur is from the police . . . You know about William – what I told you . . .'

The other nodded, though he hardly seemed to understand.

'He says yes, but he's only the vaguest idea what you say to him. Not much good at French – simply can't get the hang of it . . . He's a good lad, with a wife and kids at home . . . Show the photo, Yan. Photo . . . yes.'

Yan produced a photograph of a young woman sitting outside her front door with two babies on the lawn at her feet.

'Twins,' explained the hostess. 'Yan comes and has a meal with us from time to time. He likes it here: gives him a sort of family feeling. It's him that brought the mutton and the peaches.'

Maigret turned to the girl who hadn't yet bothered to do up her dressing-gown.

'And . . . and this . . .?'

'That's Sylvie, William's god-daughter.'

'God-daughter?'

'Oh, not in a religious way . . . He wasn't at her baptism . . . in fact, I'm not sure there ever was one. Was there, Sylvie?'

'Certainly,' answered Sylvie, still looking mistrustfully at the intruder, while she toyed with her food. She wasn't hungry.

'William took to her . . . She used to tell him all her troubles, and he'd do his best to comfort her.'

Maigret was sitting on the stool, his elbows on his knees and his chin in his hands. The stout woman got the salad ready, first rubbing the bowl with garlic. It looked a masterpiece.

'Have you had your lunch?'

He lied.

'Yes . . . I . . .'

'If not, you've only to say so. We don't stand on ceremony here . . . That's right, Yan, isn't it? . . . Look at him! He says yes, but for the life of him he couldn't tell you what I'm talking about . . . I love them all, those boys from the North.'

She tasted the salad thoughtfully and added another dash of an olive oil that smelt delicious. There was no table-cloth and the table was none too clean. The stairs came down into the kitchen itself. A sewing-machine stood in one corner.

The yard outside was bathed in sunshine, so much so that the little window made a blinding rectangle of light and in contrast to it they seemed in that room to be living in a cool semi-twilight.

'You can fire ahead with your questions. Sylvie knows as much as I do . . . As for Yan, you needn't bother about him.'

'How long have you had this bar?'

'I dare say it's fifteen years now . . . I was married to an Englishman who'd been an acrobat, so all the English sailors used to come here. Music-hall people too . . . He died nine years ago – drowned in a regatta. He was racing for a titled lady who had three yachts. I'll remember her name in a minute – you'd be sure to know it.'

'What happened then?'

'Nothing. I simply kept the place on, and here we are.'

'Do you have many customers?'

'I don't want many. What do come are more friends than customers. Like Yan, or William. They know I'm alone and that I like a bit of company, and they drop in to split a bottle with me. Or sometimes they bring a chicken or a fish or two, and we have a meal together.'

She filled up the glasses, then realized that none had been put for Maigret.

'Get a glass for the inspector, Sylvie.'

The girl got up without a word and went into the bar. Her bare feet were in slippers, and under her dressing-gown she hadn't a stitch of clothing on. She brushed past Maigret on her way without a word of excuse. The elder woman took advantage of her momentary absence to say:

'Don't take any notice ... She adored him, so it's been a dreadful blow ...'

'She sleeps here?'

'Sometimes, sometimes not.'

'What does she do?'

The woman looked reproachfully at Maigret, a look which seemed to say:

'You ask me that? ... You, an inspector of the *Police Judiciaire!*'

The next moment she was saying:

'Oh! She's a good girl. No harm in her at all.'

'Did William know?'

The same reproachful look. Had she made a mistake about Maigret? Couldn't he understand? Or must she spell it all out letter by letter?

Yan had finished eating. He seemed to be preparing a phrase, but it wasn't necessary.

'Yes, Yan. You can go now ... Will you come this evening?'

'If my people go to the Casino.'

He stood up, but hesitated to go through the customary rite. The woman, however, lifted her face, and he bent down and planted a kiss on her forehead, blushing at the same time on account of Maigret's presence. As he turned he met Sylvie returning with a glass.

'Going?'

'Yes.'

And he kissed her on the forehead too, nodded awkwardly to Maigret, tripped over the step and positively dived into the bar and out into the street, putting his cap straight as he finally hurried away.

'Yes, he's a nice boy. Doesn't like whooping it up with the other yachtsmen. Just likes to sit here quietly . . .'

She had finished eating and was leaning forward on her elbows.

'Will you make the coffee, Sylvie?'

Hardly a sound came from the streets outside. It might have been any time of the day or night, if it hadn't been for that rectangle of sunshine and the alarm-clock in the middle of the mantelpiece which ticked out the hours.

'Well now, what exactly do you want to know? . . . Here's good health to you anyhow! . . . This is some of William's whisky . . .'

'What's your name?'

'Jaja . . . Or sometimes to tease me they call me Fat Jaja.'

She looked down at her enormous bosom resting on the table.

'Have you known William long?'

'Seems like I've known him always. Yet I never knew his surname till a few days ago . . . I ought to tell you that this place was quite famous in my husband's day. Chiefly because of the music-hall fellows. People used to come to rub shoulders with them, rich people too . . .

'The yachting crowd, of course. Them more than anybody. For they're a queer lot and like out-of-the-way places like this. And they're always ready for a binge. I remember William in those days. Saw him several times. All dressed up in a white cap and with a pretty girl on each arm . . .

'Yes, those yachting folk . . . they'd be lapping up champagne into the small hours of the morning, and standing drinks to anyone that happened to be here . . .

'And then he died – I mean my husband . . . I shut the place for a month . . . Anyhow, it wasn't the season . . . And then the next winter I spent three weeks in hospital with peritonitis . . .

'When I came out I found someone had gone and opened another place bang opposite ...

'Since then it's been quiet enough here. But then I don't bother ... I'm not so keen as all that on having a lot of customers ...'

Sylvie had resumed her seat, and with her chin resting on her hand she never took her eyes off Maigret. The sleeve of her dressing-gown dipped into her plate.

'Then one day I saw William again, and it was from that time that I really got to know him ... We got tight and went on telling stories half the night. In the end I put him to bed on the divan, as he was too far gone to be able to walk home.'

'He still had his yachtsman's cap?'

'No. He was no longer quite the same, and liquor didn't take him the same way either. It no longer made him laugh. ... And ever since then he's been coming to see me from time to time.'

'Did you know his address?'

'No, and I'm not the one to ask questions. He never talked about his affairs at all.'

'How long did he stay?'

'Three or four days, mostly ... He'd bring some food with him – or sometimes he'd give me some money to go shopping with ... He used to swear he never had such good meals anywhere.'

Looking at the leg of mutton and the salad, Maigret could easily believe it.

'Was Sylvie with you then?'

'What are you thinking of? She's only twenty-one now.'

'How did you come to know her?'

A sulky look came into Sylvie's face, and Jaja said to her:

'Come along, now! The inspector knows what's what ... It was one evening when William was here. Just him and me alone. And then Sylvie came in with a couple of lads, commercial travellers or something of the sort. They were already half-soused when they arrived, and then they started swilling it down harder than ever ... As for her, you could tell at a glance she was new to it. She wanted to take them off before they were really drunk, but she didn't know how to go about it ... And of course ... You can guess what happened ... They got blind and forgot all about her. Finally they went off leaving her behind ... And then she cried ... She told us she'd come from Paris for the season and hadn't even enough money to pay for a bed ... I took her in with me ... And now she stays when she wants to – it's quite a habit.'

'Seems to be quite a common habit here!' growled Maigret.

Jaja fairly beamed.

'What do you expect? I keep open house. *C'est la maison du bon Dieu!* We're not the worrying sort. We just take each day as it comes.'

She was quite sincere. Her eyes turned slowly till they rested on the girl's chest, when she went on with a sigh:

'Pity her health isn't better. You can see her ribs sticking out. William wanted to pay for her to go into a sanatorium, but she wouldn't listen ...'

'Excuse me, but were she and William ...?'

It was Sylvie herself who answered angrily:

'Never. It's not true.'

And, as she sipped her coffee, Jaja explained:

'It wasn't in his line. Particularly with her. I won't say he didn't, once in a way ...'

'Who with?'

'Women ... women he'd pick up anywhere ... But it was rare. It didn't interest him.'

'When did he leave you last Friday?'

'Directly after lunch. We finished about two, like today.'

'Did he say where he was going?'

'He never did.'

'Was Sylvie here?'

'She'd left just five minutes before.'

'To go where?' asked Maigret, turning to the girl.

'What a question!' she snarled contemptuously.

'Down to the harbour? ... Is that where you ...?'

'There or anywhere.'

'Was there anybody else here?'

'Nobody ... It was very hot that afternoon. I fell asleep in my chair and snoozed for a whole hour.'

It was after five when William had driven up to the villa at Antibes.

'Did he go to other bars like this?'

'Not to my knowledge. Besides, there aren't any others like this.'

That was incontestable. Maigret himself, who had only been there an hour, felt as though he had known it always. It was difficult to say what gave him that impression. Was it the casual, impersonal hospitality? Or the atmosphere of indolence and indifference that reigned there?

It was the kind of place where you had to make an effort of will to get up and go.

Time passed slowly. The hands of the alarm-clock moved over its drab-white face. The rectangular sunbeam shifted.

'I read about it in the papers. The name of Brown meant nothing to me, but I recognized his photograph ... We cried over it, Sylvie and me ... What could he want with those two women? ... But of course in our situation it's best to keep clear of trouble. Out of sight, out of mind! ... But I thought the police would turn up sooner or later, and when I saw you coming out of the *Vrais Marins* I spotted you at once.'

She spoke slowly. She filled up the glasses, and sipped at hers.

'The chap that did it's a skunk, for there aren't many men in the world like William – and I know what I'm talking about.'

'He never talked to you about his past?'

She sighed. How obtuse he was! Didn't he realize that

this was just the very house where you *didn't* talk about the past? Where pasts were taken for granted?

'All I can tell you is that he was a gentleman, a man who's been very rich, and still was, maybe . . . I really don't know. He'd had a yacht and lots of people to wait on him.'

'Did he seem sad?'

Again she sighed.

'Can't you understand? . . . You've seen Yan – would you call him sad? . . . In any case, Yan's different . . . Would you say I was sad? Perhaps you would; perhaps you wouldn't. What one likes here is to have a booze, talk a lot of nonsense, and then have a good cry . . .'

Sylvie looked at her disapprovingly. But then she was only drinking coffee while La Grosse Jaja was already at her third glass of whisky.

'I'm glad you've come. We've had it all out now. We've nothing to hide and nothing to reproach ourselves with . . . All the same, that's not saying that the police'll take our word for it . . . Now, if it had been the Cannes police, they'd have taken away my licence as sure as I'm sitting here.'

'Did William spend a lot of money?'

Was it hopeless to try and make him understand?

'He did and he didn't. He certainly never grudged it – but it wasn't really such a lot. Enough for the shopping, and now and again he'd pay the gas or the electricity. Or he might give Sylvie a hundred francs to buy stockings with.'

Maigret was hungry, and that delicious leg of mutton was only a foot from his nostrils. Two slices were still lying on the dish. He picked one up in his fingers and ate it as he went on talking, just as if he'd been one of the household.

'Does Sylvie bring her customers here?'

'Never. It would give them a good excuse to shut the place up . . . There are hotels enough for that in Cannes ! . . .'

And looking into Maigret's eyes, she added:

'You really think it's those two women that . . .'

But she broke off and looked round. Sylvie also peered

through the muslin curtain of the glass-panelled door. The street door had been opened and someone crossed the bar and came to the kitchen, halting suddenly in the doorway at the sight of a stranger.

Sylvie had stood up. Jaja, rather pink in the face perhaps, said to the newcomer:

'Come in ... This is the inspector who's seeing about William.'

And then to Maigret:

'A friend of ours ... Joseph. He's a waiter at the Casino.'

Visibly a waiter. For with his grey suit he wore a white collar, white dicky, and black tie – also black patent-leather shoes.

'I'll look in later,' he said.

'No, no. Come in.'

Joseph couldn't quite make up his mind.

'I just dropped in to say *bonjour* as I was passing ... I've got a good tip for the ...'

'So you back horses?' asked Maigret, turning slightly towards him.

'Now and again. Sometimes a customer gives me a tip – but I must be running now.'

And he beat a hasty retreat, though not without making a signal to Sylvie – or so Maigret thought. The girl sat down again.

'He'll lose once more,' sighed Jaja. 'He's not a bad fellow, you know.'

'I must get dressed,' said Sylvie, standing up again, disclosing as she did so the greater party of her body. It wasn't intentional. It wasn't meant to be seductive. It simply didn't matter, and that was all.

She went upstairs and they could hear her moving about overhead. It seemed to Maigret as though Jaja was pricking her ears.

'She backs horses too, sometimes ... It's she who's lost most by William's death ...'

A moment later Maigret jumped from his seat, rapidly

crossed to the bar, and opened the door to the street. But he wasn't quick enough. Joseph was striding off as fast as he could, without a look behind him. From above came the sound of a window being shut.

'What's the matter?' asked Jaja when he returned.

'Nothing. Just an idea.'

'Another drop of whisky? And if you like the mutton, go ahead and help yourself.'

Sylvie came down transformed, indeed almost unrecognizable in her navy-blue tailored suit, looking altogether fresh and girlish. Under her white silk blouse her little breasts looked more than attractive – yet Maigret had been staring at them previously without the smallest concern. Her skirt, fitting neatly over the haunches, and her tautly stretched stockings made her figure look light and lithe.

'See you this evening.'

And she too kissed Jaja's forehead. Turning towards Maigret she hesitated. Did she want to ignore him? Or on the contrary, did she want to spit in his face?

In any case there was no doubt about her attitude. She was hostile and made no bones about it.

'Good afternoon,' she said at last, frigidly, 'I suppose you won't be wanting me any more.'

She stood there stiffly for a moment and then stalked out.

Jaja laughed as once again she filled up the glasses.

'Don't take any notice of her. These young things haven't learnt much sense . . . Shall I give you a plate, and you can try my salad?'

The empty bar below street level, the half-lit kitchen lower still . . . upstairs a bedroom which was probably in disorder . . . and the little window on to the back yard from which the sun had almost disappeared . . .

It was a strange world, and in the middle of it sat Maigret finishing up the remains of a perfect salad. In front of him was La Grosse Jaja, who seemed to be supported by her immense bosom which spread over the table, and who sighed once more:

'When I was her age I had to mind my p's and q's . . .'

She didn't need to say more, for he could very well imagine her in a loud silk dress going up and down her beat somewhere in Paris – near the Porte Saint-Martin perhaps, or the Porte Saint-Denis, while from the window of some bar her exacting 'protector' would keep a watchful eye on her.

'But nowadays . . .'

She had done too much honour to William's whisky. It was with wet eyes that she looked at Maigret, and her almost childish mouth puckered. Was she going to have a good cry?

'You remind me of William. That's where he always sat. And he used to put his pipe down beside his plate when he ate – just like you . . . And then his shoulders . . . do you know, you look like him?'

She merely wiped her eyes. She didn't have her cry after all.

CHAPTER IV

The Taste of Gentian

THE day was drawing in. That subtle hour had come when the quality of light is indescribable, when the warm breath of the setting sun is turned cool and lucid by approaching night. Maigret slunk out of *Liberty Bar* much as one might leave a house of ill repute, his hands deep in his pockets, his hat pulled down over his eyes. And then after a dozen steps he couldn't help turning round, as though to make sure the place he had come from really existed.

Yes, there it was! – a narrow frontage squeezed between two houses, the woodwork painted an ugly brown with yellow lettering. Behind the window of the bar some plant was flowering, and beside it on the windowsill, a sleeping cat.

Jaja was no doubt dozing too in the kitchen behind, all alone with the alarm-clock which counted out the minutes.

At the end of the lane he found himself back once more in the everyday world – shops, people dressed just like everybody else, cars, a tram, and a policeman . . .

And there on the right was the Croisette, looking exactly like those water-colours which the *Syndicat d'Initiative* made use of to illustrate their pamphlets boosting Cannes.

It was all so gentle and peaceful. People strolling along: no fuss, no hurry. Cars gliding as though propelled by something far subtler than machinery. And all those white yachts floating in the harbour.

Maigret felt tired, worn out, and yet he hadn't the least desire to go back to his hotel. He walked about aimlessly hither and thither, stopping without knowing why, and then wandering on again no matter where. It was as if the conscious part of his being had remained behind in Jaja's bosom. Only his body was here, while the rest was by the table still littered with the remains of the midday meal, by the table where a smart Swedish steward had sat facing Sylvie's naked breasts.

For the best part of ten years William Brown had lived there, three or four days a month, browsing in that warm laziness, keeping Jaja company – Jaja who after a glass or two would talk a bit, and after a few glasses more would have her cry, and then fall asleep in her chair.

'*La gentiane, parbleu!*'

Maigret was delighted. He'd got it at last. Gentian – that was it. That's what he'd been looking for all this time without knowing it. Ever since he'd left *Liberty Bar* he had been trying to define the place, trying to strip it of all its picturesque accessories till only its essence remained. And now he'd got it: gentian. He remembered what an old friend had said to him once when he'd offered him a drink.

'What's yours?'

'A gentian.'

'What's that? A new fashion?'

'No, old man, it's not a fashion at all. It's merely the drunkard's last resource. Have you never tried it? It's bitter. It's not even strong in alcohol. And when you've soaked yourself for twenty years in every drink imaginable, that's all that's left to you. That queer bitter taste is the one thing you can still get a kick out of.'

Liberty Bar tasted the same. A place without vice, or at least without malice, where nothing had to be explained. A bar you went straight through, into the kitchen, and sat down like one of the family.

And after a drink or two you'd go round to the butcher's and bring back a hunk of meat, and then you'd drink some more while Jaja put it on to cook. Sylvie would come down with sleepy eyes, half-naked, and you'd kiss her on the forehead without so much as a glance at her poor little breasts.

The room was dingy and none too clean. You wouldn't talk a lot. The conversation would drag on idly, without conviction, like the lives that were spent there.

The busy world was shut out ... Only that little rectangle of sunlight ...

To eat, to drink, to doze ... And then to start drinking again while Sylvie went upstairs to dress ... Dragging her stockings tight over her thighs before going off to work ...

'So-long,' she'd say to her 'god-father' as she went out: '*À tout à l'heure, parrain!*'

What would William Brown find in it? Exactly what Maigret's pal had found in gentian. *Liberty Bar* was his last resource – the last refuge of a man who had sampled everything, who had known every excitement and every vice.

Women without beauty, and who did not even try to look beautiful ... women without desire and who were not desired ... women you'd kiss gravely on the forehead and give a hundred francs to for stockings ... And when they came home you'd ask them:

'Done a good day's work?'

Maigret was oppressed by the thought of it. He wanted to think of something else. He stopped and stood facing the harbour. A thin sheet of mist was spreading, only a few inches above the water.

He had already passed the racing yachts and come to the big cruising ones. Only a few paces from him a sailor was hauling down a red flag with a white crescent belonging to a huge white steam yacht, obviously owned by some Pasha.

Next to it was a yacht not much under a hundred and fifty feet long, round whose stern in gilt letters ran the name – *Ardena*.

He thought at once of the Swedish steward at Jaja's, and almost at the same moment, raising his head, he caught sight of him on deck. His white-gloved hands were carrying a tray which he put down on a wicker table.

The owner of the yacht was leaning over the side with two girls. As he laughed he disclosed a splendid set of teeth. There was only the short gangway between them and Maigret, and the latter, with a shrug of his shoulders, walked up it and went on board. He almost burst out laughing at the expression on the steward's face.

There are moments like that, when you do something just for the sake of something to do, not because it's useful but to take your mind off other things:

'*Pardon, monsieur . . .*'

The yachtsman stopped laughing. All three turned towards Maigret and waited for him to go on.

'Might I inquire whether you know a certain William Brown?'

'Has he a yacht?'

'He had one . . .'

Maigret hardly bothered to listen for the answer. He gazed at the Swede in front of him, a really aristocratic-looking man who must have been about forty-five. And seeing him there with those two women he thought:

'Brown was like that! He too had been surrounded with beautiful girls whose pretty dresses showed just enough of their figures to excite desire. To amuse them he would take them to some little out-of-the-way bar, and the whole place would soon be swimming in champagne . . .'

With a strong accent the Swede answered:

'If it's the Brown I'm thinking about, he once owned that big yacht there, the last of the line: the *Pacific* . . . But she has changed hands two or three times since then.'

'Thank you.'

The man and his two companions were at a loss to know the meaning of Maigret's visit. They watched him as he walked away, and he heard a little giggle from the two girls.

There was only one other yacht in the harbour as big as the *Pacific*, the one that had been flying the Turkish flag. But, in contrast to the latter, the *Pacific* showed every sign of neglect. Rusty patches of the hull were showing, where the paint had flaked off, and all the brasswork was green.

A pathetic little notice was hanging from the side rails: *To be sold*.

Washed and trim in their tight-fitting jumpers, sailors were coming ashore from the yachts, and wandering off in twos and threes towards the town.

When Maigret passed the *Ardena* on his way back he was conscious of three pairs of eyes on him, and he felt sure there must be another pair peering at him from some strategic point where Yan had taken cover.

*

The streets were all lit up. Maigret had some difficulty in finding the garage again. There were one or two more questions he wanted to ask.

'What time last Friday did Brown come for his car?'

They had to call the mechanic.

'At ten to five.'

In other words, just in time to get back to the Cap d'Antibes. A little after five, they'd said.

'Was he alone? . . . And nobody was waiting for him

outside? ... You noticed nothing wrong with him – he wasn't wounded?'

William Brown had left *Liberty Bar* about two o'clock. What was he doing between two and five?

There was nothing more for Maigret to do in Cannes. He waited for his bus, and then tucked himself into a corner, and sat there gazing idly at the head-lamps of the cars that followed each other in procession along the main road to Nice.

The first person he saw as he alighted in the Place Macé was the detective, Boutigues, sitting on the terrace of the *Café Glacier*. Boutigues jumped up and ran to meet him.

'We've been looking for you ever since this morning ... Sit down. What'll you have? ... Waiter! ... Two Pernods ...'

'Not for me, thanks. I'll have a gentian,' said Maigret, who was keen now to know what it tasted like.

'First of all I questioned all the taxi drivers. As none of them had driven you anywhere I tried the bus conductors. That's how I knew you had gone to Cannes.'

He spoke quickly, eagerly, one might even say passionately. Maigret looked at him with some astonishment, but the little man went on unabashed:

'There are only five or six restaurants there where you can have a decent meal. I rang up every one of them ... Where the devil did you have lunch?'

Boutigues would have had the surprise of his life if Maigret had told him the truth, had told him of the wonderful leg of mutton and the salad flavoured with garlic ... of the glasses of whisky ... of Sylvie ...

'The examining magistrate won't take any step without consulting you first. And now that the son has arrived on the scene ...'

'Whose son?'

Maigret made a grimace. He had swallowed a mouthful of gentian!

'Brown's son. He's come from Amsterdam.'

The trouble was – Maigret had a headache. He tried to concentrate, but succeeded only with an effort.

'Brown has a son?'

'Several. That's to say, three. By his real wife who lives in Australia . . . Only one of them is in Europe. He sees to the wool . . .'

'The wool.'

At that moment Boutigues could hardly have had a very high opinion of the inspector who had come from Paris. The fact is, the latter was still in *Liberty Bar*. To be more precise, he was thinking about the waiter who backed horses and to whom Sylvie had spoken from the upstairs window.

'Yes. The Browns are the biggest wool people in Australia. They breed sheep and export the wool themselves. One looks after the livestock, while another at Sydney sees to the shipping. The third handles the stuff at this end. He travels from place to place according to where they ship the wool to. Mostly Liverpool, Havre, Hamburg, or Amsterdam. He's the one that . . .'

'And what does he say?'

'That his father must be buried as quickly as possible. He'll pay everything . . . He's in a hurry. Says he has to catch the aeroplane which leaves tomorrow night.'

'Is he staying at Antibes?'

'No. At Juan-les-Pins. He wanted a big hotel where he could have a whole suite of rooms. He's asked the exchange to keep his line through to Nice all night long, as he's expecting calls from Antwerp and Amsterdam, and God knows what other places too.'

'Has he been to the villa?'

'I suggested it, but he wouldn't hear of it.'

'What's he come for, then?'

'He has seen the examining magistrate. That's all. Merely says things must go quickly. And he asks how much!'

'How much what?'

'How much it'll cost.'

Maigret looked absently round the Place Macé, while Boutigues continued:

'The magistrate was waiting for you in his office all the afternoon. He couldn't very well refuse to allow the burial now that the post-mortem is finished. Brown's son rang him up three times, and in the end he was told the funeral could take place first thing tomorrow morning.'

'First thing in the morning?'

'Yes, to avoid having any crowd. That's why I wanted to get hold of you . . . They're closing the coffin this evening, so if you want to see the body . . .'

'No.'

That was quite definite. Maigret had no wish to see the corpse. He knew William Brown well enough as it was.

There were a lot of people sitting in front of the café, and Boutigues noticed that eyes were turned towards him and Maigret. He rather liked it; nevertheless he whispered:

'We'd better speak more quietly.'

'Where is he to be buried?'

'But . . . at the cemetery here, of course. The hearse will be at the mortuary at seven. Everything's arranged. I mustn't forget to let Mr Brown know the exact time.'

'And the two women?'

'Nothing's been decided about them. It may be that Mr Brown would prefer . . .'

'Where did you say he was?'

'The *Provençal* at Juan-les-Pins. Do you want to see him?'

'Good-bye,' said Maigret. 'I'll see you at the funeral.'

He was in a most unaccountable mood. An almost savage mood – yet at the same time he wanted to laugh. A taxi took him to the *Provençal*, where he was received by the hall porter, passed on to a messenger in gold-braided uniform, and finally ushered into the presence of a young man in a black suit sitting at a desk.

'Mr Brown? I'll see if he's disengaged . . . May I ask your name?'

Bells rang. Clerks and secretaries came and went, and

after a good five minutes Maigret was led along interminable corridors to a room marked No. 37. From behind the door came the sound of a typewriter and an irritable voice saying:

'Come in.'

And Maigret found himself face to face with the son of William Brown, the wool-merchant in charge of the department known as Europe.

*

From the point of view of years, he was completely nondescript. Being the son of William Brown, he was probably quite young. But you might easily have taken him for thirty, or possibly even forty. A tall, thin, clean-shaven man whose face was already lined. Perfectly groomed, he wore a black tie with narrow white stripes, in which was a pearl tie-pin.

Impossible to imagine him either untidy or spontaneous. Every hair was in its place, every gesture premeditated.

'Take a seat, will you? ... And if you'll excuse me a moment ...'

A typist was sitting at the Louis XV table. A secretary was speaking English into the telephone. And Brown's son finished dictating a cablegram in English about some damages that were being claimed on account of a dockers' strike.

'It's for you, sir,' said the secretary, handing him the telephone receiver.

'Hallo! Speaking! What is it?'

He listened for a long time without putting in a word, then simply rang off after saying:

'No.'

He pressed an electric bell, asking Maigret:

'A glass of port?'

'No, thanks.'

When the waiter came, he ordered it none the less.

He did everything calmly, but with a careworn air as if

the fate of Europe depended on the most trivial of his acts, a nod of his head, or a stroke of his pencil.

'Type that out in the next room, please.'

Finally he sat down with a sigh and crossed his legs.

'I'm afraid I'm tired. Are you handling this case?'

The waiter returned with the port, and Brown Junior pushed it over towards the inspector.

'It's an absurd affair, isn't it?'

'Not so absurd as all that,' growled Maigret.

'I mean annoying.'

'Certainly. It's always annoying to get a knife between your shoulder-blades. Still more if you die of it.'

The wool-merchant stood up. His patience was wearing. Opening the door to the next room, he gave some orders in English, then coming back to Maigret he held out his cigarette-case.

'No, thanks. I keep to a pipe.'

Mr Brown reached for a box of English tobacco that was standing on a little table.

'*Du gris*, if you don't mind,' said Maigret, producing his own – a little grey packet of common tobacco.

Mr Brown was pacing up and down the room with long strides.

'You know, perhaps, that my father led a ... a rather wild life.'

'He certainly had a mistress.'

'That's not all. Far from it. I'm sorry to have to speak like this, but if you don't understand the situation you may put your foot in it, you may make ... what do you call it? ... a *gaffe*.'

The telephone interrupted him. The secretary dashed in to take it, answering this time in German. Mr Brown, listening, signalled to him to say no. The call went on, however, until Brown could stand it no longer. He snatched the receiver and hung up.

'My father came to Paris many years ago ... without my mother. He nearly ruined us ...'

The Australian couldn't keep still. While speaking he had shut the door behind the departing secretary. Returning he pointed to the glass of port.

'You're not drinking?'

'No, thanks.'

At which the other shrugged his shoulders impatiently:

'Well, my mother managed to take the business out of his hands ... She suffered a lot. And worked like a slave ...'

'It was she who put the business on its feet again?'

'With my uncle, yes.'

'Her brother, I suppose?'

'Yes. My father seemed to have lost all ... all sense of dignity. We don't need to go into detail, for I'm sure you'll understand.'

Maigret's eyes had been fixed on him steadily the whole time, and it seemed to put the wool-merchant out of countenance. It was a heavy look, utterly unfathomable. Perhaps it didn't mean anything at all. Perhaps it threatened a lot of trouble.

'One question, Mr Brown – Mr Harry Brown I believe, judging by the name on your luggage. Where were you last Friday?'

The answer did not come until Harry Brown had twice paced the whole length of the room.

'What's in your mind?'

'Nothing. I simply asked you where you were.'

'Has that any bearing on the case?'

'Perhaps it has; perhaps it hasn't.'

'I was in Marseilles. One of our ships was arriving ... that is, a ship with a cargo of our wool. The *Glasgow* ...'

'You didn't see your father?'

'I didn't.'

'One more question, and that will be the last. Who paid your father his allowance? And how much was it?'

'I did. Five thousand francs a month ... Perhaps you'd like to tell that to the newspapers! ...'

The typewriter was still audible through the door to the other room. You could hear the little bell at the end of each line, and the thud of the carriage as it was pulled back against the stop.

Maigret stood up and reached for his hat.

'Thank you. Good evening.'

Harry Brown was taken aback.

'Is that all?'

'Yes, that's all, thank you.'

The telephone rang again, but the Australian seemed hardly to hear it. He was staring incredulously at Maigret as the latter walked to the door.

Then in desperation he picked up an envelope from the table:

'I had this ready ... I thought some police charity might like ...'

Maigret was already in the corridor. A moment later he was walking down the sumptuous staircase and across the entrance hall, conducted by the gold-braided lackey.

At nine o'clock he was having dinner at the *Hôtel Bacon*, at the same time consulting the local telephone directory. As soon as he had finished he asked the Cannes exchange for three numbers one after the other. The third time the answer came:

'Yes. It's just over the way.'

'Good! And would you be kind enough to tell Madame Jaja that the funeral is at seven o'clock tomorrow morning at Antibes ... Yes, the funeral ... She'll understand.'

He started pacing up and down the dining-room. Through a window he could see, a quarter of a mile away, Brown's villa, two windows of which were lit up.

Could he face it?

No, he didn't feel up to it at all. Bed was what he wanted.

'Is there a telephone at the Browns'?'

'Yes, Inspector. Shall I get through for you?'

The neat little maid in a white cap ran over to the telephone. Somehow she reminded Maigret of a mouse.

'Monsieur . . . Here you are! I've got one of them.'

Maigret took the receiver.

'Hallo! . . . This is the inspector speaking . . . Yes . . . I haven't been able to come over and see you. The funeral is at seven tomorrow morning . . . What do you say? . . . No. Not this evening. I've some work to do. *Bonsoir, madame.*'

It must have been the old woman. And Maigret could see her bustling off to tell her daughter. And the two of them hurrying upstairs to get out their best black clothes, wondering if they would be ready in time.

The proprietress of the hotel came into the room all smiles.

'Did you like the *bouillabaisse*? I had it made specially for you . . .'

The *bouillabaisse*? Maigret racked his brains.

'Oh, yes. Excellent. Delicious,' he managed to say with a polite smile.

But for the life of him he couldn't remember it. It had got mixed up with so many other things. It was all a jumble – Boutigues, the bus, the garage . . .

As for food, two things floated on the surface: Jaja's leg of mutton and the garlic-flavoured salad.

There were other things too, but deeper down. The sickly smell of the port he hadn't drunk, and no less sickly the smell of Harry Brown's brilliantine.

Beneath them all, a bitter undercurrent – the taste of gentian.

'Bring me up some mineral water – Vittel for preference,' said Maigret as he turned to go upstairs.

CHAPTER V

The Funeral of William Brown

THOUGH it was only spring, the early morning sun was quite heavy. The streets were empty and all the shutters closed; there was life, however, in the market, the light, easy-going life of people who get up early and have a long day before them; and the shouting from stall to stall, some of it in French, some in Italian, seemed to take precedence over all other activities.

Right in the middle of the market-place rose the yellow frontage of the Town Hall with its double perron. In its basement was the mortuary.

At ten to seven a hearse drew up, a distressing black thing in the middle of all the fruit and flowers. At the same time Maigret arrived, and a moment later Boutigues, hurrying, buttoning up his waistcoat, having only left his bed ten minutes before.

'There's no sign of Mr Brown yet, so we've just time for a drink,' he said, pushing open the door of a little bar, where he ordered two glasses of rum.

'This funeral's been enough to turn my hair grey . . . To start with, he never said what sort of price he wanted to pay for the coffin. I rang him up at the *Provençal* in the evening, and he said it was all the same to him, only it must be of good quality. Then the trouble began, for there wasn't a single solid oak coffin to be had in Antibes at such short notice, so I had to have one sent over from Cannes. It didn't get here till eleven o'clock . . . Then about the service: I didn't know whether we ought to have one or not. I rang up the *Provençal* again, but they said he'd gone to bed . . . So I simply had to do my best . . . There you are!'

He pointed to a church a hundred yards away, whose doorway was draped by the conventional silver-fringed black curtains.

Maigret preferred to make no comment, though young Brown had certainly struck him as being more like a Protestant than a Catholic.

The bar was at the corner of a little street and had a door at the side as well as in front. As the two policemen left by one door a man entered by the other, and Maigret caught his eye.

It was Joseph, the waiter at the Casino in Cannes. He hesitated a moment, not knowing whether to recognize Maigret or not. Finally he decided on a non-committal nod.

Maigret guessed that he had escorted Jaja and Sylvie to Antibes, and he was not mistaken. There they were, walking just in front of him, towards the hearse. Jaja waddled along, panting for breath, dragged by the girl, who was apparently afraid of being late.

Sylvie had her blue suit on and looked quite the proper *jeune fille*. As for Jaja, she was obviously unused to walking. Very likely she had bad feet or swollen legs. She wore shiny black satin.

They must have got up at half past five to catch the first bus. A unique event in *Liberty Bar*!

'Who are they?' asked Boutigues.

'I don't know,' Maigret answered evasively.

But at the same moment the two women, having reached the hearse, stopped and turned round. And as soon as Jaja saw Maigret she bustled up to him.

'We're in good time, aren't we? ... Where is he?'

Sylvie had rings under her eyes. She showed Maigret the same hostile reserve as before.

'Joseph came with you?'

She was on the point of lying, but thought better of it.

'Who told you so?'

Boutigues stood to one side. A taxi appeared. Unable to make its way through the market, it stopped at a street corner.

The two women who alighted created quite a stir. They

were in the deepest mourning, so deep that their heavy
crêpe veils almost touched the ground. They looked altogether incongruous in the sunshine and the busy strident
crowd.

Maigret said to Jaja:

'Excuse me, will you?'

Boutigues was getting anxious. He asked the undertaker
to wait a few minutes longer before fetching the coffin.

'We're not late, I hope?' asked Madame Martini. 'I
thought we should be when our wretched taxi didn't turn
up at the right time.'

She was not long in spotting Jaja and Sylvie.

'Who are those people?'

'I don't know.'

'We don't want *them* butting in . . .'

Another taxi. The door opened before it had quite
stopped, and out jumped Harry Brown, impeccably dressed
for the occasion, his hair beautifully brushed, his face
freshly shaved. His secretary accompanied him, also dressed
in black, carrying a handsome wreath.

At the same moment Maigret noticed that Sylvie had
vanished. Looking round, he spied her among the stalls
of the market, standing by some baskets of flowers. When
she returned it was with a huge bunch of Nice violets.

The two be-crêped women were not to be outdone, and
they too moved off, hurriedly consulting one another. The
elder one fumbled in her purse, while the other picked out
a bunch of mimosa.

With a nod to Maigret and Boutigues, Harry Brown took
up his stand, a few paces from the hearse.

'I'd better tell him about the service,' sighed Boutigues.
'I hope he'll approve.'

Close to them in the market, activity subsided. People
stood still to watch the spectacle. Twenty yards farther,
however, the animation was undiminished: cries and
laughter, among a sea of flowers, fruit, and vegetables; the
sunshine; the smell of garlic; the scent of mimosa.

Four men carried the enormous coffin, furnished with a profusion of bronze ornaments. Boutigues returned.

'He doesn't seem to care a scrap – simply shrugged his shoulders . . .'

The crowd made way, and the horses stepped off. Harry Brown advanced stiffly, hat in hand, looking at the toes of his patent-leather shoes.

The four women hesitated, exchanging glances. As neither pair abdicated, they fell automatically into a single row, immediately behind Harry Brown and his secretary.

The church doors were wide open. It was quite empty inside, and its coolness was delicious.

Harry Brown waited at the top of the steps for the coffin to be lifted out of the hearse. He was used to ceremonies. To be the centre of all eyes caused him no embarrassment whatever. In fact, he calmly scrutinized the four women, though without showing any undue curiosity.

The funeral had been arranged hurriedly at the last minute, and it was not surprising that the organist had been forgotten. The priest whispered to Boutigues and drew him aside into the sacristy. The latter was thoroughly put out when he rejoined Maigret.

'There'll be no music. We should have to wait a quarter of an hour. That is if the chap's at home, but he might equally well be out mackerel-fishing.'

A few strangers came into the church, cast a look round, and then went out again. And all the time Harry Brown stood rigidly, but quite at ease, looking about him with detached curiosity.

Without organ or choir, the service was soon over. The aspergillum sprinkled its holy water, and the four men carried out the coffin.

Outside, the day's heat was already beginning. The *cortège* passed in front of a hairdresser's, where a man in a white coat was taking down the shutters. Farther on, a man was shaving at an open window. Men and women, going to work, turned round to stare at so incongruous a funeral – the merest handful of people following a coffin fit for a prince.

The two women from Cannes and the two from Antibes were still in line abreast, though separated by a gap a yard wide. An empty taxi followed in the rear. Boutigues' responsibilities weighed rather heavy on his shoulders.

'I do hope there won't be a scene,' he said.

There was none. All went smoothly. The cemetery, with all its flowers, was almost as gay as the market. The priest was there already, standing beside the open grave, with the little choir boy who carried the holy water.

Harry Brown was invited to throw in the first handful of earth. There was a moment's hesitation over who should be the second; then Madame Martini pushed her daughter forward and followed in her wake.

The wool-merchant, with his long strides, had already reached the cemetery gates, where the taxi was awaiting him. Maigret and Boutigues were still by the grave, standing a little to one side.

Another hesitation. Jaja did not want to leave without saying good-bye to the inspector. But the Antibes couple cut in in front of her. Gina was weeping, pressing her handkerchief into a ball under her veil and dabbing her eyes.

With an air of mistrust, the mother asked:

'That's his son, isn't it? ... I suppose he'll be wanting to come to the house ...'

'He may, but I don't know.'

'Are you coming today?'

She was speaking to Maigret, but her eyes were on Jaja and Sylvie, who engrossed all her attention.

'Where do they spring from – those creatures? ... They oughtn't to have been allowed ...'

Birds were singing in every tree. The sextons were busy and shovelfuls of earth fell in steady rhythm, the sound becoming gradually fainter as the grave filled up. Sylvie stood staring at them fixedly, her lips pale. The wreath and the other flowers had been put on the next grave for the time being.

Jaja was waiting impatiently for the others to go. She was hot, and wiped her face. She had been on her feet long enough already.

'Yes,' said Maigret to Madame Martini. 'I'll be coming along presently.'

The black veils withdrew towards the gates. Jaja approached with a sigh of relief.

'So they're the ones! . . . Was he really married?'

Sylvie was still standing apart, her eyes on the grave that was almost filled in. It was now Boutigues' turn to be impatient. He stood by himself, not quite daring to come up and listen to the conversation.

'Is the son paying for that coffin?'

Jaja was visibly ill at ease.

'A funny funeral,' she went on. 'I don't know why, but I'd never have thought it would be like that . . . I couldn't have cried if I'd tried to . . .'

It was only now that her feelings were coming to the surface. She looked round the cemetery disconsolately.

'A funny funeral indeed! Why, it wasn't even sad . . . one might have thought . . .'

'One might have thought what?'

'I don't know . . . It's as if it wasn't a real funeral at all . . .'

She stifled a sob, dabbing her eyes, and turned to Sylvie.

'Come on. Joseph's waiting.'

The gate-keeper, on the doorstep of the cemetery lodge, was cutting up a conger-eel.

*

'How does it strike you?'

Boutigues was worried. He too felt vaguely that things were not going right, and that he was out of his depth. Maigret lit his pipe.

'It strikes me that William Brown was murdered,' was all he answered.

'Certainly.'

They wandered along the streets, where the awnings were already lowered over the shop-windows. The barber they had passed before was now sitting outside his door reading his paper. In the Place Macé the two women from Cannes were standing with Joseph, waiting for their bus.

'Let's sit down and have a drink,' suggested Boutigues.

Maigret didn't say no. An overwhelming lassitude had taken hold of him. A succession of confused images flitted across his retina. He let them pass without attempting to sort them out.

On the terrace of the *Café Glacier*, he sat with his eyes half shut. The sun scorched his eyelids. His overlapping lashes made a shadowy curtain through which things and people looked hardly real.

Dreamily he watched Joseph hoist Jaja into the bus, and then a dapper little man in whites and a sun-helmet, who slowly walked by, leading a purple-tongued chow.

Superimposed upon the real ones were the other images: an unshaven William Brown at the wheel of an old car, driving his two women from shop to shop, with the collar of his night-shirt showing at the neck.

His son, Harry, would now be back in his grand suite at the *Provençal*, dictating cablegrams, telephoning, and pacing up and down with long, regular, forceful strides.

'It's a strange business,' sighed Boutigues, who did not care for long silences.

He uncrossed his legs and crossed them the other way before adding:

'A pity we forgot about the organist.'

'Yes. William Brown was murdered . . .'

It was really for his own benefit that Maigret repeated the words. He was trying to convince himself that, after all, something very serious had occurred. His collar was too tight and his forehead glistening with sweat. He gazed greedily at the lump of ice that floated in his Pernod.

Brown was murdered . . . He left home, as he did every month, and drove over to Cannes. Leaving the car at the garage, he went to the bank or wherever it was where they paid him his allowance. Then he spent a week at *Liberty Bar*.

A week of warm laziness such as had now overcome Maigret. A week in slippers, shifting from one chair to another, eating and drinking with Jaja and watching Sylvie lolling about half-naked . . .

'On Friday afternoon at two he left. At ten to five he fetched the car, and a quarter of an hour later he reached the villa wounded and fell down dead on the doorstep, while Gina, thinking him drunk, scolded from an upstairs window. He had the usual two thousand francs 'on him . . .'

Maigret had not spoken. It was only a reverie that floated through his brain as he watched the passers-by, or the lump of ice in his glass, through the curtain of eye-lashes.

It was Boutigues who muttered:

'I can't imagine who could have the slightest interest in his death.'

That, of course, was the whole crux of the matter. Indeed, who could?

Brown's two women, for instance? On the contrary, they had every reason to keep him alive as long as possible. For, out of the two thousand francs he brought home every month, they always managed to put a little by.

The other two, in Cannes? They had nothing to gain and everything to lose. Wasn't Brown one of the few customers of *Liberty Bar*, and one that kept the whole household in food and drink so long as he stayed? Didn't he sometimes pay Jaja's electric light and gas bills? Didn't he pay for Sylvie's silk stockings?

No. The only one who stood to gain anything was Harry Brown – or rather the Brown family, who would no longer have to pay the truant father his five thousand francs a month.

But what are five thousand francs a month to people who sell wool by the ship-load?

Boutigues sighed again.

'I'll finish up by thinking, like the public, that it's a spying affair.'

'*Garçon!*' called Maigret. 'The same again.'

He regretted it instantly. He wanted to cancel the order, but it would have looked too silly. It would have been a confession of his weakness.

For years he remembered this hour spent on the terrace of the *Café Glacier* in the Place Macé at Antibes ... It was one of his rare moments of weakness, or rather of complete surrender.

Certainly the surroundings were not being helpful ... the soft warm air, and the little girl at a street corner selling mimosa. She was barefoot and her legs were bronzed by the sun.

A grey sports car with chromium-plated fittings slid past towards the sea with three girls in beach-pyjamas and, at the wheel, a young Romeo with a little moustache.

It was much too like a holiday. That had been the trouble from the start. It had been the same the evening before in Cannes – the harbour at sunset, and the *Ardena*, and its owner swanking in front of his two girls whose dresses showed off their supple bodies.

Maigret was dressed in black, exactly as he always was in Paris, with a bowler which was altogether out of place down here.

There was a poster with blue letters in front of him, saying:

> *Casino de Juan-les-Pins.*
> *Grand gala de la pluie d'or.*

Fireworks! Golden rain! ... And the lump of ice slowly melted in his second milky-green Pernod.

Holidays! To lean over the side of a green or orange boat, and stare at the bottom, mottled by the rays of sunshine that were broken by the ripples above ... To lie down under a pine tree and listen to the buzzing of a bumble-bee ... To ...

Anyhow, not to bother about a man he hadn't known from Adam a week before, who had had the misfortune to get a knife stuck in his back!

Nor to bother about those two women of *Liberty Bar* whose faces haunted him, though he hadn't known them twenty-four hours. What were they to him?

Inspector of the *P.J.*! A rotten job, and that's all there was to say about it! A smell of melting tar drifted over the Place Macé. Boutigues had bought another red carnation and was sticking it into his buttonhole.

And William Brown ... He was buried, wasn't he? What more could he want? Why should Maigret bother about him any longer? *He'd* never owned one of the biggest yachts in Europe. *He* hadn't got mixed up with those two Martinis – the fearsome old hag and her fifth-rate vamp of a daughter. *He* hadn't sunk waist-deep in the slovenly forgetfulness of *Liberty Bar*.

Little puffs of warm air caressed his cheeks. More holiday-makers passed. Everybody seemed to be on holiday. Even Boutigues, who couldn't keep silent and who now murmured:

'Anyhow, I'm very glad they didn't leave me the responsibility of ...'

Maigret stopped looking at the world through his eyelashes and turned towards his companion. He was rather red in the face from the heat and his two Pernods. His eyes looked sleepy, but the effort of a second or two was sufficient to bring them back to normal.

'Exactly!' he said. 'Here! Waiter! How much is that?'

'You leave it to me.'

'Nothing of the kind.' And Maigret threw some money on to the table.

Yes, it was an hour which was long to be remembered. He had actually been tempted to let things slide, as many others would have done, and let the evil of the day suffice ... No, that wasn't quite right. The day had no evil in it; it was simply glorious.

'Are you going? ... Have you got an idea to work on?'

No. His head was much too full of sunshine for that. There was no room in it for the least shred of an idea. But as he did not want to discuss the matter, he merely muttered:

'William Brown was murdered.'

Though to himself he added:

'And what the hell does it matter to anybody?'

Indeed, what did it matter to all these people who basked in the sun like lizards during the day and then went to the *gala de la pluie d'or* in the evening?

'I must do some work,' he said, holding out his hand to Boutigues.

He slowly walked off, then stopped to allow a car to pass – one that might have cost anything up to three hundred thousand francs. It was driven by a girl of eighteen who looked straight in front of her with a frown.

'Brown was murdered.' He kept on repeating the words over and over again.

He was beginning to realize that the lure of the South was not to be snorted at. His back was turned to the *Café Glacier*, and to make sure of no backsliding he started giving himself orders just as if he was speaking to a subordinate:

'Find out what Brown was doing between two and ten to five last Friday.'

For that he'd have to go to Cannes, and for that he'd have to take the bus.

So there he stood under a lamp-post waiting for it, his hands in his pockets, his pipe between his teeth, and a look on his face that was none too agreeable.

CHAPTER VI

A Round of Hotels

AT Cannes, Maigret plodded on for hours doing the dreary job that was generally given to an underling. But he needed to act, or at least to create some illusion of action.

At the *Police des Mœurs* he learned that Sylvie was on the register and was well known.

'I've never had any bother with her,' said the sergeant. 'She behaves herself, and comes up pretty regularly for inspection.'

'And *Liberty Bar*?'

'So you've heard of it? A funny place that kept us guessing a long time, and keeps a lot of people guessing still. So much so that hardly a month passes but what we get an anonymous letter about it ... At first we thought La Grosse Jaja might be trading in drugs. We kept her under observation, and I can assure you there's nothing of that kind ... Then people have hinted that it was a haunt of perverts ...'

'I know that's not the case,' said Maigret.

'No, it's really quite harmless. Old Mother Jaja has an irresistible attraction for a certain type: elderly men who no longer care for anything but simply to sit and tipple with her. Apart from the bar, she has a small pension, as her husband died accidentally.'

'I know.'

In another department Maigret inquired about Joseph.

'We keep an eye on him because he's always at the races. But nothing has ever been brought up against him.'

So it went on: results nil all along the line. As Maigret strode through the town, his hands in his pockets, his look of obstinate ill-humour became more and more accentuated.

He started on the big hotels, examining the registers. He stopped to have lunch in a restaurant near the station, and then went on again. By three o'clock he was reasonably sure that Harry Brown had not spent the previous Thursday night in Cannes, nor that of Friday either.

It was preposterous – simply being busy for the sake of being busy.

'Harry Brown could just as well have driven over from Marseilles for the day. Why should he spend a night in Cannes?'

Maigret returned to the *Police des Mœurs* and borrowed the photograph they had of Sylvie. He already had one of William Brown, the one he'd taken from the villa.

Another round of hotels, this time of quite a different order. Little hotels, particularly those round the harbour, where you could take a room, not only for the night, but by the hour.

The proprietors of these places knew at a glance that he belonged to the police. It was their business to, for they feared the police more than anything.

'Wait a moment, will you? I'll ask the chambermaid.'

There would be hurried footfalls on dark staircases. This was a world where you didn't have to probe very far to find the seamy side of life.

'That big man? No, but I don't think I've ever seen him here.'

It was the photograph of William Brown that Maigret showed first, after which he would produce Sylvie's.

Hers was recognized almost every time.

'Yes, she's been here, though we haven't seen her lately.'

'Did she come at night?'

'Oh, no! Not particularly. If she comes with somebody it's always *pour un moment*.'

Hôtel Bellevue . . . *Hôtel du Port* . . . *Hôtel Bristol* . . . *Hôtel d'Auvergne* . . .

And any amount more, most of them in little streets. Discreet places too, most of them, that you'd hardly think were hotels at all if it wasn't for the open corridor at whose entrance was a marble plaque inscribed: *Eau courante. Prix modérés.*

Sometimes Maigret would strike a rather better-class place with a carpet on the stairs . . . In others he'd meet a furtive couple in the passage who would look the other way.

And again and again as he went to and fro he'd find himself facing the harbour where some six-metre racing yachts had been hauled up on the slips. Sailors were painting them with careful brushwork, while little groups of idlers stood watching them.

In Paris they had talked about 'tactful handling', but it didn't look as though tact would be needed after all. If things went on like this there wouldn't be anything to be tactful about.

He smoked pipe after pipe, filling a fresh one before the other had gone. He always carried two or three about with him. He had made a practice of it ever since the Radek case, during which he'd found himself without a pipe just when he was most in need of one.

He was fed up with Cannes, furious with a woman who persisted in trying to sell him some winkles, and then with a little barefoot boy who got in his way and nearly tripped him up. And when Maigret swore at him, the little devil laughed in his face.

*

'Do you know this man?'

For the twentieth time he held out William Brown's photograph.

'I don't recognize him. There's so many that come and go.'

'And this woman?'

'Sylvie? . . . She's upstairs.'

'Alone?'

The landlord shrugged his shoulders, and called out:

'Albert! . . . Come down a moment, will you?'

The *valet de chambre* came down. He was a grimy individual, and he looked sideways at the inspector.

'Is Sylvie still upstairs?'

'In No. 7.'

'Have they ordered drinks?'

'Nothing at all.'

'Then they won't be long,' said the landlord to Maigret. 'If you want to speak to her, you've only to wait . . .'

It was called the *Hôtel Beauséjour*, and was in a street running parallel to the harbour, just opposite a baker's.

Did Maigret want to see Sylvie again? Had he anything to ask her if he did?

He really didn't know himself. He was tired. But by dint of plodding along unwillingly there was something determined and even menacing in his attitude. You might have thought he was hot on the trail.

Anyhow he wasn't going to wait in front of the hotel, for the baker's wife opposite was looking at him through the shop-window. A sarcastic look.

Was Sylvie in such demand that people queued up for her favours? That was it! And it made Maigret boil with rage to think he was being taken for one of her clients.

He strolled to the next corner, intending to walk round the block to fill in the time. When he got to the quay, he turned to study a taxi that was drawn up by the kerb, and whose driver was pacing up and down on the pavement.

Something had attracted his attention, though he couldn't tell what. He looked away, but his eyes were drawn back to it. As a matter of fact, it was not the taxi itself but the driver that somehow recalled . . . Yes! He'd got it! Recalled the funeral that morning . . .

'You come from Antibes, don't you?'

'From Juan-les-Pins.'

'And you followed a funeral this morning at Antibes?'

'Yes. Why?'

'Who's your fare? The same chap?'

The driver looked the inspector over from head to foot, without knowing what to answer.

'What do you want to know for?'

'Police! . . . Come on! Out with it.'

'Yes. It's the same one. He's hired me by the day. Since lunch-time yesterday.'

'Where's he now?'

'I don't know . . . He went off that way.'

The driver pointed to a street, then suddenly turned to Maigret, asking anxiously:

'Look here! You're not going to arrest him before he pays the bill?'

For a good minute Maigret stood stock still, forgetting to smoke, staring at the taxi's clumsy old hood. Then suddenly he remembered the couple in the hotel, and hurried back there fearing they might have gone.

The baker's wife saw him coming, and called her husband. A moment later a white floury face joined hers at the window.

No matter! Maigret no longer cared. His thoughts were focused on Room No. 7. Looking up at the hotel, he wondered which window belonged to it.

He was trying not to crow too soon. What right had he to suppose? . . .

And yet . . . No, it couldn't be a coincidence. On the contrary, it was the first time that two links had actually come together to make the beginning of a chain . . .

Sylvie and Harry Brown! A clandestine meeting in a low hotel!

Five times he walked past the *Hôtel Beauséjour* to the corner of the little street leading to the quay. Five times he saw the taxi standing in the same place. As for the driver, he had advanced to the corner, to be able to see what happened.

At last someone opened the glass-panelled door in the passage, and the next moment Sylvie stepped briskly into the street, almost bumping into Maigret.

'*Bonjour!*' he said.

She stopped dead. He had never seen her so pale, and when she opened her mouth she was unable to utter a sound.

'Your friend's dressing?'

She looked wildly about her, and even dropped her bag. When Maigret picked it up she snatched it out of his hand as if terrified he would open it.

'One moment, please.'

'Excuse me ... Someone's expecting me ... Do you mind if we walk? ...'

'That's just what I don't want to do, particularly in that direction.'

She was more touching than pretty. Her huge eyes seemed to swallow up the rest of her face. In an agony of dismay, she almost panted with fear.

'What do you want with me?'

She looked as though she might take to her heels. To prevent anything of the kind, Maigret took her hand and held it, in such a way that the bakers over the way could easily have taken it for an affectionate gesture.

'Is Harry still there?'

'I don't understand ...'

'Very well. We'll wait for him together ... And mind what you're about! No nonsense! ... And leave that bag to me ...'

Maigret took it out of her hand. Through the silky material he could feel something which suggested a wad of bank-notes.

'Come on now! We don't want a scene. There are people watching.'

'Please ... please!'

'No.'

And then, as there were people passing, he added in a whisper:

'Any more fuss and I'll put you in handcuffs.'

She looked at him with eyes whose pupils were dilated

with fright, and then, discouraged or tamed, she hung her head. .

'Harry's in no hurry to come down.'

She made no attempt to persuade him he was wrong. She said nothing.

'Did you know him before?'

They were standing right in the sun. Sylvie's face was moist with sweat.

She appeared to be groping desperately for an inspiration. Was there no means of escape?

'Listen . . .'

'I'm listening.'

But no. She changed her mind and said nothing, merely biting her lip viciously.

'Is Joseph waiting for you somewhere?'

'Joseph?'

The name seemed to unnerve her still further. And all at once they heard steps on the stairs of the hotel. Sylvie trembled. She dared not look down the dark corridor of the *Hôtel Beauséjour*.

The steps approached, changing their note as they advanced along the tiled passage. The glass-panelled door opened, then quickly closed again. Silence.

They could not see Harry Brown in the shadow inside, but surely he had seen them. His hesitation was brief, however. The door opened a second time and he emerged into the sunshine. No hang-dog looks for Harry Brown! Straight as a poker, without the least sign of misgiving, he walked past Maigret with a casual nod of recognition.

The latter was still holding Sylvie's unresisting hand. Harry Brown strode off towards his taxi. To catch him Maigret would have had to let her go. Two such different birds made rather an awkward handful. And with the baker and his wife looking on!

Abandoning the wool-merchant, he hurried off in another direction, dragging Sylvie along.

'Come along.'

'Are you arresting me?'

'Don't bother about that.'

He had to telephone at once, but nothing would induce him to let go of Sylvie for a second. There were some cafés in the neighbourhood. He entered the first he came to and dragged her with him right into the telephone-box.

A moment or two later he was speaking to Boutigues.

'Run as quick as you can to the *Hôtel Provençal*. Ask for Harry Brown and request him politely but firmly not to leave Antibes until I've seen him. If necessary, *stop him going.*'

Sylvie listened limply. There was no fight left in her, no spark of revolt.

'What would you like?' he asked, sitting her down at a table.

'It's all the same to me.'

She was carrying her bag now, but Maigret kept an eye on it all the time. The waiter looked at them inquisitively, sensing something unusual. A little girl was going from table to table selling violets. Maigret took the bunch she offered and presented it to Sylvie. He groped in his pockets for some money, his face clouding. Suddenly, when it was least expected, he seized Sylvie's bag, saying:

'You don't mind, do you? . . . I've no small change . . .'

It was done so quickly and so naturally that she had no time to protest. Her fingers clenched slightly, but not till the bag was already out of her grasp.

The little girl waited gravely, selecting another bunch from her basket, while Maigret under a fat bundle of thousand-franc notes was looking for some small coins.

'And now let's go,' he said, standing up.

He was rather nervy himself and was longing to be out of range of staring eyes.

'Supposing we paid a call on that kind Mother Jaja . . .?'

Sylvie followed obediently. She was beaten. And as they

walked along they looked like any other couple, except that the gentleman was carrying the lady's bag.

*

'You go in first.'

She went down the two steps into the bar, and then walked over to the other door. Through its muslin curtain a man's back was visible as he jumped abruptly from his seat.

It was Yan the Swedish steward, who blushed to the roots of his hair as Maigret followed Sylvie into Jaja's kitchen.

'You again?... Look, my friend, I'd be grateful if you'd kindly clear out.'

Jaja couldn't make out what was happening, though she could see from Sylvie's face that something was up. She asked for nothing better than to be rid of the Swede.

'Come tomorrow, Yan, will you?'

'I don't know.'

Cap in hand he did not know how to take his leave, disconcerted as he was by the inspector's heavy stare.

'Yes,' said the latter, 'that's all right ... Good-bye.' And he opened the door for the steward and shut it again behind him.

He gave a sharp turn to the key in the lock, then turning to Sylvie he said:

'You can take your hat off.'

In a timid voice Jaja ventured:

'So you met?...'

'Exactly! We met.'

The air was so charged with thunder that she didn't even dare offer him a drink. To regain her composure she picked a newspaper up from the floor and folded it. Then she went to the stove and looked at something that was stewing.

Maigret filled his pipe slowly and carefully. He too went up to the stove, rolled a bit of newspaper into a spill, and lit it from the fire.

Sylvie remained standing at the table. She had taken off her hat and put it down in front of her.

Then Maigret sat down, opened her bag, and started counting out the bank-notes, laying them one after the other in a pile among the dirty glasses on the table.

'. . . eighteen . . . nineteen . . . twenty,' he counted. 'Twenty thousand francs.'

At the sound of his counting, Jaja had spun round. She looked wildly at the notes, then at Sylvie, then at the inspector. She racked her brains to understand.

'What does it mean?'

'Oh, nothing extraordinary,' growled Maigret. 'Only Sylvie caught a bigger fish than usual today. That's all. And what do you think his name was? . . . Harry Brown!'

He was making himself quite at home, with his elbows on the table, his pipe in his mouth, his bowler shoved on to the back of his head.

'Twenty thousand francs for *un petit moment* as they'd say at the *Hôtel Beauséjour*.'

To cover her confusion, Jaja wiped her podgy hands on her apron. She couldn't find a word to say. She was dumbfounded.

Deathly pale, her features drawn, Sylvie looked at neither of them. She gazed into vacancy, expecting the worst and waiting for the next blow to fall.

'You can sit down,' said Maigret.

She sat down.

'And you too, Jaja . . . But wait a moment . . . Bring some clean glasses.'

Sylvie was sitting in the same place as the day before. She looked different now.

Jaja put a bottle of wine and glasses on the table and sat down on the edge of her chair.

'And now, my children,' said Maigret quietly, 'you can fire away.'

The smoke of his pipe drifted slowly towards the little blue window – for the sun no longer reached it. Jaja looked at Sylvie, who for her part, whether from obstinacy or because her thoughts were far away, neither looked at anything nor said anything.

'I'm waiting.'

But it was no good. He could have repeated it a hundred times: he could have waited ten years. It was only Jaja, her chin sinking into her bosom, who sighed:

'*Mon Dieu!* . . . I'd never have thought . . .'

As for Maigret, he could hardly contain himself. He got up and started pacing up and down.

'She'll have to cough it up sooner or later,' he muttered.

But she just sat there lifeless, staring . . . He was on the verge of losing his temper. Twice, three times he passed close to her.

'There's plenty of time . . . But all the same . . .'

The fourth time he could stand it no longer. It was automatic. His hand seized the girl's shoulder, without realizing the force of his grip.

She lifted up an arm as though to ward off a blow, like a little girl who fears a beating.

'Well?'

She broke down, he hurt her so. Bursting into sobs, she cried out:

'You brute! . . . You dirty brute! . . . I'll tell you nothing . . . nothing! . . . Absolutely nothing! . . .'

Jaja was too miserable for words. Maigret, frowning, sank on to a chair. And Sylvie went on crying, without hiding her face or wiping away her tears, but she was crying from rage more than from pain.

The door of the bar opened and a customer came in, an event which hardly happened once a day. He leaned an elbow on the counter and began fiddling with the slot-machine.

CHAPTER VII

William's Will

WITH a scowl, Maigret rose from his chair. He was anxious to intercept any possible manoeuvre of the two women. Supposing, for intance, the customer was really an emissary of Joseph's . . . ? The idea decided him at once, and he quickly unlocked the door and went into the bar to serve the fellow himself.

'What do you want?'

The other was so taken aback that, in spite of his bad temper, the inspector nearly laughed aloud. He was a seedy wretch, a dull, greying, middle-aged man, who had no doubt slunk round to *Liberty Bar* by back streets with erotic visions in his mind. But instead of Jaja or Sylvie it was Maigret at his gruffest who came to the counter.

'*Un bock*,' he stammered, ordering the smallest measure of beer.

Through the muslin curtains the inspector could see the two women now sitting side by side. Jaja was asking questions, Sylvie answering dully.

'There isn't any beer.'

That is to say, Maigret couldn't see any and didn't trouble to look farther.

'Then give me something else . . . Anything you like . . . Some port . . .'

Maigret picked up a bottle at random and poured some of its contents into the first glass that came to hand. The other took a gulp and then hastened to say:

'How much is it?'

'Two francs.'

Maigret glanced from time to time into the room behind, where Jaja had resumed her seat, and at the bar opposite, where he could hardly make out the figures inside.

His customer slouched off, bewildered, while Maigret returned to the other room, sitting down astride his chair.

Jaja's attitude was slightly changed. She had been anxious before chiefly because she couldn't guess what the trouble was. Now her anxieties had taken shape. She looked thoughtfully at Sylvie – with pity certainly – but also with a touch of reproach. A look which seemed to say:

'You've done a fine day's work, getting yourself into a mess like that! And it's not going to be so easy to get out of it.'

Out loud she ventured cautiously:

'You know, Inspector, men are strange creatures . . .'

But the words lacked conviction. She was conscious of it herself. Sylvie too, who shrugged her shoulders. Nevertheless Jaja laboured on:

'He saw her this morning at the funeral and took a fancy to her . . . And being as rich as all that . . .'

Maigret sighed, filled another pipe, and gazed gloomily out of the window. An atmosphere of mournfulness filled the room. Jaja decided to hold her tongue for fear of making matters worse. Sylvie was no longer crying. Motionless, she waited for whatever was to come.

Only the alarm-clock went busily on with the day's work, pushing over its pasty face its black hands that seemed too heavy for it.

Tick tack, tick tack, tick tack . . .

At times the sound seemed to fill the place, almost unbearably loud. A white cat in the back yard came and sat down outside the window.

Tick tack, tick tack, tick tack . . .

Jaja wasn't built to stand tense situations. She got up and fetched a bottle of spirits from the kitchen cupboard. Pouring out three glasses, just as if nothing was the matter, she pushed one over to Maigret without a word, and another to Sylvie.

The twenty thousand francs still lay on the table beside Sylvie's open bag.

Tick tack, tick tack . . .

It lasted a whole hour and a half. An hour and a half of silence, except for the ticking and the tacking and an occasional sigh from Jaja, who drank on, her eyes getting brighter and brighter.

Sometimes the noise of children playing in the streets; now and again the insistent bell of a distant tram; and once the door of the bar opened and an Arab stuck his head in, calling out:

'Monkey-nuts!'

He waited a moment, but, as there was no response, he shut the door again and moved on.

It had gone six before the door opened again. This time there was a faint stir in the kitchen which told Maigret that it was what they were expecting. Jaja made a move, but a look from him was enough to keep her in her place. Sylvie, assuming indifference, looked into the farthest corner of the room.

The kitchen door opened and Joseph came in. The first thing he saw was Maigret's back – then the table, the glasses, the bottles, the open bag, the money.

The inspector slowly turned round, and the newcomer, brought to a standstill, could only find one word to utter: the famous *mot de Cambronne*, the five-letter word that is spelt with four letters in English!

*

'Shut the door . . . And sit down . . .'

The waiter shut the door but remained standing. He frowned and looked thoroughly put out, but did not lose his presence of mind. On the contrary, he mustered all he had – which was plenty.

He went up to Jaja and kissed her on the forehead.

'*Bonjour.*'

Then he did the same to Sylvie, who did not even raise her head.

'What's the matter?'

From that moment Maigret realized that he'd got hold of the sticky end. But, as always happened in such cases, he gripped it all the tighter.

'Where have you come from?'

'Guess,' answered Joseph, taking out his pocket-book and producing a *carte d'identité* such as all foreign residents in France are provided with.

'I'd left it rather late . . . I've been to the Préfecture to get it renewed.'

The date that was stamped on the outside confirmed his story. Opening it, Maigret read: *Joseph Ambrosini*; *born at Milan*; *profession, waiter.*

'You haven't been to see Harry Brown?'

'Me?'

'And you didn't see him on the Thursday or Friday of last week?'

Joseph looked at him with a smile, as much as to say:

'What on earth are you babbling about?'

'Look here, Ambrosini! I suppose you'll admit being Sylvie's lover?'

'It depends what you mean by that. I won't say I've never . . .'

'Come on, come on! You're what is politely called her protector . . .'

Poor Jaja! She had never been so unhappy in her life. She had drunk so much she couldn't see quite straight. Now and again she opened her mouth to put in a word of reconciliation. It was obvious what she wanted to say.

'Now, now, children! Why don't you shake hands and be friends? Life's too short to waste it arguing. Let's have a drink together and forget all about it.'

As for Joseph, in spite of what they'd told Maigret about him, this didn't look as though it was his first tussle with the police. He never dropped his guard. He kept his head perfectly and never tried to be too clever.

'You have been misinformed,' was all he answered.

'So you've no idea where those twenty thousand francs came from?'

'I take it Sylvie earned them ... She's pretty enough for ...'

'That'll do!'

Maigret was on his feet again, pacing up and down the room. Sylvie looked at her feet, but Joseph was ready to look anybody in the face.

'You'll have a drop of this anyhow,' said Jaja to him, taking the opportunity of filling her own glass.

It took Maigret quite a time to make up his mind. He stood facing the alarm-clock, whose hands were now at a quarter past six. When he turned round it was to say:

'The two of you can come with me. I arrest you both.'

Ambrosini did not wince. With the merest touch of sarcasm he muttered:

'Very good.'

The inspector put the bank-notes in his pocket. Then, after handing Sylvie her hat and bag, he turned to Joseph.

'Shall I use handcuffs? Or will you give me your word you won't ...?'

'All right. We'll keep you company.'

Sobbing, Jaja threw her arms round Sylvie, and the latter had a job to free herself. In fact, Maigret and his two prisoners had their work cut out to prevent her following them to the police station.

Lamps were being lit. Once more, Cannes in the light of the evening. They passed near the street of the *Hôtel Beauséjour*, but Joseph didn't so much as glance at it.

At the police station night duty had begun, and the men who had been relieved were strolling off. The sergeant bustled about and gave Maigret the necessary papers to sign.

'Lock them up separately ... I'll probably be coming to see them tomorrow.'

Sylvie had sat down on a bench. Joseph started rolling a cigarette, but was not allowed to finish. Maigret moved off without a word to them. At the door he turned to look at Sylvie. She was staring at the ground, however, and made no response. Finally, with a shrug of the shoulders, he walked out, muttering:

'Never mind!'

*

Having stowed himself away in a corner of the bus, he never noticed that it filled up to overflowing, and that when they drove off an old lady was standing almost next to him. Looking out of the window, he watched the head-lamps of the passing cars, and, quite oblivious of its being forbidden, puffed away furiously at his pipe, until the old lady, bending forward, said:

'*Pardon, monsieur . . .*'

The words brought him back to earth. He sprang to his feet, did not know where to knock his pipe out, and presented such a picture of discomfiture that a young couple behind him burst out laughing.

At half past seven he pushed his way through the revolving doors of the *Provençal*, to find Boutigues talking to the manager from one of the easy-chairs of the lounge.

'Well?'

'He's upstairs,' answered Boutigués, who looked worried.

'You told him what I said?'

'Yes. But he didn't seem surprised at all. I was expecting him to make a row.'

The manager was waiting for an opportunity to put a word in; as soon as he opened his mouth, however, Maigret made for the lift.

'Shall I wait for you?'

'If you like.'

He was only too familiar with the state of mind he had been in for the last few hours. It made him furious. It always did, though fury did not help matters at all.

That confused sensation that you're floundering, that everything's going wrong – he'd had it ever since Joseph had said so glibly:

'What's the matter?'

No. Longer than that. He had shut his eyes to it, or tried to, but he'd really had it ever since Harry Brown had walked off with such self-assurance from the *Hôtel Beauséiour*. But it hadn't stopped him floundering on.

That's how it always was. If he felt he was getting in a mess, he was so determined to prove himself right that he simply waded in all the deeper.

The lift carried him up in a slither of well-greased steel, while Maigret savagely repeated his instructions:

'. . . a case for tactful handling!'

That's what he'd been sent to Antibes for. So that there should be no awkward revelations and nobody rubbed up the wrong way.

At other times he would have entered Harry Brown's suite with his pipe in his pocket. This time he lit it deliberately. He knocked, and without waiting, burst straight in.

The scene he came upon was practically identical with the one the day before. Harry Brown, perfectly groomed, was pacing up and down giving orders to his secretary, then with a leisurely movement picking up the telephone receiver:

'Excuse me a moment, will you?' he said to Maigret.

No trace of anxiety. Was it possible to be more imperturbable than that? It's true Maigret had seen him a bit rattled the evening before. But it must have been a very rare occurrence in the life of this Australian wool-merchant. Certainly that morning he had been marvellous. He had followed his father's coffin, in company with four impossible women, without turning a hair. And that afternoon: following Sylvie out of a disreputable hotel! Not so easy to get away with that! Yet, after only a moment's hesitation, he had carried it off superbly.

He was dictating now. Another of those cablegrams. Without pausing, he picked up a box of cigars and placed it on a little table by Maigret's side. Then he rang a bell.

'That's all, James. You can take the telephone into the next room.'

And when the waiter appeared:

'A whisky, please.'

How much of it was real? How much of it acting?

'A matter of education,' thought Maigret. 'He must have gone to Oxford or Cambridge.'

That was an old grudge of his! The grudge of a pupil of the *Lycée Stanislas*. A grudge, however, that was not unmixed with admiration.

'You can take the typewriter into the next room too, Miss Bingham.'

But no. Seeing her encumbered with a fat note-book and a pencil, he picked the thing up himself and carried it for her.

He said nothing till the waiter had poured Maigret out a glass of whisky and left the room. Then he locked the door, and coming over to Maigret he took out his pocket-book, from which he produced a stamped document. After glancing at it, he handed it to the inspector.

'Read this. You understand English?'

'No more than a few words.'

'That's what I bought for twenty thousand francs at the *Hôtel Beauséjour* this afternoon.'

He sat down. Despite his self-possession he must surely have felt easier now that his visit to Sylvie was presented in a different light.

'I must first of all explain a few things to you. You don't know Australia, do you? It's a pity . . . My father before his marriage owned a very large estate. Enormous. Big as one of the Departments of France. When she married him my mother brought with her an estate that was not much smaller, and with the union of the two properties my father became the biggest sheep-breeder of the country.'

Harry Brown spoke slowly, taking pains to make himself clear, yet without wasting words.

'Are you a Protestant?' asked Maigret.

'We all are, on both sides of the family.'

He was going on, but Maigret interrupted him:

'Your father was not educated in Europe, was he?'

'No. It wasn't done so much in those days . . . He never came here till after his marriage. Several years after, and he already had three children.'

In his mind's eye, Maigret reconstructed the whole situation. Perhaps it wasn't correct in every detail, but he didn't care. He felt sure he was right in the essentials.

He imagined a huge, severely built house, standing in the middle of a vast estate, and inhabited by grave people, looking like Presbyterian ministers.

William Brown succeeds his father, marries, has children, and beyond that thinks only of breeding sheep and selling wool . . .

'There was a lawsuit on, here in France,' went on Harry. 'And he came over to see it through.'

'He came alone?'

'Alone.'

How obvious it was. Paris and the Riviera. London and Berlin. William Brown suddenly waking up to the fact that, with his colossal fortune, he could cut a brilliant figure in a more brilliant world than he had ever dreamt of.

'And he never went back?' asked Maigret with a sigh.

'No. Proceedings dragged on . . .'

Why indeed should he hasten them? Wasn't he being shown round, shown everything and introduced to every-body? High life. Low life too. Women . . .

'For two years he kept putting off his return.'

'Who looked after things out there?'

'Everything was going to pieces till at last my mother took things in hand. Her brother came and helped her. She felt obliged to step in, as she received letters telling her . . .'

It was enough. More than enough. Maigret could see it only too clearly. Brown, who had only known a world of sheep and Presbyterian ministers, had kicked over the traces and plunged into the wildest of orgies.

He put off his return, then put it off again. He let the lawsuit drag on, and when it did finish, found other excuses to stay.

He had bought a yacht and entertained guests by the dozen. Smart people, rich people, people who could afford to laugh at every social convention.

'So your mother and your uncle had him put under *conseil judiciaire* ?'

'Well, that's what you do in France. Things are a bit different with us. Put it this way: that we took the business out of his hands.'

How did they do it? That wasn't quite so clear. Was it done legally or illegally? Had they made him out insane? Anyhow, that didn't alter the fact that one fine day William Brown must have woken up at Nice or Monte Carlo to find that he was no longer a rich Australian wool-magnate, but a poor relation living on an allowance.

'For a long time he lived on credit, and we paid his debts.'

'And then you stopped paying?'

'We never left him destitute. But the more we paid the more he spent, and there was nothing for it but to cut him right down to five thousand francs a month.'

Maigret had been seeing it all so clearly, but now he felt that there was something unspoken which he could not grasp. And suddenly he asked:

'Apart from the allowance you made your father, did you have any contact with him?'

'Not directly.'

'Indirectly?'

'Any communication was sent through the bank that paid the money.'

'A bank in Cannes?'

'Yes.'

'And did you communicate with him just before his death?'

It was in vain that the inspector watched the Australian for any signs of nervousness. With perfect composure, Harry answered:

'The bank manager saw him on our behalf.'

'Last time he drew his money?'

'Yes . . . Allow me to explain . . . The situation between my father and the family was never really cleared up. He was still fighting for what he claimed were his rights. And, pending a final settlement, we have been under an injunction not to dispose of any of the property. It has tied our hands and more than once prevented us doing some very good business.'

'So there's a lawsuit still on?'

'Yes. It's been going on these last ten years.'

'There are lawyers out there defending your father's interests?'

'Shady lawyers.'

'Of course! And it's been costing a lot of money?'

'A lot. What with solicitors and barristers we've been employing five lawyers ever since I can remember.'

'And all the family was against him?'

'All, without exception.'

'And what were you offering him to fade away and leave you in peace?'

'Ten thousand pounds.'

'Would he have been better off with that than with his allowance?'

'Decidedly. Particularly if he'd bought an annuity.'

'Then why did he refuse?'

'To annoy us. It had become an obsession with him. He was absolutely determined not to leave us in peace.'

'I see . . . He refused . . .'

'Not only that. He also told the bank manager that he had taken steps to ensure our troubles continuing if he died.'

'What troubles?'

'The lawsuit. It's not so much the cost: it's been doing us a lot of harm.'

It surely would. To win their case they would have to sling mud at William Brown – still worse, at his memory – and it would stick to all of them. Mud. There was plenty of it. *Liberty Bar*, Jaja, Sylvie in her dressing-gown which didn't half serve its purpose . . . Then the villa at Antibes – the two women he'd take shopping, with his night-shirt showing at the neck.

And the Browns didn't like mud. No doubt about that. One had only to look at Harry, capable, methodical, virtuous Harry, whose hair was so beautifully smoothed down, and whose politeness was so perfect and just sufficiently aloof . . .

To annoy them!

Yes, that was William all over. The enemy of order and respectability. A man who could go for days without washing. And to think he'd started life just like his son Harry!

They had disowned him, taken his goods and chattels, cast him out.

But he went on fighting. He must have known he could never get the better of them. There was, however, one thing he could do . . .

Annoy them!

He could annoy his wife and her precious brother and his three sons who no longer looked upon him as a father. It was the one satisfaction left him. Perhaps the one thing that was worth taking a bit of trouble over – to get a little of his own back on all those good people who went on working, making money, and more money . . .

'If he died intestate there would be nobody to take up his claims. The lawsuit would die a natural death, and with it all the scandal and tittle-tattle that some people seem to enjoy . . .'

'Of course.'

'So he didn't die intestate. He had made a will. And who do you think were his heirs? . . . Four women.'

Maigret could hardly keep a straight face at the thought of those four women – Madame Martini, Gina, Jaja, Sylvie – stepping off a liner at Sydney or Melbourne to claim each of them a quarter of the Brown estates.

'And that will,' went on Harry, 'is the document you're holding in your hand.'

It was long. Maigret could not read it, but it looked authentic enough, and he spotted the name of the notary who had drafted it.

'That's what my father was referring to when he said he had "taken steps".'

'Did you know the terms of the will?'

'Until today I knew nothing about it. Soon after I got back from the funeral, a man asked to see me . . .'

'Was his name Joseph?'

'He didn't say. He looked like a waiter. He showed me a copy of the will and said that I could buy the original for twenty thousand francs if I went to a certain hotel in Cannes . . . People of his sort don't lie about such things.'

A frown had gathered on Maigret's face.

'Do you mean to tell me you have been conspiring to destroy a will?'

The accusation did not appear to trouble Harry in the slightest.

'I know what I'm doing,' he answered calmly. 'And I think I know how to deal with women of that kind.'

He stood up, and catching sight of Maigret's full glass said:

'You're not drinking?'

'No, thank you.'

'Any court of justice would understand that . . .'

'That the Brown family must win in the end!'

What possessed Maigret to say a thing like that? Had he completely lost his head?

But the Australian showed no sign of annoyance. He moved towards the door through which came the clicking of the typewriter.

'The will is not destroyed,' he said quietly. 'It's in your possession. Do as you think fit. I shall be staying here until . . .'

By this time he had opened the door, and his secretary dashed forward with the telephone.

'Here's London, sir. They're asking . . .'

Harry took the receiver and plunged into conversation with the London office.

Maigret thought it a suitable moment to go. He stuffed the will into his pocket and made his way to the lift, only to find it was not working. Finally, as he went downstairs, he grunted:

'A case for tactful handling!'

In the lounge Boutigues and the manager were drinking port from handsomely cut glasses, with the bottle standing between them.

CHAPTER VIII

The Four Legatees

BOUTIGUES bounced along by Maigret's side, and they hadn't taken twenty steps before he announced:

'I've made a discovery. The manager there – has to keep an eye on another hotel that belongs to the same company. The *Hôtel du Cap* at Cap Ferrat.'

They were leaving the *Provençal* behind them. In the moonlight the sea before them was nothing but an enormous, lifeless pool of ink.

West of them the lights of Cannes. East of them those of Nice. And over the latter Boutigues pointed towards the darkness.

'You know Cap Ferrat? . . . Between Nice and Monte Carlo . . .'

Maigret knew. By this time he had a pretty good idea of the French Riviera, that long, hardly interrupted esplanade called the Côte d'Azur which starts at Cannes and finishes at Mentone.

An esplanade forty miles long, with its villas, great and small, its luxury hotels, and here and there a casino. The sea, so famous for its blueness . . . The mountains behind . . . A land fulfilling every promise – orange trees, mimosas, sunshine, palm trees and cactuses, tennis, golf, *salons de thé*, and American bars . . .

'And the discovery?'

'Nothing less than that Harry Brown has a mistress on the Riviera. At Cap Ferrat. The manager knows her by sight. She's a woman about thirty, either a widow or divorced. A most quiet, respectable sort of person. He has taken a villa for her . . .'

Was Maigret listening? Sulkily he stared round him at the spread of sea and mountains. Boutigues went on:

'He goes to see her about once a month. And it's the greatest joke at the *Hôtel du Cap*, as he takes absurd precautions to hide what everybody knows. When he sleeps out, he sneaks back into the hotel by the servants' entrance.'

'How funny!' said Maigret, but with so little sign of being amused that Boutigues was quite crestfallen.

'Are you going to have him watched?'

'No . . . Yes . . . Perhaps . . .'

'Will you go and see his lady friend at Cap Ferrat?'

Maigret hadn't the faintest idea whether he would or not. He couldn't think of half a dozen things at once, and for the moment he wasn't thinking of Harry Brown, but of his father William. When they arrived at the Place Macé, he perfunctorily shook Boutigues' hand and jumped into a taxi.

'Take the road to the Cap d'Antibes. I'll tell you when to stop.'

Then, leaning back in his seat, he sighed and repeated once again:

'William Brown was murdered.'

*

The little garden gate, the gravel path, a ring at the bell. A light switched on inside, steps in the hall – and then the front door opened a few inches.

'Oh, it's you!' said Gina Martini, relieved to see who it was.

She opened the door wide and stood aside to let the inspector pass. A man's voice could be heard in the drawing-room.

'Come in, will you?' said Gina. 'You'll understand . . .'

The man was standing with a note-book and pencil in his hand. Only half of Madame Martini was visible, the other half being in a cupboard.

'Monsieur Petitfils . . . We asked him to come and help us.'

Monsieur Petitfils was thin, with a long mournful moustache and tired eyes.

'He's one of the biggest estate agents round here. We wanted his advice and . . .'

Still the same smell of musk. The two women had discarded their dressing-gowns and slippers. The house was untidier than ever. Were the lights working properly? Certainly the room seemed dingier than before. The old woman emerged from the cupboard and started to explain.

'From the moment I saw *those two* at the funeral I haven't had a moment's peace. In the end we called in Monsieur Petitfils . . . He agrees with me that it would be best to make an inventory.'

'An inventory of what?'

'Of all the things that belong to us, and those that were William's. We've been at it ever since two o'clock this afternoon.'

There were signs of their activity: piles of sheets on the

table, incongruous objects on the floor, more linen in baskets.

Monsieur Petitfils was making a list of everything, putting a cross opposite each item the Martinis claimed. There were plenty of crosses.

There was nothing for Maigret to do here. Useless to look for memories of William Brown in this house that was no longer his. In their sortings and classifyings his women had obliterated all trace of him.

'As for the stove,' said the old woman, 'it's always been mine. I had it twenty years ago in my flat in Toulouse.'

'Can we offer you anything, Inspector?' asked Gina.

On one of the tables stood a dirty glass – the estate agent's. And as he made out his list he smoked one of Brown's cigars.

'No, thank you. I only came to say ...'

What had he come to say?

' ... that I hope tomorrow to lay hands on the murderer.'

'Already?' asked Gina. But they were obviously not interested at all, and her mother hastened to turn the conversation back to more important matters.

'You've seen the son, haven't you? ... What does he say? ... What's he going to do? ... Is he coming here to take possession?'

'I don't know ... I hardly think he is.'

'It would be disgraceful if he did ... People as rich as that ... But they're often the worst when it comes to ...'

She really suffered. The suspense was a torture to her. She looked round at her wretched knick-knacks in an agony of fear at the thought of losing them.

And Maigret had only to put his hand in his pocket, draw out a piece of paper, unfold it, show it to them ...

What would it do to them? Wouldn't it send them delirious with delight? Mightn't it even be too much for the old one and finish her off altogether?

Millions and millions of francs. Millions, admittedly, that were not theirs for the asking. They'd have to do much more than ask. They'd have to go out to Australia and fight for them.

And go they would; fight they would. He could see them! Sailing off to the Antipodes with all their airs and graces!

It wouldn't be Monsieur Petitfils whose advice they would be asking, but solicitors, barristers, K.C.s.

'I won't interrupt you any longer. I'll come again to-morrow.'

His taxi was waiting for him. He got in without giving any address. The driver held open the door and waited.

'Cannes,' said Maigret at last.

*

They were always the same, the thoughts that kept chasing each other through Maigret's musings.

'Brown was murdered.'

'Tactful handling . . .'

That blessed William! If he'd been stabbed in front, one might almost have thought he'd done it himself. Just to annoy them. But it wasn't so easy to stab yourself between the shoulder-blades.

William was no longer a puzzle to Maigret. On the contrary, he had the impression he'd known him always. Australia. William as a boy, well brought up, rather shy, watched over by religious parents. Then William as a young man, coming into the family estates, marrying a girl of his own class, the father of three boys . . .

That Brown was just like this other Brown – the one in the *Provençal*. Sometimes perhaps his thoughts would wander unaccountably and he would be a prey to an obscure restlessness. But when that happened he'd say he was out of sorts and take a cascara.

The same William coming to Europe. The dykes bursting. A flood of pleasures of every description. And he became a familiar figure all along that esplanade that stretches from Cannes to Mentone. A yacht at Cannes . . .

baccarat at Nice . . . and all the rest of it . . . And an intolerable lassitude at the thought of going back 'out there'.

'Next month, perhaps.'

And next month the same words would be repeated.
Till at last they took action 'out there', his wife, his
brother-in-law, his sons, all the big Browns and the little
Browns. They hit back. They seized his property.

Things looked different then, though credit lasted a
while. Then they struck again: they stopped paying his
debts. An allowance of five thousand francs a month.

No more yachting; no more *baccarat* . . . A modest villa
at Antibes . . .

In the matter of women, too, he came down in the
world – right down to Gina Martini.

But, if he'd come down a long way, there was still
farther to go. The villa at Antibes was more or less respectable. He had to go *the whole way*. So he found *Liberty Bar* . . .
Jaja . . . Sylvie . . .

Meanwhile the eternal lawsuit dragged on over there, his
suit against the good, wise, proper Browns. A hopeless
case . . .

Just to annoy them!

And he even made a will – just to annoy them.

It wasn't Maigret's business to decide who was right and
who was wrong. Yet there he was with the will in his
pocket. He had it in his power to . . .

Why should he judge between them? It was the last
thing he wanted. Yet he couldn't help comparing the
two parties: William on the one hand and on the other
that son of his, so proper, so self-controlled, knowing
just how to take care of himself and the good name of
Brown.

Harry disliked disorder in every shape and form. His
thoughts had wandered too, but he had tackled the question
methodically. He had a mistress tucked away in a villa at
Cap Ferrat . . .

'A most quiet, respectable sort of person,' Boutigues

had said. And he always used the staff entrance when he came back to his hotel in the early morning.

Order versus disorder – that was the case that had come up for trial with Maigret on the bench. He had only to produce the will from his pocket to send two women packing – off to Australia. And would the other two allow themselves to be outdone? Wouldn't they pack up and go too?

It was fascinating to think of them, all four perhaps on the same ship. Jaja with her tender feet, her swollen ankles and drooping breasts; Sylvie who couldn't bear to wear anything at home except a dressing-gown loosely floating around her naked body ... And then the other pair. Madame Martini with her cheeks plastered with make-up. Gina leaving a trail of musk down the Suez Canal.

Meanwhile Maigret was being driven along the forty-mile esplanade with the lights of Cannes approaching.

'A case for tactful handling!'

The taxi stopped opposite the *Ambassadors*, the driver asking:

'Where shall I take you?'

'Nowhere. This'll do.'

Maigret got out and paid. The Casino was ablaze with lights. Smart cars were arriving. It was close on nine.

At the same time half a dozen other casinos between Cannes and Mentone would be blazing with lights too, and fifty luxurious cars would be gliding towards them.

When Maigret reached his destination, he saw at a glance that *Liberty Bar* was shut. It would have been pitch-dark inside but for the street lamp which dimly lit up the zinc-covered bar and the slot-machine.

He knocked, and was astonished at the way the sound echoed in the alley. A moment later a door opened behind him, and a man appeared in the entrance of the other bar, asking:

'Is it for Jaja?'

'Yes.'

'Who wants her?'

'I do. Inspector Maigret . . .'

'In that case I've a message for you . . . She'll be back in a few minutes and she asked if you'd mind waiting . . . If you like to wait inside . . .'

'No, thanks.'

He preferred to walk up and down. In the *Vrais Marins* were some customers he didn't like the looks of. A window opened in one of the neighbouring houses, and a woman's voice called out cautiously:

'Is that you, Jean?'

'No.'

And Maigret, pacing up and down the alley, said to himself:

'First of all I must find out who killed William.'

*

Ten o'clock. Jaja had not appeared. Each time he heard steps Maigret started, thinking his watch was at an end. Each time he was disappointed.

His beat was fifty yards of irregular cobble-stones between walls hardly more than six feet apart. Old houses with bulging walls, and windows that were no longer rectangular. The two bars. On the one hand *Aux Vrais Marins*, on the other *Liberty Bar*, dark and lifeless.

Maigret opened the door of the *Vrais Marins*.

'She didn't say where she was going?'

'No. Won't you take something while you're here?'

The customers, who had been told who he was, examined him from head to foot.

'No, thanks.'

He walked to the corner of the alley and stood for a moment at the frontier between the two worlds, the world of normal respectability and the world of disrepute.

Half past ten . . . Eleven . . . Not far from the corner of the alley was the café called *Harry's Bar*, where Maigret had been to telephone that afternoon, dragging Sylvie behind him. He walked over to it and went into the telephone-box.

'Give me the police . . . Hallo! . . . Is that the police? . . . Inspector Maigret speaking . . . Those two birds I brought round to you this afternoon – has anyone been to see them?'

'Yes. A fat woman.'

'Who did she see?'

'The woman first. Then the man . . . We didn't know . . . as you didn't leave any instructions . . .'

'When was it?'

'She came the best part of two hours ago. She brought some cakes and cigarettes.'

Maigret rang off irritably. Then immediately lifted the receiver again. This time he asked for the *Provençal*.

'Hallo! Police . . . Yes, I'm the inspector who called this evening. Will you tell me whether Monsieur Brown has received any visitors?'

'A woman came about twenty minutes ago . . . Fat. Poorly dressed.'

'Where did he see her?'

'She was shown up to his room.'

'Has she gone?'

'She went a moment ago.'

'A common-looking woman, wasn't she? And very fat?'

'That's right.'

'Did she have a taxi?'

'No. She left on foot.'

Maigret rang off, sat down and ordered some *choucroute* and some beer.

So Jaja had seen Sylvie and Joseph. Of course she had. Why hadn't he thought of it before? They had given her some message or other for Harry Brown . . . She'd be coming back by bus, so she couldn't be expected for another half-hour.

He picked up a paper that was lying on the table and read it as he ate. Two lovers had committed suicide at Bandol. The man had a wife somewhere abroad.

'What will you have to follow?'

'Nothing, thank you. How much is that? No, wait a moment. Give me another glass of beer.'

A little later he was once more in the alley, passing and repassing the dark window of *Liberty Bar*. He thought of the Casino. It was a gala night. Gala nights appeared to be an everyday matter in this part of the world. Opera and ballet. Then supper and dancing. And all the time the gambling: *boule* and *baccarat*.

The same thing all along the coast. Forty miles of it! Hundreds of *croupiers* scanning the gamblers; hundreds of women scanning the men; hundreds of waiters and gigolos scanning the women.

And hundreds of estate agents, like Monsieur Petitfils, with their lists – villas for sale, villas to let – scanning the lists of new arrivals on the Riviera.

But here and there, at Cannes, Nice, or Monte Carlo, a quarter darker than the rest. Back alleys; queer places; people who slunk along in the shadows; old women and young women; slot-machines; a kitchen-parlour behind a bar . . .

The dregs . . .

Still Jaja did not come. Ten times Maigret swung round at the sound of steps . . . He felt uncomfortable each time he passed the *Vrais Marins*, whose barman kept looking at him with a sneer on his face.

At that very moment there were thousands, tens of thousands, of sheep on the Brown estates, munching the Browns' grass, herded by the Browns' men . . . Or perhaps the Browns' men were shearing them, for it would be broad daylight over there . . .

Wagons of wool; cargoes of wool; captains, officers, crews. Ships putting to sea; officers checking the temperature in the holds . . . Then the brokers hob-nobbing in Amsterdam, Liverpool, Havre, talking over the price of wool.

And Harry Brown in his suite at the *Provençal*. Cablegrams from Australia. Telephone-calls to the London Office . . . In the paper just now he had read:

Daughter of Mohammedan Ruler Married at Nice ...

and it went on to say:

In honour of the occasion elaborate festivities have been taking place in India, in Afghanistan, in ...

and then farther on:

A dinner was given in Nice in the *Palais de la Méditerranée*. Prominent among the guests were ...

A Moslem princess marrying at Nice, and champagne flowing all along the forty-mile esplanade . . . While out East, devil knows where, hundreds of thousands of people were . . .

Still Jaja did not come. Maigret knew pretty well every cobble-stone by this time and every detail of the houses in the alley. A young girl with plaited hair was sitting at one of the windows struggling to finish her homework.

Had Jaja's bus met with an accident? Had she gone on somewhere else? Or perhaps taken flight? Peering in through the window at *Liberty Bar*, he could see the cat licking its paws.

Scraps from the newspaper kept coming back to him. Sport, Society Gossip, a King visiting the Riviera:

Travelling incognito, His Majesty arrived yesterday at Ville-franche, from whence he proceeded to his Cap Ferrat estate.

While in another column:

Early this morning Monsieur Graphopoulos was arrested in Nice, shortly after winning five hundred thousand francs in a *salle de baccarat*. He is accused of cheating.

This was followed by a short paragraph:

It seems that the assistant director of the *Police des Jeux* is likely to be inculpated.

Of course! If William Brown crumbled before temptation, how could one expect a wretched devil earning two thousand francs a month to be a hero?

Maigret was fed up to the teeth. Fed up with waiting. Fed up with a case that was not in his line at all.

Why had they sent him there with such absurd instructions? Tactful handling. No awkward revelations. No stirring up a hornet's nest . . .

Wasn't every case a hornet's nest? Only, of course, some hornets mattered more than others!

And suppose he wasn't tactful? Suppose he produced the will? Suppose those four women did go to Australia? . . .

Steps . . . This time he didn't bother to look round, until a key turned in a lock and a plaintive voice said:

'So you're there!'

It was Jaja. Jaja tired to the point of dropping, and whose hand trembled as she removed the key. Jaja in all her finery: mauve overcoat and dark red shoes.

'Come in . . . Just a moment and I'll switch on the light.'

The cat promptly began purring and rubbing against her swollen legs. She groped for the switch.

'When I think of that poor child, Sylvie . . .'

At last she switched on the light and they could see their way. The barman opposite had his unholy face right against the window. Jaja led the way into the room behind.

'Do come in . . . My legs will hardly hold me up . . . And what with my feelings . . .'

She went straight to the stove, where the fire was glowing, poked it up, and shifted a saucepan on the hotplate.

'Sit down, Inspector. I'll just get changed, but I'll be down again in a moment.'

She had not once looked at Maigret. With her back to him, she went on:

'To think of the poor child . . .'

She went upstairs and began taking her things off, talking all the time.

'A real good girl . . . If she had wanted . . . It's always those that pay for the others . . . Again and again I've told her . . .'

Maigret sat down by the table, on which were some

cheese and some sardines. He could hear every movement
Jaja made as she waddled to and fro in the room above.
Particularly the jig she danced, trying not to lose her
balance, as she took her shoes off.

CHAPTER IX

Broken Glass

'IF it had only been the walking . . . But you can't imagine
all I've been through . . . What my feet'll be like tomorrow
morning . . .!'

Jaja had stopped waddling hither and thither in the bedroom. Sitting in a chair, she was woefully caressing her
bare feet as she spoke.

She raised her voice so that Maigret could hear in the
room below; and she was astonished, on looking up, to see
him standing by the top of the stairs, outside the bedroom
door.

'Oh! . . . I didn't know you were there . . . I'm afraid the
place is in an awful state – but don't take any notice of that.
Since all this trouble began . . .'

Maigret would have found it hard to say why he'd gone
up. Listening to her chatter, it had occurred to him, though
only half-consciously, that he had never seen the upstairs
room.

Coming into the doorway, he stood looking round
him, while Jaja talked on, becoming more and more
voluble.

'God alone knows if I've had any dinner . . . I don't think
I have . . . It fairly turned me up to see Sylvie there. What a
mess it all is!'

She had slipped her dressing-gown loosely over her
bright pink underclothes, fringed with lace, which con-
trasted with her inordinately white skin. The bed was still

unmade, and Maigret could not help thinking that nobody seeing him there would have believed he had come only to talk.

The room was quite ordinary, apart from its untidiness, and better furnished than one might have expected. The mahogany bed looked thoroughly *bourgeois*. A round table. A wardrobe. A chest of drawers. On the other hand, the slop-pail was in the middle of the room, and the table was littered with powders, face-creams, and dirty towels.

Jaja sighed as she finally put on her slippers:

'I wonder how it'll end up.'

'It's here that William used to sleep?'

'I've only this room beyond what's downstairs.'

In a corner was a divan, upholstered in shabby velveteen.

'He slept on that divan?'

'Sometimes . . . Sometimes I did.'

'And Sylvie?'

'Whenever she was here. William would have the divan and she'd share the bed with me.'

The room was so low that Maigret's hat touched the ceiling. The window was narrow, the curtains of green velveteen. The electric lamp had no shade.

Maigret could imagine William and Jaja, having drunk all they could hold, tottering up to bed. William on the divan – then Sylvie coming in and slipping into bed beside Fat Jaja.

The latter had never been so talkative as she was now. She spoke plaintively, as though wanting Maigret's pity.

'I'm that upset. I'm sure to fall ill. I always do. It took me that way when the sailors had a fight just outside the bar . . . it's three years ago now . . . and one of them got slashed with a razor . . .'

She stood up and began to look for something, then forgot what it was.

'And what about you? Have you had anything to eat? Come down and we'll see what we can find.'

Maigret led the way down. Jaja went to the stove, put some more coal on, and stirred something in a saucepan.

'I haven't the heart to cook a supper when I've no one to cook for ... And when I think of where Sylvie is ...'

'Look here, Jaja!'

'What?'

'What was it Sylvie said to you while I was serving that chap in the bar?'

'Oh! ... Yes ... I asked her what the twenty thousand francs were, and she said she didn't know except that it was Joseph's doing.'

'And this evening?'

'What do you mean: "this evening"?'

'When you saw her at the police station?'

'Just the same. She didn't know, and she was wondering what Joseph had been up to.'

'Has she been a long time with Joseph?'

'She's with him, and at the same time she's not ... they don't live together ... She met him somewhere – at the races, I suppose – anyhow it wasn't here. He said he could do her a good turn, put her in the way of business ... Of course, he could, being a waiter ... He's been well brought up. Educated too. Though that doesn't alter the fact that I've never taken to him.'

There were some lentils in one of the saucepans. Jaja poured them out on to a plate.

'Wouldn't you like some? ... Really? ... Well, help yourself to some drink ... I don't feel up to cooking. Haven't the heart to ... Is the door of the bar shut?'

Maigret was sitting astride his chair, as he had done that afternoon. He watched her eating, listened while she talked.

'You see, those people – and the Casino waiters most of all – are a clever lot. They'd think of things we could never understand ... And if anything goes wrong, it's sure to be a woman that gets pinched ... Now if Sylvie had listened to me ...'

'And what was the business Joseph sent you on this evening?'

She stared at Maigret with her mouth full, as though unable to understand. But after a moment she went on:

'Oh, yes! . . . To Harry Brown.'

'What was it you were to say to him?'

'That he was to get Sylvie released, otherwise . . .'

'Otherwise what?'

'Oh, I know you won't give me a moment's peace. Though you must admit I've treated you fair and square . . . I'm doing my best, aren't I? I've nothing to hide.'

He guessed why she was so talkative, and in such a tearful voice – also why he'd had so long to wait. She had stopped more than once by the way to buy herself a drop of courage to face him with.

'It was me that was always holding Sylvie back, and stopping her from hooking up with Joseph altogether. . . . And then when I understood he'd been up to something . . .'

'Well?'

It was really more funny than pathetic. Still going on with her supper, she began to cry. It was a preposterous sight: a fat woman in a purple dressing-gown sitting over a plate of lentils, whimpering like a child.

'Don't hustle me so. Give me time to think. With all this trouble, my head's spinning . . . Come on! Give me something to drink . . .'

'In a minute.'

'Let me have something to drink, and I'll tell you everything.'

He gave way and poured her out a small glass of spirits.

'Now, what is it you want to know? . . . What was I saying? . . . Oh, yes! . . . When I saw the twenty thousand francs . . . Were they in William's pocket?'

It cost Maigret an effort to keep his head from spinning too as he listened to Jaja's tortuous ramblings, for at the same time a gleam of enlightenment was dawning in his mind.

'In William's pocket? . . . You mean: were they stolen from him when he was killed? . . . Is that what you thought?'

'I really don't know what I thought . . . There! I can't eat another mouthful . . . Have you got a cigarette on you?'

'I only smoke a pipe.'

'There ought to be some somewhere. Sylvie always has some.'

She poked about here and there, but couldn't find any.

'Do they always send them to Alsace?'

'Who? . . . What? . . . For heaven's sake, what are you talking about?'

'Women . . . What's the place called? . . . That prison. I know it begins with "Hau" . . . In my time . . .'

'When you were in Paris?'

'Yes. They were always talking about it. They used to say it was a hell, and any amount of them tried to kill themselves . . . And not so long ago I read about it in the paper. It seems there are even convicts there who've turned eighty . . . No, I don't believe there's a cigarette in the place. I suppose Sylvie took them with her.'

'And Sylvie's afraid of going there – is that it?'

'Sylvie? . . . I don't know . . . I was thinking about it in the bus. There was an old woman in front of me, and . . .'

'Sit down.'

'Yes . . . Don't take any notice . . . I'm not quite myself this evening . . . What were we talking about?'

A look of wild anxiety came into her eyes. She ran her hand across her forehead. A wisp of hair – there was a tinge of red in it – fell down over her cheek.

'It makes me feel so sad . . . Pour me out another drink, will you?'

'When you've told me what you know.'

'But I don't know anything. What should I know? . . . First of all I saw Sylvie. And even so there was a chap

standing over us all the time listening to what we said . . .
And I did so want to cry . . . But as she kissed me good-bye
she whispered in my ear that it was all Joseph's fault.'

'Then you saw him?'

'Yes. I told you that before. He sent me off to Juan-les-
Pins to warn Harry Brown that if . . .'

She was groping for her words. Sometimes her mind
seemed to slip, as it does with some drunkards. And at such
moments she would look at Maigret as though she was
drowning and longed to catch hold of him.

'Don't worry me any more. I can't stand it . . . I'm just a
poor wretched woman who's always tried to have a kind
word for everybody.'

'No! Not yet!'

Maigret snatched away the bottle she had picked up. He
could see what would happen – all of a sudden she'd
be dead-drunk and he wouldn't get another word out of
her.

'You saw Harry Brown?'

'No . . . Or rather, yes . . . He said if I crossed his path
again he'd have me locked up too.'

Then, suddenly, exultant:

'Hossegor . . . No, that's not right either . . . Hossegor's
something else – it comes into a story . . . Hagueneau! There
you are! That's the place!'

It was the name of the prison that had been preying on
her mind.

'They say they're not even allowed to speak. Do you
think that could be true?'

Maigret had never known her so inconsequent. It was
enough to make one wonder whether her mind was not
going altogether.

'Of course,' he said, 'if Sylvie's an accomplice she'll be
sent to . . .'

Jaja interrupted him hurriedly, talking faster than ever,
feverishly, while the blood mounted to her face.

'All the same, I've come to understand a thing or two

this evening . . . Those twenty thousand francs, for instance
– I know now what they were for. It's William's son – that
fellow Harry – that gave them to her to pay for . . .'

'To pay for what?'

'Everything!' said Jaja triumphantly, throwing a look
of defiance at her visitor before going on:

'You see, I'm not so green as I'm cabbage-looking . . .
And when that young man heard there was a will . . .'

'One moment! You knew about it?'

'It was last month that William spoke of it . . . We were
here, all four of us . . .'

'You and he, Sylvie and Joseph?'

'Yes. We'd been hitting it up a bit extra, as it was
William's birthday . . . And we got talking of all sorts of
things. He even said something about Australia.'

'What did he say?'

'That he was tickled to death to think of what they'd
say out there . . . And he whipped the will out of his pocket
and started reading it aloud. He didn't read it all, as he
didn't want to speak of the other two women . . . He said
he'd been and had it all drawn up by a lawyer.'

'A month ago, you say? . . . At that time did Joseph know
of Harry Brown?'

'You can never tell with him. Being a waiter like that,
he picks up all sorts of things.'

'And do you think he might have told Harry?'

'I didn't say that. I didn't say anything of the kind . . .
Only, you can't help thinking, can you? . . . You know,
those rich people are no better than any others . . . And just
supposing Joseph had been and told him all . . . And
supposing young Brown had said in a casual sort of way
that he'd like to have that will. But what use would the
will be to him so long as William was alive? Couldn't he
easily make another?'

For a moment Maigret was off his guard, and she had
poured herself out a glass and swallowed it before he could
stop her. She leaned over towards him, puffing her alcoholic

breath right into his face. Lowering her voice dramatically, she continued:

'And once he was dead . . . You see what I was coming to . . . Then there'd be the price to discuss . . . For twenty thousand francs, or it might have been double . . . He might have paid Joseph twenty thousand in advance. You never know . . . I'm only saying what comes into my head, of course. But things like that aren't usually paid for in one go . . . As for Sylvie . . .'

'She wouldn't know anything about it?'

'If she'd known, I'd have known . . . Was that someone knocking?'

She sat petrified with fear. To reassure her, Maigret had to go to the street door. When he returned he found she had taken the opportunity to have another tot.

'Don't go thinking I've told you anything; I haven't. I don't know anything to tell you . . . You see what I mean? . . . I'm only a miserable . . . a poor woman who's lost her husband, who . . .'

And once more she burst into tears. This time it wasn't funny at all. It was merely painful.

'According to you, Jaja, what would William have been doing that Friday afternoon between two o'clock and five?'

She looked at him without answering, still crying. But her sobs soon lacked conviction.

'Sylvie had left just before him,' Maigret went on. 'Don't you think they might have . . . ?'

'Who?'

'Sylvie and William?'

'That they might have done what?'

'How should I know? . . . Met somewhere, perhaps? . . . After all, Sylvie's young and nice-looking . . . And William . . .'

He was watching Jaja closely. Feigning indifference, he continued:

'They might have met somewhere. Joseph would be in hiding. And at the right moment he'd spring out and stab William in the back.'

Jaja said nothing. She merely gaped at him with a frown on her forehead, as though making a tremendous effort to follow what he was saying. It wasn't so easy in her condition. Her eyes were vague and her thoughts were no doubt wandering all over the place.

'Harry Brown, hearing of the will, suggests the crime. Sylvie decoys William to the spot. Joseph does the deed. Then Harry is told to bring the money to the hotel . . .'

Jaja didn't move a muscle. Was she too taken aback to speak? Or didn't she understand a single word?

'Joseph arrested sends you off with a message for Harry, to say he'll spill the beans if he's not set free.'

Jaja literally shouted:

'That's it! Yes, that's it!'

She stood up. She panted. She was apparently torn between a desire to cry and to burst out laughing.

Suddenly she put both hands to her head convulsively. Her hair fell down. She stamped with impatience.

'Yes, that's it . . . And me thinking . . . I don't know . . . I . . . I . . .'

Maigret sat still, looking at her with some astonishment. Was she going into a fit of hysterics? Or to faint?

'I . . . I . . .'

It was quite unforeseen. She seized the bottle and threw it on the floor, where it smashed to pieces.

'And me thinking . . .'

The light in the alley outside was faintly visible through the two doors. The barman opposite could be heard putting up the shutters. It must have been very late. The trams had stopped ages ago.

'I can't bear the thought of it,' she shrieked. 'I can't . . . I won't . . . Anything but *that* . . . It's not true . . . It's . . .'

'Jaja!'

But the sound of her name did nothing to calm her. She was worked up into a frenzy. With the same impetuosity with which she had seized the bottle she stooped and picked up something from the floor.

'Not Hagueneau – anything but that . . . It's not true. Sylvie didn't . . .'

In all his years of service, Maigret had never witnessed so sorry a spectacle. It was a bit of glass that she had picked up, and, talking all the time, she cut into her wrist, right down to the artery.

Her eyes were almost popping out of her head. She looked raving mad.

'Hagueneau . . . I . . . It wasn't Sylvie . . .'

A gush of blood spurted out just as Maigret reached her. His right hand was covered with it and it even splashed on to his tie. He seized her by both arms.

For a few seconds Jaja looked at the blood – her own blood – as it trickled wantonly on to the floor. Then her whole being went soft. Maigret held her for an instant, then let her sink gently down.

His fingers felt for the artery and pressed it. But that was no good – he must find something to tie it up with. He hunted anxiously round the room, and, finding an electric cord, he wrenched it away from the iron it belonged to.

Jaja lay motionless on the floor. Coming back to her, he wound the cord round her wrist, pulling it with all his might.

He went out into the cool night air. On the threshold he hesitated. The *Vrais Marins* was dead and shuttered. Then he strode down the alley to the street at the end.

There were no lights anywhere, except for the street lamps and the Casino, which was still illuminated. Looking along the street, he could see where the cars were parked, chauffeurs standing in groups by the harbour, where the masts of the yachts pointed up, straight and motionless, to the sky.

Not far off, at the cross-roads, a policeman was on duty.

'Fetch a doctor! Quick! To *Liberty Bar*!'

'Is that the little place down the alley, where . . .?'

'Yes. The little place where . . .!' answered Maigret testily. 'And for the love of God get a move on.'

CHAPTER X

The Divan

THE two policemen did their best not to be rough as they carried the body up the narrow stairs. But Jaja was heavy. Sometimes she was bumped against the wall, sometimes the banisters, and once or twice she was almost bent double, with her hind-quarters dragging over one stair on to another.

The doctor, waiting for the way to be clear, looked round him with curiosity in the room below. A gentle whimpering moan filled the rooms both upstairs and down, seeming to come from nowhere, though in fact it came from Jaja.

In the low bedroom Maigret opened up the bed and helped the other two to hoist Jaja on to it. She was quite limp, a dead weight, though she looked more like a stout doll stuffed with bran.

Did she know what was going on? Did she know where she was? From time to time her eyes opened, but they didn't look at anything or anybody.

And the moan she uttered came out gently, regularly, without the slightest grimace of pain.

'Is she suffering much?' asked Maigret of the doctor, a little old man, kind and punctilious, who was astonished to find himself in such surroundings.

'She oughtn't to be suffering at all. Perhaps she's easily upset – or maybe she's frightened.'

'Is she conscious?'

'She doesn't look it. And yet . . .'

'She's pretty near dead-drunk,' said Maigret with a sigh. 'I was only wondering whether the pain would have sobered her up.'

The two policemen waited for further instructions. They too looked round the room with curiosity. The curtains

were not drawn, and behind a window opposite Maigret
could see the faint white splodge of a face. He drew the
curtains, then beckoned to one of the policemen.

'I want you to fetch the girl I had locked up this evening. Sylvie she's called . . . But not the man.'

And, turning to the other:

'Wait for me downstairs.'

The doctor did what was necessary to the severed artery,
and then stood by the bed looking at the fat woman, who
was still moaning. He seemed at a loss to know what to do
next. To cover his indecision, he took her pulse, felt her
hands, her forehead.

'Can I have a word with you, Doctor?' said Maigret
from his corner.

When the doctor came over to him, he went on in an
undertone:

'I'd like you to take the opportunity to look her over.
If you could give me a rough idea . . .'

'Certainly, if you wish it.'

The little doctor seemed more and more ill at ease. He
was probably wondering whether Maigret was a relation
of Jaja's. He opened his bag and took out some apparatus.
Methodically, but without much conviction, he set about
taking her blood-pressure.

Dissatisfied, he took it three times. Then he opened her
dressing-gown to listen to her heart. As is so common with
French doctors, he did not use a stethoscope, and he looked
round for a clean face-towel to put between his ear and her
chest. There wasn't a clean one in the room, so in the end
he had to use his handkerchief.

At last he returned to Maigret.

'Undoubtedly . . .'

'Undoubtedly what?'

'She'll never know old age! The heart's enlarged and
almost worn out. As for the blood-pressure, it's positively
terrifying.'

'How long do you give her?'

'That's another question . . . If she was one of my patients I'd send her into the country. Complete rest, absolute quiet, a very strict diet . . .'

'No alcohol, of course.'

'That's the most important thing of all.'

'And you'd save her?'

'I wouldn't say that. But I might keep her going for a year or two . . .'

They both pricked their ears, suddenly conscious of the silence around them. Something was lacking. Jaja's moaning.

When they turned towards the bed they saw her, raised on an elbow, a fierce look in her eye, her chest heaving.

She had heard. She had understood. And she looked at the little doctor as though holding him responsible for her condition. The latter groped for something to say.

'Do you feel better?'

Her lips curled contemptuously. Without a word she lay down and closed her eyes.

The doctor was not sure whether he was wanted any longer. But he started putting his instruments away. As he did so, he must have been holding an inward conversation, for every now and again he nodded approvingly.

'I suppose that's all,' said Maigret when everything was put away. 'There's nothing to fear, is there?'

'Not for the moment, anyhow.'

As soon as he had gone, Maigret placed a chair by the foot of the bed, sat down, and lit his pipe to overcome the smell of antiseptics which disgusted him. Nor did he like the look of the basin of water that had been used to wash the wound. For want of a more suitable place, he pushed it out of sight under the wardrobe.

He was calm. Quietly, ponderously, he looked at Jaja's face, which seemed all curves. Round cheeks – and now her hair thrown back revealed a large rounded forehead with a little scar on one of the temples.

To the left of the bed, the divan.

Jaja wasn't sleeping. Of that he was sure. Her breathing was irregular, and the eyelids quivered frequently.

What was she thinking about? She knew he was there, looking at her. And she knew now that her works were running down, and that she had not much longer to live.

What was she thinking about? What images were fluttering to and fro behind that rounded forehead?

And there she was, suddenly frantic again, sitting up with a jerk, looking at Maigret with wild eyes and crying out:

'Don't leave me! . . . I'm frightened . . . Where's he gone to? Where's that little man? . . . I don't want to . . .'

Maigret stood up and bent over her. He couldn't help a tender note coming into his voice as he said:

'That's all right, old thing. Just be quiet.'

And that's what she was – an old thing. A poor old thing soaked in alcohol, with legs so swollen that she walked like an elephant.

Yet in her day she had walked miles and miles, up and down the same bit of pavement near the Porte Saint-Martin.

She let him push her head gently back on to the pillow. She was sober now. The policeman downstairs had found a bottle and was pouring himself out a drink. Jaja pricked her ears, asking anxiously:

'Who's that?'

But other sounds were approaching – steps in the alley and the voice of a woman – breathless from walking so fast – asking:

'Why is there no light in the bar? What's the . . .?'

'Hush! Don't make a noise.'

The policeman downstairs opened the door. Steps across the bar, across the kitchen, then up the stairs. Jaja looked at Maigret in consternation. She almost screamed as he went towards the door and opened it.

'You can go – the rest of you,' he said, standing aside to let Sylvie pass.

The girl came in and then halted abruptly in the middle of the room, putting her hand to her thumping heart. She had no hat on. She had no idea what was the matter. Her eyes were set in a fixed stare on the bed.

'Jaja! . . .'

Downstairs, the one who had had a drink was pouring out another for his mate. There was a clink as their two glasses touched. Then the door of the bar opened and shut; steps gradually faded away towards the harbour.

So still and silent was Maigret that his presence was hardly noticeable.

'My poor Jaja . . .'

Yet Sylvie came no nearer. Something held her back: the stony stare with which the older woman greeted her.

Turning to Maigret, Sylvie stammered:

'Is it . . .?'

'Is it what?'

'Nothing . . . I don't know . . . What's the matter?'

Maigret made no answer.

Silence. A strange silence, for, in spite of the distance and the closed door, the ticking of the alarm-clock below was distinctly audible. And in the tense atmosphere upstairs the ticking was strange too – a feverish, jerky, headlong ticking, as though in a moment the clock, in its giddy haste, would lash itself to pieces.

*

Jaja was working up to another crisis. You could feel it coming, stirring her limp body, kindling her eyes, parching her throat. But she held tight. She tried all she could to keep it back. Meanwhile Sylvie remained standing in the middle of the room, utterly bewildered, with her head lowered and her hands clasped across her chest. She knew neither what to say, what to do, nor how to hold herself.

Maigret smoked, calmly letting things take their course. He knew it was the end.

For there was no longer any mystery. No unforeseen element could crop up now. All the characters had fallen into their right places: the two Martinis, Gina and her mother, who were perhaps still making their inventory with the help of Monsieur Petitfils; Harry Brown at the *Provençal* waiting unperturbed for the case to be wound up, and in the meantime running the wool business by cable and telephone; Joseph under lock and key . . .

At last Jaja could hold it back no longer. With a look of hatred she raised herself and pointed at Sylvie with her unwounded hand.

'It's her! . . . It's her fault, the filthy little —'

She had brought it out: the worst word of her vocabulary. Tears ran down from her eyelids.

'I hate her! . . . Do you hear? I hate her. A snake in the grass! Making up to my face, and then behind my back calling me the old woman. Yes, the old woman. And hadn't I . . . ?'

'Lie down, Jaja,' said Maigret. 'You'll make yourself ill.'

'You leave me alone.'

And with a renewed burst of energy she went on:

'But I shan't let her get away with it. I won't go to Hagueneau – do you understand? . . . Or if I do, she'll have to come with me . . .'

Her throat was so dry that she looked round instinctively for something to drink.

'Go and fetch her something,' said Maigret to Sylvie.

'But . . . she's already . . .'

'Go!'

He walked over to the window to make sure the curtains were properly drawn. There was nobody visible now in the window opposite. The street lamp shone on the sign of the bar opposite: *Aux Vrais Marins*.

'Of course you'll stand up for her because she's young. I shouldn't be surprised if she'd already tried to get off with you.'

Sylvie came back, dragging her drooping body. There were deep shadows under her eyes. She handed Maigret a half-full bottle of rum.

Jaja sneered.

'Now that it's all up with me you don't care how much I drink. I heard what the doctor said – every word of it.'

And the thought of it made her more agitated than ever. She was scared to death of dying. Her eyes grew haggard.

All the same, she took the bottle and greedily gulped down a few mouthfuls, looking from one to the other of her two companions.

'The old woman who's going to snuff out! . . . But I won't. Anyhow not before she does. For it's all her fault.'

She broke off like someone who has lost the thread. Maigret sat quite still, waiting.

'She's talked. I know she's talked, or they wouldn't have let her out . . . And wasn't I all the time doing my best for her? . . . For it's not true that Joseph sent me off to Antibes. I went all on my own. Do you understand?'

Of course! Of course Maigret understood. He had understood for the last hour or more. He pointed to the divan.

'It wasn't William that slept there, was it?'

'No. Indeed it wasn't. He slept here in my bed. In *my* bed, do you understand? . . . He came to *Liberty Bar* for my sake and nobody else's. And that creature – she's the one that slept on the divan. You might have guessed that long ago.'

She shouted it out in a hoarse voice. She only had to be left alone now and it would all come out. It had to. It was welling up from her innermost being – all that she had been hiding and suppressing. This was the real Jaja, Jaja stripped of the last shreds of reserve.

'The truth is, I loved him, and he loved me . . . He understood. He knew that if I'd never been educated or taught fine manners it wasn't my fault . . . He was happy here. Many's the time he's told me so. It hurt him to leave me, and when he came back he was like a schoolboy come home for the holidays.'

She was crying as she spoke. Her face was piteous in the hard light of the unshaded lamp . . .

And one arm all swathed in bandages . . .

'I never suspected a thing. I've been a fool. But one always is a fool in such cases . . . She'd nowhere to go, and I took her in out of the kindness of my heart. And I kept her here, thinking it would brighten the place up to have some young blood about.'

Sylvie did not move.

'Just look at her . . . Stands there as meek as a lamb, but she's sneering at me all the time. She's always been the same, and, idiot that I was, I thought she was shy and frightened. It used to go straight to my heart . . . And to think it was with my dressing-gowns she got him – by showing all she had to show . . .

'She wanted to get him. And Joseph wanted her to – that pimp of hers. It didn't take him long to guess that William had money somewhere or other . . .

'If he hadn't thought of it before, there was the will . . .'

She snatched up the bottle and drank so avidly that they could hear her throat gulping it down. Sylvie took the opportunity to cast an imploring glance at Maigret. She swayed slightly from side to side, hardly able to stand.

'It was from this room that Joseph stole it. I don't know when. No doubt some night we'd had a drop too many. William had talked about it, and Joseph knew well enough that with almost any will you can do a bit of blackmail.'

Maigret listened without excitement. Once again he looked round the room. The bed, the divan . . .

William and Jaja . . .

And Sylvie on the divan . . .

Poor William – he couldn't help comparing them.

'No. I never suspected a thing till I saw Sylvie give him a queer look as she went out after lunch. Even then I couldn't believe ... But she'd hardly been gone a minute when up jumps William too. In the ordinary way he never thought of going till much later ... I didn't say anything, but as soon as he'd left I went and put my things on.'

She was coming to the critical part. It was she who told the story, but Maigret already knew the plot. And with the few details she gave him, he could see it all ...

Sylvie dressing before lunch so as to go out directly after. A significant look in William's direction as she goes.

And Jaja sees it.

She says nothing and goes on eating and drinking. But no sooner has William gone than she slips her overcoat over her indoor clothes.

Nobody left in the bar. An empty house, the door locked ... They chase one after the other, with Joseph hovering somewhere in the background with the will in his pocket ...

'Do you know where she waited for him? ... At the *Hôtel Beauséjour*. And I was left standing in the street not knowing what to do with myself ... I wanted to go in and knock on their door and beg Sylvie to give him back to me ... There was a cutler's at the corner. And while they were ... while they were up there, I stared into the shop-window ... I hardly knew what I was doing. I was aching in every limb ...

'I went in ... I bought a knife ... I think I was crying ...

'Then they came out, those two. William was glowing: he looked ten years younger ... I saw him taking her into a *confiserie* to buy her some chocolates. And the sight of it made me sick – I couldn't bear it any more. I rushed as fast as I could to get outside the town before he passed. I knew he'd be coming along the road to Antibes ...

'As soon as he saw me he stopped the car and opened the door ...

'And I shouted at him: "I've got something for you. There you are! And it's for her too!" ...'

Jaja fell back on to her pillow, her shoulders heaving, her face bathed in tears and sweat.

'I don't even know what happened next. I suppose he pushed me out and slammed the door. There was no knife in my hand. I must have dropped it in the car.'

That was a detail Maigret had not thought about. William, with the mists already closing in on him, must have had the presence of mind to throw the knife into some bushes.

'It was late when I got back.'

Of course. She must have stopped at many a bar on the way.

'When I woke up next morning, I could hardly believe it . . .'

She sat up once more.

'But I won't go to Hagueneau. I won't . . . You can do your worst. The doctor said so – my number's up . . . And it's this little slut . . .'

A chair scraped on the floor. Sylvie had dragged it to her just in time to sink into it sideways, fainting.

She fainted gently, progressively, but it wasn't put on. Her nostrils were pinched and there was a yellowish tinge about them. The orbits of her eyes were dreadfully hollow.

'Serve her right,' cried Jaja. 'Let her be . . . At least . . . I don't know . . . My mind's in a whirl . . . Perhaps it's all Joseph's fault after all . . . Sylvie! My little Sylvie! . . .'

Maigret bent over the girl and tapped her hands and her cheeks. He saw Jaja seize the bottle and drink again, fairly swilling the raw liquor down her throat, after which she broke into a desperate fit of coughing.

At last she sighed and buried her face in her pillow.

Maigret picked Sylvie up and carried her downstairs, where he splashed her face with cold water.

The first thing she said when she opened her eyes was: 'It isn't true.'

A voice of utter, absolute despair.

'It isn't true . . . I *must* make you understand . . . I don't want to make myself out any better than I am. But I'm not as bad as that. I love Jaja, and I'd never have done it if he hadn't begged me and begged me. It's months since he began looking at me differently. And he kept on begging me . . . And how could I refuse him, when every night . . . with other men . . . ?'

'Shhh! Speak quietly.'

'Let her hear. If she thinks it over she'll understand . . . And when I did give in I didn't even want Joseph to know, as I was afraid he'd take advantage of it . . . We arranged to meet at . . .'

'Was that the first time?'

'The only time. So you see . . .

'It's quite true about the chocolates . . . He was mad, so mad that it made me frightened . . . He treated me as if . . . as if I hadn't been a . . .'

'And that's all?'

'I'd no idea it was Jaja. No, I swear I hadn't. I only thought it might be Joseph . . . I was afraid . . . He told me to go to the *Beauséjour*, where somebody was to bring me some money. I didn't know who it was until he came . . .

'What else could I have done?'

The moaning started again upstairs – the same gentle high-pitched moaning as before.

'Is she badly hurt?'

Maigret shrugged his shoulders and went upstairs. Jaja was in a deep heavy sleep, moaning faintly with every other breath. He came down again to find Sylvie, who was sitting with all her nerves taut, listening to every sound.

'Don't make a noise,' he said. 'She's sleeping.'

There was something in Maigret's voice that puzzled her. She watched him anxiously as he filled another pipe.

'Stay with her. And when she wakes up you'll tell her that I've gone – for good.'

'But . . .'

'You'll tell her she's been dreaming, that she's had a nightmare, that . . .'

'But . . . I don't understand . . . And Joseph?'

Standing with his hands in his pockets, he looked into her eyes. Then from one of the pockets he drew out a bundle of bank-notes – twenty thousand francs – and put them on the table.

'You love him?'

'You know well enough one has to have a man. Otherwise . . .'

'And William?'

'That was different. He wasn't one of us. He was . . .'

Maigret walked towards the door. As he gripped the handle he turned round.

'Lie low. *Liberty Bar* had better be forgotten about. See?'

Sylvie followed him across the bar. As the outer door opened the early morning air blew in. A damp chill was rising from the ground – almost like a mist.

'I never thought you were like that,' stammered the girl. 'I . . . Jaja . . . I tell you she's the best woman in the world.'

He turned to her, nodded, then walked down to the harbour, where he stopped to relight his pipe.

CHAPTER XI

'*Morue à la Crème*'

MAIGRET uncrossed his legs and, leaning forward, handed the document to the Australian.

'I can . . .?' asked Harry Brown, throwing a cautious glance towards the door, behind which was his secretary.

'It's yours.'

'We're only too anxious to treat them liberally. I was thinking of a hundred thousand francs to each of them. I hope you understand. It's not the money we're concerned about. It's the scandal. If those four women came *out there* . . .'

'I understand.'

Through the window Maigret could see the beach of Juan-les-Pins. A hundred people in bathing-costumes lying on the sand. Three girls doing physical exercises under the eye of a tall, thin instructor. An Algerian going from group to group with a basket of monkey-nuts . . .

'What do you think of a hundred thousand each?'

'Excellent!' said Maigret, rising.

'You haven't touched your glass.'

'No, thanks.'

The well-dressed, well-groomed Harry Brown hesitated.

'Do you know, Inspector,' he ventured at last, 'for a moment I thought you were an adversary. In France . . .'

'Yes?' said Maigret, moving towards the door. Harry Brown followed him. There was less assurance in his voice as he went on:

'In France scandal doesn't matter so much as in . . .'

'Good morning.'

Maigret bowed, without offering his hand, and turned his back on the temporary headquarters of the wool business.

'In France! . . . In France! . . .' he muttered as he walked down the purple-carpeted stairs.

What about France? What did Frenchmen call Harry Brown's goings-on with that quiet, respectable woman at Cap Ferrat?

A love-affair!

And wouldn't the same expression do just as well for William's affair with Jaja, with Sylvie?

*

Walking along the beach, Maigret had to thread his way between half-naked bodies. All round him were bronzed skins, set off by coloured bathing-suits.

Boutigues was waiting for him by the physical-culture instructor's hut.

'Well?'

'It's all over. William Brown was killed by some person or persons unknown, who robbed him of his pocket-book . . .'

'But . . . All the same . . .'

'But what? . . . No stirring up a hornets' nest! So there we are.'

'All the same.'

'No stirring up a hornets' nest,' said the inspector once again, staring at the blue water, calm as a mill-pond, and the little boats . . . No. This was certainly not the place to make trouble.

'You see that girl in the green bathing-costume?'

'The one with the thin hams?'

'You'd never guess who she was,' said Boutigues triumphantly. 'Morrow's daughter.'

'Morrow?'

'You know. The diamond man. One of the dozen richest men in Europe.'

The sun was hot. Maigret in his black suit and bowler hat made the one dark spot on the landscape. The sound of music drifted down from the Casino.

'Shall we have a drink?'

Boutigues, of course, was wearing his light grey suit with a carnation in his buttonhole.

'As I said before, down here we . . .'

'Yes . . . Down here . . .'

'You don't like it?'

With a lyrical sweep of his arm, the young detective pointed to the bay, so wonderful a blue, to the Cap d'Antibes with its white villas half hidden by the trees, to the Casino, yellow as custard, and to the palms along the promenade.

'That stout man over there in the striped bathing-suit – he's editor of one of the biggest papers in Germany.'

After a sleepless night, Maigret's eyes were a glaucous grey. All he could do in response was to grunt:

'And what if he is? . . .'

*

Salt cod doesn't sound very grand, but, when you know how to make it, it's quite another matter. And Madame Maigret certainly did.

'I've made you some *morue à la crème*,' she said, as they sat down to lunch in the flat on the Boulevard Richard-Lenoir, through whose windows a few scraggy chestnut trees were visible. 'Are you glad to be back?'

'I should think I am!'

'What was it all about?'

'A love-story. But since they'd told me to be tactful . . .'

With both elbows on the table, he was thoroughly enjoying the *morue à la crème*. He spoke with his mouth full.

'An Australian who'd had enough of Australia and its sheep . . .'

'What do you mean?'

'An Australian who kicked over the traces, and did it pretty thoroughly . . .'

'And then?'

'Then . . . Nothing much. He had a glorious binge until his wife, and his brother-in-law, and his children put a spoke in his wheel by cutting off supplies.'

'That's not very interesting.'

'Not in the least. That's what I was trying to tell you . . . He went on living on the Riviera . . .'

'It must be beautiful down there.'

'Magnificent! . . . He took a modest villa, and not to be too lonely he had someone to live with him.'

'A woman! I begin to understand.'

'I wonder? . . . Pass the sauce, will you? . . . You might have put a bit more onion in it.'

'It's these onions you get in Paris. They've got no flavour at all. I used a whole pound . . . But go on . . .'

'So the woman came, but she brought along her mother.'

'Her mother?'

'Yes ... And it rather spoilt the charm. So he began to look for amusement elsewhere.'

'He took a mistress?'

'He's already had one – with an old hag of a mother thrown in! What he found was a low-class bar with a nice, fat, kind woman to drink with him.'

'She drank?'

'Yes. They both did. And after a bit they'd talk a lot of nonsense, and then she would have a good cry ...'

'She was unhappy?'

'It wasn't that. On the contrary, she thought something marvellous had happened.'

'What?'

'That somebody loved her, that she'd found a kindred spirit, and all the rest of it.'

'All the rest of what? ...'

'Nothing ... They made a good couple. Both getting elderly. And they could keep in step with each other – glass for glass.'

'What happened?'

'She'd taken in a little *protégée*, a girl called Sylvie. And in the end the Australian fell for Sylvie.'

Madame Maigret looked reproachfully at her husband.

'It's not a very pretty story you're telling me.'

'Can't be helped. It's the truth. He fell for her, but Sylvie wasn't having any, because of the old woman. But in the end she gave in, as, after all, the Australian was the principal character.'

'I don't follow that ...'

'It doesn't matter. So the two of them met in a hotel.'

'Behind the old woman's back?'

'Exactly. You follow me perfectly. But the old thing found out. And when she realized she was being left in the cold, she killed her lover ... Really, this *morue* is a triumph ...'

'I don't understand, all the same.'

'What don't you understand?'

'Why you didn't arrest the old woman. After all ...'

'Not a bit of it!'

'What do you mean?'

'Give me some more first ... Thanks ... That's not what I was sent for. I wasn't sent to make trouble. You know what a hornets' nest is! And the wife and the brother-in-law and the sons in Australia are very big people indeed, and rich enough to pay a lot of money for a will.'

'A will? Where are we getting to now?'

'It's rather complicated. Let's call it a love-affair and leave it at that. A woman getting on in years who kills her lover because he goes off with a young one.'

'And what's become of them – the women?'

'The old one has a few more months to live. It depends on how much she drinks.'

'How much she drinks?'

'Yes. Don't forget, it's not only a love-story. A drink-story too.'

'You're right. It is complicated.'

'Even more than you think. The old woman who killed her lover will die in three or four months, or five, or six, with her legs swollen and her feet in a basin of hot water.'

'How do you know?'

'Look up in your medical dictionary how people finish when they're suffering from dropsy.'

'And the young one?'

'It's worse for her, because she loves the old one like a mother. And besides that, she loves her wretched pimp.'

'Her what? You've a queer way of expressing yourself today.'

'And the pimp will lose the twenty thousand francs at the races,' went on Maigret imperturbably, eating all the time.

'What twenty thousand francs?'

'Never mind. Only there'll be more than twenty thousand if a certain wool-merchant keeps his word.'

'I'm altogether out of my depth now.'

'So am I . . . Or rather, I understand it all too well. I was told to be tactful, and that's all. It's over and done with . . . A poor little love-story with a rotten ending.'

Then suddenly looking up:

'There's no vegetable?'

'I wanted a cauliflower, but . . .'

And Maigret couldn't help thinking:

'Jaja wanted love, but . . .'

THE MADMAN OF BERGERAC

—

CHAPTER I

The Restless Traveller

IT all came about by the merest chance. The day before, Maigret hadn't even known he was going on a journey, although it was just the time of year when he had usually had enough of Paris. A month of March spiced with a foretaste of spring. The sun bright, eager, almost warm.

Madame Maigret was spending a fortnight in Alsace with her sister, who was expecting a baby.

But the post this Tuesday morning brought the inspector a letter from an old friend who had retired two years previously from the *Police Judiciaire* to settle down to country life in the Dordogne.

And don't forget: if ever a good wind should blow you into this part of the world, I count on you to spend a few days under my roof. My old servant is never so happy as when there's a guest to be made a fuss of ... The salmon fishing has begun ...

It was written on printed notepaper:

LA RIBAUDIÈRE
PAR VILLEFRANCHE-EN-DORDOGNE

But it wasn't so much the address that set Maigret dreaming. Beside it was stamped the outline of a little manor house, flanked by two round towers.

At twelve Madame Maigret rang up from Alsace to say the child was expected some time during the night.

'It's quite like summer weather,' she added, 'and the fruit trees are in blossom . . .'

Yes, it was the merest chance. A little later Maigret was in his chief's room, chatting, when the latter said:

'By the way, you might take a trip to Bordeaux some time to clear up that question we were discussing the other day.'

It was a matter of no great importance and of no urgency whatever: one of those questions that could be settled in no time on the spot, but which were troublesome to deal with by correspondence.

Bordeaux . . . Dordogne. The association was all the more natural as they were not far apart on the map.

Maigret stared at the ray of sunshine that shone on to the glass ball that the director of the *Police Judiciaire* used as a paper-weight.

'It's not a bad idea,' he said. 'I've nothing on at the moment.'

*

Late that afternoon, he took the train at the Gare d'Orsay, choosing a corner seat in a first-class carriage.

'Villefranche?' he asked.

'Change at Libourne.'

'I thought it was a through train.'

'Only the sleeping-cars.'

Maigret thought no more about it, looked through two or three newspapers, and then made his way to the dining-car, where he lingered over his coffee till nearly ten o'clock.

When he returned to his carriage he found the curtains drawn and the light dimmed. An elderly couple were stretched full length on the two seats.

An attendant passed along the corridor.

'Is there a *couchette* free?'

'There's nothing first-class. But I think there's one second. If you don't mind . . .'

'Not the slightest.'

And Maigret took his bag down from the rack and followed the man to the *wagon-couchette*, where the latter peeped through door after door till he found a compartment in which only the upper *couchette* was occupied.

Here too the curtains were drawn, and only the dim light was burning.

'Shall I switch on the light?'

'No, thanks.'

The air inside was hot and steamy. From somewhere or other came a faint hiss as if one of the joints of the radiator pipes was leaking. The man in the upper *couchette* could be heard breathing heavily and tossing about.

Sitting on his bunk, the inspector quietly took off his shoes, jacket, and waistcoat, and lay down. His head was in a thin draught. He couldn't tell where it came from, but by balancing his bowler over one side of his face he was able to ward it off.

Did he fall asleep? Hardly. But at any rate he dozed. Perhaps an hour. Perhaps two. Or it could have been even longer. But however that might be, he never completely lost consciousness.

And in this semi-consciousness the dominant sensation was discomfort. Was it the heat? Or was it the draught, which succeeded after all in getting round the bowler?

They were bad enough, but what really bothered him was the restlessness of the man above.

He couldn't keep still for a minute, nor even for a fraction of a minute. And with every movement there was a creaking and a grinding within three feet of Maigret's head. Besides, the man's breathing was irregular as though he was feverish.

At last Maigret could stand it no longer. Putting on his shoes and clothes, he went out and started pacing up and down the corridor. There, however, it was too cold.

Back again in the carriage, he lay down as he was. Only now he was too hot and had once more to discard his jacket and waistcoat.

Another spell of troubled somnolence, writhing with sensations and ideas – a nightmare mood, though without an actual nightmare.

The man above – had he not leant over the side of the upper *couchette* and peered into the shadow in which Maigret lay? Certainly he was never a moment still. Maigret, on the contrary, lay still as a corpse. The half-bottle of claret he had drunk at dinner and the two brandies he had had after it lay heavy on his stomach.

The night dragged slowly on. Now and again the train stopped. There would be voices on the platform, steps in the corridor, the slamming of doors. And each time it seemed as though they were never going to start again.

Was the man weeping? There were moments when his breathing stopped. Then a snuffle. He would turn over and blow his nose.

Maigret regretted his first-class carriage. Why hadn't he stayed there in spite of the elderly couple? He could easily have asked one of them to move.

He dozed, woke, dozed, woke again, until finally he could contain himself no longer. He coughed to clear his throat.

'Excuse me, monsieur, but would you please try to keep still?'

Having said that, he felt more uncomfortable than ever, for his voice had been much gruffer than he had intended. And, after all, the man might be ill . . .

There was no answer. No response whatever, except that the movements overhead ceased. The man must be making a frantic effort not to budge an inch. Then it suddenly occurred to Maigret that it might not be a man after all. Suppose it was a woman? He had never had a real view of the person above him, who was now no doubt lying rigidly, staring up at the the ceiling.

And the heat, which was rising, must be fearful up there. Maigret tried to turn it half off, but the lever was jammed. It was three o'clock. Would the night never come to an end? He tried being severe with himself.

'I really must get to sleep.'

But he wasn't in the least sleepy now. In fact, he felt almost as jumpy as his fellow-traveller. He listened intently.

'There we are! He's starting again.'

He tried to take no notice, forced himself to breathe regularly, counted up to a hundred and then began again.

There was no doubt about it now – the man was weeping. Maigret had decided after all that it was a man. Probably someone who had been to Paris for a funeral. Or the contrary: some poor devil who worked in Paris, who had received a sudden call to his native town. His mother ill, or perhaps dead. Or it might be his wife. Maigret was sorry he had spoken so roughly. There might even be a coffin in a special wagon attached to the train. Why not?...

And then there was his sister-in-law in Alsace . . . She might at any moment be giving birth to her third baby . . . Her third baby . . . Three in four years . . .

Maigret slept.

The train stopped, then went on . . . It raced over a steel bridge, making an infernal din. He opened his eyes abruptly.

The first thing he saw was a pair of legs that dangled from the upper berth. He lay still, watching them. The man was sitting, leaning forward, lacing up his boots, obviously taking infinite pains to make no jerky movement. In spite of the dimness of the light, Maigret noticed that the boots were of patent leather. The socks, on the other hand, were of thick grey wool, the sort of socks that are generally hand-knitted.

The man stopped what he was doing. Was he listening? Had he noticed a change in Maigret's breathing?

Maigret started counting again. But there was no question of his going to sleep now. He was fascinated by the hands that once more went on cautiously lacing up the boots. They trembled. In fact, they shook so much that when the man tried to tie a bow he had to make four shots at it.

They ran through a little station. Lights flicked past, showing faintly through the curtains.

The stranger's feet felt for the little ladder and he started to come down. Such precautions! It was quite ridiculous. Every movement was a caricature. Was he as scared as that of Maigret? Scared of waking him up and being ticked off again.

He opened the door very slowly, inch by inch, then crept out and hurried along the corridor. Either he forgot to shut the door or thought it more prudent to let it be.

Chance again! If it hadn't been for that open door, Maigret would have turned over with a sigh of relief and gone to sleep at last. But he had to rouse himself to shut it.

As he did so he looked out.

The result was surprising. He was on his feet in a second. He just had time to slip on his jacket, not bothering about the waistcoat.

He had seen the man open the door at the end of the corridor and put one foot on to the step outside, as though waiting to make a jump. And it was certainly no accident: the train was slowing down.

They were going through a wood. The clouds overhead were lit up by an invisible moon. The brakes went on. A minute or two before, they had been doing fifty miles an hour. They had come down to twenty, or even less, when suddenly the man disappeared.

He jumped well clear of the train and rolled down the railway embankment. Maigret did not stop to think what he was about. He simply made a dash for the door and jumped out after him.

He too cleared the track and rolled down the embankment. Over and over he rolled – three times in all – before coming to rest at the bottom.

The train rattled on, the red glow from the engine fading away in the distance.

Maigret picked himself up, a little shaken, but with nothing sprained or broken. The other man's fall must have been worse, for he was only now beginning to get to his feet, slowly and painfully.

It was an absurd situation. Ruefully, the inspector wondered what had possessed him to throw himself out into the night like that, leaving his bag and his waistcoat to complete the journey to Villefranche-en-Dordogne. He hadn't even the faintest notion where he was.

Apart from the railway embankment, he could only see trees, except in one place where there was a pale streak of road.

Why didn't the man move? He had risen no farther than to his knees. Was he really hurt? Or had he seen Maigret?

'*Hé! là-bas*,' called out the latter, feeling for his revolver.

He had hardly grasped it, however, when he saw a flash. He felt a stab in his shoulder even before he heard the bang.

It was all over in a moment. The man was on his feet now, and running. Maigret saw him cross the strip of road and disappear into the darkness beyond.

The inspector swore. His eyes were wet, not with pain, but with vexation. It had happened so quickly. He had been outmanoeuvred, routed, and was in a thoroughly sorry plight.

The revolver fell from his hand. He stooped to pick it up, and swore again because his shoulder hurt.

As a matter of fact it was not so much pain as a horrid feeling of blood flowing abundantly, welling out with every pulse.

He stood there at a loss, not daring to run or even to move, no longer bothering about picking up his gun. His temples were moist, and it was difficult to swallow. When he put his hand to his shoulder, it was, as he expected, instantly sticky with blood. He felt for the exact position of the wound and pressed it to stay the bleeding.

Half-stunned as he was, he was conscious of the train stopping at some distance, perhaps as much as a mile. He listened hard for it to start again, but it seemed as though it never would.

Why should he mind whether it started or not? He simply couldn't help it — he longed for it to start. The empty silence around him was agonizing.

At last! Thank God! The puffing and rumbling began again. Turning towards it, he could just make out the faint red glow moving behind the tree-tops.

Then nothing. Silence once more. Only Maigret. There all by himself, holding his right shoulder with his left hand. Yes, it was the right shoulder that was wounded. He tried to move the arm, but it was too heavy: he could only raise it a few inches.

Not a sound from the wood. Was the man already out of earshot? Or was he lying low amongst the bushes? Waiting perhaps to finish Maigret off as soon as he reached the road?

'You fool! . . . You fool! . . .'

Maigret cursed himself, feeling utterly forlorn. What on earth had made him think of jumping out of the train? Or rather, why hadn't he thought? . . . At dawn, his friend Leduc would be waiting for him at the station. There'd be salmon for lunch . . .

He started to walk, dragging his feet, stopping every few yards, then staggering on again. He made for the road, that white strip of road. It was the only thing to make for. When he reached it, he found it dusty as in mid-summer.

Blood still oozed from the wound. Not so much as at first, because he pressed it all the time as hard as he could. As the blood dried on it, his hand became stickier and stickier.

You wouldn't have thought he'd already been wounded three times in the course of his career. He would have suffered any downright pain rather than feel his blood oozing away like that. He felt as bad about it as if he was being wheeled into an operating-theatre.

And, after all, it would be pretty stupid, wouldn't it? To die all alone on that dusty road in the middle of the night! Not even knowing where he was! And with a bag and a waistcoat to represent him at Villefranche-en-Dordogne!

Was the man there behind the bushes? Never mind! Let him shoot! Maigret plodded on, leaning forwards, his head swimming. He came to a milestone, but most of it was in shadow. All he could read by the moonlight was 3 km. 5.

What would it be at three and a half kilometres? What town? Or perhaps a village? Was he going towards where the train had stopped! He couldn't tell. All he knew was that the sky was a little paler in that direction. So that was where the day would soon be dawning. He must be walking eastwards – not that he was any the wiser for that. A cow mooed somewhere ahead.

His fellow-traveller did not seem to be there. Or, if he was, he must have abandoned the idea of finishing Maigret off. The latter thought he could hold out for a few minutes more. Determined to make the best of them, he plodded on like a tired soldier struggling to keep in the ranks. Left, right! . . . Left, right! . . . He counted his steps to prevent himself thinking.

That cow must belong to a farm, and farmers were early risers. So there was a chance of finding somebody about.

His shirt was all wet. The blood was trickling right down to his waist, under his belt, and he could feel it on his thigh . . .

Was that a light between the trees? Or was he becoming delirious? . . .

'If I lose a quart of blood . . .' he thought.

Yes, it was a light. Only, he had to cross a ploughed field to reach it. It was heavy going. He could hardly make it. He bumped into a tractor that had been left ready for the next day's work . . .

'Hallo! . . . Anyone there? . . . Quick! . . .'

In that 'quick' was a despairing note. He was leaning against the tractor now . . . Slipping . . . Sitting on the

ground . . . He heard a door open, saw another light – a
lantern . . . Someone holding it up . . .

'Quick! . . .'

A man was approaching. Would he be able to stop the
blood? Perhaps he wouldn't think of it. Maigret's hand
was losing its grip. His left arm fell limply by his side, like
the other.

'One, two . . . one, two . . .'

With each pulse the blood oozed from the wound.

*

Confused images with blanks of unconsciousness between
them. Tortuous images with the oppressive quality of a
nightmare.

A rhythm . . . the steps of a horse . . . straw under his
head . . . trees going by . . .

That at any rate was understandable. He was lying on
straw in some kind of a cart. It was broad daylight, and
they were going slowly along a road bordered by plane trees.

Maigret lay still, with his eyes open. Within his field of
vision was a man who strolled along waving a whip.

Nightmares again . . . He had not had a good look at the
man in the train. All he had seen clearly were the trembling
hands, the patent-leather boots, and the thick grey socks.
And even so, it was only in the dim light of the sleeping-
compartment. As for the rest of him, it was no more than
a vague outline.

And yet . . . Somehow he couldn't help feeling that this
peasant was the man who had tossed about in the upper
couchette. The face he saw was lined and weather-beaten. A
long grey moustache. Thick eyebrows. Pale blue eyes which
looked straight ahead without so much as a glance at him.

Where were they? . . . Where were they going? . . .

Moving a hand, the inspector was conscious of some-
thing strange pressing on his chest. Of course! Bandages . . .
Then one idea ran into another and all was confusion again.
A ray of sunshine struck his face, making him blink.

Presently there were houses. Houses with white fronts. A wide street bathed in bright light ... Steps behind the cart. People following ... And voices ... But the words were only a jumble ... The bumping of the cart over the cobbles hurt ...

The bumping had stopped. He was floating in the air, rocked on something soft, then gliding along with unaccustomed smoothness.

They were wheeling him on a stretcher. In front was a man in a white coat. Gates were shut. Noise of a crowd fading away ... Someone came running.

'Take him straight into the theatre.'

Maigret didn't move his head. He didn't think. He just lay looking at whatever passed before his eyes.

They were out of doors again now, going through a garden. A number of small buildings, very clean, built of white brick. People in grey, all dressed alike, sitting on seats. Some had bandaged heads or arms in slings ... Nurses going to and fro.

He was thinking now, or trying to, groping for a word that kept on eluding him. There it was – hospital!

Where was that peasant who was so like the man in the train? ... Whew! ... The deuce of a twinge! ... They were carrying him upstairs ...

When Maigret woke next, it was to see a man washing his hands, at the same time looking gravely at him.

It gave him quite a shock. This man had a little goatee and thick eyebrows. Was he like the peasant? Perhaps. Perhaps not. But he was certainly like the man in the train.

Maigret opened his mouth, but no words came. The man with the goatee gave orders quietly:

'Put him in Number 3 ... Better keep him isolated on account of the police.'

What? On account of the police? What was the fellow talking about?

White people wheeled him away. Back through the

garden. The sun – he had never seen such a sun before. Bright, jubilant, blazing into every corner.

They put him to bed. The walls were white. It was almost as hot here as in the train . . . Somewhere a voice saying:

'It's the inspector who wants to know . . .'

The inspector? That must mean him . . . But he hadn't asked anything . . . How absurd it all was! Particularly this business of the peasant, who was like the doctor, who was like the man in the train . . .

Had the man in the train a beard or a moustache? Or neither? Were his eyebrows thick?

'Force his mouth open . . . Right! . . . That'll do.'

It was the doctor pouring something down his throat . . . Of course! To finish him off. To poison him! . . .

*

Towards evening, when Maigret came to his senses again, the nurse who was watching by his bedside went to the door. Outside, five men were waiting in the corridor. They were: the public prosecutor of Bergerac, the examining magistrate and his clerk, an inspector, and a police pathologist.

'You can come in now, but the doctor says he's not to be tired. By the look in his eyes, I shouldn't be at all surprised if he's mad.'

The five men nodded and exchanged glances.

CHAPTER II

Five Disappointed Men

IT was like a badly acted melodrama. The nurse, after a final glance at Maigret, smiled at the five men as she withdrew. A smile which meant:

'I'll leave him to you.'

And the five men took possession of the room. They all smiled too, each in his own peculiar way. But all the smiles were equally menacing – so much so that they looked put on for a special purpose. You might have thought they had plotted together to play some practical joke.

'After you, *Monsieur le procureur* . . .'

The prosecutor was a very short man with hair standing up *en brosse*, with a fierce expression on his face that had no doubt been studiously adopted to fit his profession, and a look of cold disdain that was no less carefully assumed.

He passed the bed with the merest glance at Maigret, then posted himself with his back to the wall not far from the window, where he stood rigidly, hat in hand.

The examining magistrate followed. This time the glance at Maigret was accompanied by an unmistakable sneer. Then the clerk . . . They were now three in line abreast, backs to the wall. Finally, the police pathologist joined them to make a fourth. It was almost as though they had been lined up for an inspection.

That left only the police inspector with the bulging eyes, who in the badly acted melodrama appeared to be cast for the role of saviour of the righteous.

With a glance at the others he approached the bed and slowly lowered a hand on Maigret's unbandaged shoulder.

'Caught you this time! What?'

It ought to have been extremely funny, but Maigret didn't even smile. On the contrary, he frowned anxiously.

For he was anxious, anxious about himself. The line between dream and reality was already vague enough, and the way these men were carrying on made it vaguer every moment.

The police inspector was obviously thinking himself very smart.

'I must say . . . I'm not sorry to have a look at that mug of yours at last!'

And those four men against the wall, who simply stared and said nothing . . .

Maigret was surprised to hear himself heave a deep sigh. He gazed at his left hand as he drew it from under the bedclothes.

'Who were you after last night? A woman? Or a young girl?'

At that, Maigret was overwhelmed – overwhelmed by the thought of all the talking that would have to be done to put matters straight. It was awful to think of. He was sleepy. His whole body was aching.

'Better . . .' he began with a limp movement of his hand.

They didn't seem to understand, and in a faint voice he repeated:

'Better . . . tomorrow . . .'

He shut his eyes, and in a second all was confusion, until the four men against the wall were all rolled into one person . . . a peasant who was like the doctor . . . who was like the peasant . . . who was like the man in the train . . .

*

The next morning he was sitting up in bed, or rather propped up by a couple of extra pillows. From that position he watched the nurse as she pottered about in the sunshine, tidying up the room.

She was a fine-looking girl, big and strong, strikingly fair. The glances she kept on throwing at Maigret were at the same time both challenging and nervous.

'Tell me! It was *five* men that came to see me yesterday, wasn't it?'

She answered haughtily:

'You know perfectly well.'

'All right . . . Well, tell me what they wanted.'

'I've orders not to speak to you. And I'd better warn you that I'll repeat anything you say.'

Maigret was very much better. In fact, he was well enough now to derive a subtle pleasure from the situation, much as one enjoys continuing a dream even after one knows it's really over.

The sun was as bright as in illustrated fairy-tales. From somewhere outside came the sound of passing cavalry, and suddenly a triumphant blare of trumpets.

At the same moment the nurse passed close to the bed, and Maigret, wishing to attract her attention, plucked at her dress.

She spun round, uttered a piercing shriek, and fled.

It was not till midday that the mists began to lift. The surgeon was busy dressing the wound when the police inspector arrived in a brand-new straw hat and a royal-blue tie.

'You haven't had the curiosity to look in my pocket-book?' asked Maigret gently.

'You know very well you haven't got one.'

He must have lost it rolling down the railway embankment.

'All right. Telephone to the *Police Judiciaire* . . . They'll tell you I'm Divisional Inspector Maigret. Or it might be quicker still to ring up my former colleague, Leduc, who's living at Villefranche . . . But first of all, for the love of God, tell me where I am.'

The other was not so easily convinced. There were supercilious smiles, and now and again he nudged the doctor.

The last suspicions were only broken down when Leduc drove up in his old Ford. Then at last, to many people's disappointment, it had to be admitted that Maigret was really Maigret and not what he was supposed to be – the Madman of Bergerac.

*

Leduc had the ruddy complexion of a man who leads an easy-going life in the open air. Since leaving the *Police Judiciaire* he had adopted a meerschaum pipe, whose cherry stem could be seen projecting from his pocket.

'Here's the story in a nutshell. I've naturally heard all about it, as I drive into the market here every Saturday, and I take the opportunity to have a good meal at the *Hôtel d'Angleterre* ... Well, it must have been about a month ago that they found a woman's body on one of the main roads. Strangled. But that wasn't all. Having killed her that way, the sadist stuck a long needle right through her heart.'

'Who was she?'

'Léontine Moreau. She lived at a farm called Moulin-Neuf. She wasn't robbed.'

'Was she ... ?'

'No, she wasn't tampered with, though she was a good-looking woman of thirty ... The crime took place at night-fall as she was returning from her sister-in-law's ... That's the first ...'

'There were two?'

'Two and a half ... The second was a girl of sixteen, the station-master's daughter, who had been out for a ride on her bicycle. She was found in the same state.'

'At night?'

'She wasn't found till next morning, but she had been killed the evening before ... Then lastly there was one of the maids of the *Hôtel d'Angleterre*, who had been to see her brother, a road-mender, who was working three or four miles away. She was on foot. And suddenly someone seized her from behind and threw her down ... But she's a strapping girl, and she caught hold of the man's hand and bit into his wrist. He swore and made off. She only saw his back as he ran into the bushes.'

'Is that all?'

'It's all so far. But the people here are convinced there's a maniac roaming about in the woods. They refuse to believe it could be one of themselves. When the news got around that you'd been found shot, everybody thought you were the murderer and that you'd been after someone again, but had met more than your match.'

Leduc spoke gravely. He didn't seem to see the comic side of it at all.

'And what's more,' he went on, 'they won't get the idea out of their heads in a moment.'

'Who's in charge of the case?'

'The local people.'

'If you don't mind, I think I'll go to sleep now.'

He was very weak and had an inexhaustible capacity for dozing. He didn't really want to sleep, but to doze, to lie in semi-consciousness with his eyes shut. Most of all, he liked to have his head turned towards the window, with the sun shining through his eyelids.

His fancy had now three new characters to play with, to put through their paces like a child drilling his multi-coloured tin soldiers.

A woman aged thirty from the Moulin-Neuf Farm . . . The station-master's daughter . . . The chambermaid of the hotel.

He could remember the wood. Tall dark trees with a white strip of road. And he could imagine the victim lying in the dust while the murderer thrust the long needle through her heart.

It was a fantastic image. All the more so for being evoked in this spotless private ward, from which the peaceful sounds of the street were clearly audible. He listened to a man, right under his window, who was a full ten minutes trying to get his car started. The surgeon arrived in a smooth, powerful car, which he drove himself. But it was eight o'clock before Maigret saw him.

'Is it serious?'

'It will take some little time to heal. We'll have to keep you in bed for a fortnight.'

'Could I be moved to a hotel?'

'Aren't you comfortable here? . . . Of course, if you had someone to nurse you . . .'

'Look here, Doctor! Between ourselves, what do you think of this Madman of Bergerac?'

The doctor stood lost in thought so long that Maigret asked again:

'Do you think, like the others, that there's some sort of wild man living in the woods?'

'No.'

Of course he didn't. Maigret, in his musings, had recalled several similar cases. Some of them he'd handled himself.

'A man who, in ordinary life, would behave just like you or me – isn't that more likely?'

'Probably,' answered the doctor.

'So, as likely as not, he lives in Bergerac, and may easily be a respectable professional man?'

The surgeon looked at him queerly, hesitating. He seemed to have something on his mind.

'Have you any idea?' went on Maigret, watching him closely.

'I've had a great many, one after the other. I pounce on them, and then reject them indignantly ... But only to come back to them later. If you clear your mind of all prejudices, practically anyone may be suspected of mental derangement.'

Maigret laughed.

'So we'd better have the whole town put under observation, from the mayor downwards. And of course we'd have to include the whole staff of the hospital.'

But the surgeon did not smile.

'Just a moment – keep still!' he said as he probed the wound with some delicate instrument. 'It's a more terrible business than you think.'

'What's the population of Bergerac?'

'Sixteen thousand ... But to my mind everything points to its being someone of the upper classes ... Even ...'

'Exactly! The needle ...' said Maigret, screwing up his face as the doctor hurt him.

'What do you mean?'

'Stuck each time through the middle of the heart – do you think that would imply some knowledge of anatomy?'

The doctor did not answer, and nothing more was said while he replaced the bandages. His face looked careworn. At last he straightened himself with a sigh.

'You say you'd rather be in a hotel?'

'Yes. My wife could come and see to me.'

'Are you going to interest yourself in these murders?'

'And how!'

*

Rain would have spoilt everything. But for over a fortnight not a drop fell.

And there was Maigret installed in the best bedroom on the first floor of the *Hôtel d'Angleterre*. His bed had been shifted over towards one of the windows, and from where he lay he could look down on the Place du Marché and watch the sun as it alternately lit up and threw into shadow each row of houses in turn.

Madame Maigret accepted the situation as she accepted everything, without either astonishment or fuss. Within an hour of her arrival she had arranged the room according to her own ideas. It ceased to be the impersonal hotel bedroom and became definitely hers.

Two days before, she had been quietly asserting herself in much the same way by her sister's bedside in Alsace.

'A grand girl! If you only could have seen her! Ten pounds: I weighed her myself.'

She took the surgeon aside.

'What can he eat, Doctor? Some good strong chicken broth?... There's one thing you ought to forbid, and that's his pipe. He'll be asking for it before the day's out, as sure as I'm alive. And you should keep him off beer too...'

The wall-paper was a marvellous red-and-green affair. Blood-red and the crudest of greens, in stripes which fairly hummed in the sunshine.

And horrid little hotel furniture of varnished pitch-pine. Nothing which stood squarely on all four legs at once. An immense room with two beds. A mantelpiece two centuries old, in front of which stood a cheap radiator.

'What I'd like to know is what possessed you to do such a thing. Suppose you'd fallen under the train!... By the way, I think I'll make you a *crème au citron*. I take it they'll raise no objection to my using the kitchen.'

The semi-conscious reveries were becoming rarer now. Even with the sun shining through his closed eyelids, Maigret's ideas were fairly logical. Nevertheless he still went on with his puppet-show, playing with the characters his imagination had elaborated.

The first victim . . . the woman from the Moulin-Neuf Farm . . . What was it they had told him?

'She had married a farmer's son and lived with the family. She didn't get on any too well with her mother-in-law, who accused her of thinking too much about her looks and wearing silk underclothes – even for milking the cows . . .'

It was something to go on, and Maigret went patiently to work, painting her portrait in his mind as lovingly as any artist could manipulate his brushes. He saw an attractive, buxom, well-washed young woman introducing new-fangled ideas into the farmer's household, consulting catalogues that would be sent her from Paris.

She was returning home from the town . . . Maigret could see the road perfectly. It must be, like all the roads round Bergerac, overshadowed by a row of plane trees on either hand . . . And the white, dusty, chalky surface – white even at night under the shadow of the trees . . .

And then the flapper on her bicycle.

'Sixteen. Old enough to have a boy friend. There was no mention of one, however. Once a year she used to have a fortnight's holiday in Paris, staying with an aunt . . .'

The surgeon came twice a day. The public prosecutor called, and taking Madame Maigret for a servant, he handed her his hat and stick, and was then profuse in his apologies. In any case, he had come to apologize.

'You see, your not having any papers on you . . . I'm sure you'll forgive the mistake.'

'Yes, my pocket-book seems to have disappeared . . . But do sit down . . .'

Even so, the man still looked aggressive. He simply couldn't help it: it had become a habit. Added to the scowl on his face, he had a little bulbous nose and a bristling moustache.

'It's a most lamentable affair. To think that in a place like this! . . . Now, if it had been in Paris, where hooligans and madmen can be met with every day . . . But here! . . .'

Sacrebleu! Here was another man with bushy eyebrows! Like the doctor. Like the peasant. They were grey too. And whether he had seen them or not, Maigret couldn't help attributing thick grey eyebrows to the man in the train.

The head of his stick was of carved ivory.

'Well! Anyhow . . . I hope you'll soon be on your feet again and that you won't bear us a grudge.'

He had only come out of politeness and was already longing to go.

'You've an excellent doctor, at all events. A pupil of Martel's . . . As for the rest, it's a pity . . .'

'What rest?'

'Oh! Never mind. No need for you to worry . . . I'll look in again one of these days, and in the meantime they'll let me know how you're getting on.'

As soon as he had gone, Maigret started to lap up his *crème au citron*, which was a perfect masterpiece. But the smell of truffles that rose from the kitchen was rather mortifying.

'You never saw such a thing,' said his wife. 'They serve up truffles by the dishful here, just like fried potatoes. Even in the fifteen-franc dinner.'

Leduc arrived in the old Ford. Maigret could hear him backing and shunting for a long time before the car was finally parked under his window. He wore a straw hat like the police inspector's.

'Sit down . . . Like some of my *crème au citron*? . . . No? . . . Well, tell me what you know of the private life of my doctor. I haven't even heard his name.'

'Dr Rivaud. I don't know much about him really – that is, apart from gossip. He lives with a wife and a sister-in

-law. And they say the sister-in-law is just as much his wife as the real one . . . But of course . . .'

'And the prosecutor?'

'Monsieur Duhourceau. You've heard something already?'

'Go on.'

'His sister's the widow of a sea captain, and she's in an asylum. Though some say she's not mad at all, but that he had her shut up so as to get hold of her money.'

Maigret was sitting up in bed, gazing out through the window with half-closed eyes. To Leduc's surprise he beamed with satisfaction.

'And what else?'

'Nothing. In these little towns, you know . . .'

'But don't forget, my dear Leduc, that this little town is different from any other. It's a little town with a madman.'

It was quite funny to see Leduc. He seemed really rather upset.

'Yes, a madman. A madman at large. A madman who's only mad by fits and starts, while the rest of the time he's walking about and talking to people, just like anybody else.'

'How does Madame Maigret like it here?'

. 'She's been turning the kitchen upside down. She and the chef exchange recipes. When I come to think of it, perhaps it's the chef who's mad.'

There's something slightly intoxicating about a narrow escape from death. And then to lie in bed and be petted . . . Still more so if your surroundings are given piquancy by a touch of unreality . . .

To lie in bed and let your brain work of itself, just for the fun of it, studying a strange place and strange people through a sunlit window and from the scraps of information that would reach you . . .

'I suppose there's a public library in the town?'

'Of course.'

'Well, if you want to do me a great favour, you'll go and pick me out the best books on mental diseases, perversions, maniacs, and all the rest of it. And one other thing – see if you can arrange with the landlord to have a telephone fixed up here by my bed . . . And of course I must have a telephone directory – they're always most instructive books.'

That was enough for the moment. Maigret was drowsy. He could feel the somnolence welling up from the depths of his being and spreading gradually to every limb.

'Shall I see you tomorrow?'

'Of course. But I must be off now. I haven't yet done my marketing, and I have to buy a goat.'

Leduc picked up his straw hat. When he shut the door behind him, Maigret's eyes were closed and his breathing came regularly through his half-open mouth.

Downstairs, in the passage, the retired inspector ran into Dr Rivaud. Drawing the latter aside, he hesitated and shuffled and then stammered.

'You're quite sure, I suppose, that this wound . . . that it couldn't have affected my friend's intelligence? . . . I mean his . . . I hardly know how to put it . . . but perhaps you understand . . .'

The gesture with which the doctor answered might have meant anything.

'He's an intelligent man as a rule?' he asked.

'Very intelligent, even if he doesn't always look it.'

'Ah!'

And with that the surgeon turned thoughtfully and went upstairs.

CHAPTER III

The Second-class Ticket

MAIGRET had left Paris on the previous Tuesday, late in the afternoon. Wounded early on the Wednesday morning, he had spent that day and the two following in the hospital of Bergerac. On Saturday, as soon as his wife had arrived, he had been moved to the big first-floor room of the *Hôtel d'Angleterre*.

On Monday his wife suddenly said to him:

'Why didn't you use your free travelling-pass?'

It was four in the afternoon. Madame Maigret, whose hands were never idle, was tidying up the room for the third time that day.

The Place du Marché was humming with warmth and life. The outside blinds were partially lowered, giving a mellow light inside the room.

Maigret, who was smoking one of his first pipes, looked at his wife with some astonishment. It seemed to him that she avoided his eye as she waited for his answer. He even thought she was slightly flushed with embarrassment.

It was certainly an unexpected question. Every inspector attached to a flying squad had a railway pass which enabled him to travel free first-class anywhere in France. And of course Maigret had used his last Tuesday.

'Come here and sit down.'

He saw she hesitated, but he insisted.

'Now, tell me all about it.'

She became still more embarrassed under his quizzical look.

'I oughtn't to have put the question like that . . . But I can't help thinking you're a bit strange at times.'

'You too?'

'What do you mean?'

'Well, everybody else does! And they can't bring themselves to believe wholeheartedly in my story of the man in the train . . . And now . . .'

'Listen! It's like this – there's a mat in the passage, outside our door, and when I moved it just now I found this.'

Although she was living in a hotel, she wore an apron, not only because she liked to do a little house-work, but because it made her feel more at home. She now felt in its pocket and drew out a railway ticket. It was a second-class ticket from Paris to Bergerac, and was dated the previous Tuesday.

'It was under the mat?'

'Just at the edge.'

'Take a pencil and a piece of paper.'

She obeyed, licked the point of the pencil, and sat waiting.

'Now, who's been to see me here? . . . First of all, the proprietor of the hotel. I think he was the first. Then the doctor . . . Make a list of them . . . The prosecutor came to make his little apology. Then there's the local inspector who came yesterday. Who else?'

'There's Leduc,' said Madame Maigret reluctantly.

'Quite right! Put him down. Is that all? . . . Of course there are the servants. And, for that matter, anybody staying in the hotel might have dropped it as they went along the passage.'

'But there's no reason for them to be in the passage.'

'Why not?'

'Because it only leads to this room. If they came as far as our door it would be to look through the keyhole.'

'Ring up the station-master, will you?'

Maigret had seen practically nothing of the town, and he had not been anywhere near the station. But he had studied the plan in the *Guide Michelin*, and with its help he had formed a mental picture of Bergerac that was accurate in all essentials.

He knew that the Place du Marché which he surveyed through his window was at the very heart of the town. The large building on the right was for the most part out of sight, but he knew it none the less as the Palais de Justice. Under the heading . . . *Hôtel d' Angleterre*, the guide said:

Premier ordre. Chambres depuis 25 francs. Salles de Bains. Repas a 15 et 18 francs. Spécialité de truffes, foie gras, ballotines de volaille, saumon de la Dordogne.

The Dordogne which provided the salmon flowed past behind the hotel, but Maigret could not only follow its course in the plan, but could study its scenery in a series of picture postcards. Another showed him the outside of the station. As for the *Hôtel de France* on the other side of the Place du Marché, he knew it to be the rival of his own.

'Here's the station-master.'

'Ask him if any passengers alighted from the Paris train early Wednesday morning.'

'He says no.'

'That's all.'

It was impossible to come to any other conclusion than that the ticket found in the passage had been used by the man who had jumped from the train.

'Do you know what I'd like you to do? . . . Go and have a look at Monsieur Duhourceau's house – you know, the public prosecutor's. And then you might go and see Dr Rivaud's.'

'What for?'

'Nothing in particular. Just to tell me what you see.'

He took advantage of being alone to exceed the number of pipes he was allowed. The day was closing in, the Place du Marché rose-coloured with evening light. The commercial travellers, having finished their rounds, drove up one after another, parking their cars in front of the hotel. From downstairs came the clack of billiard balls. Others would no doubt be drinking their *apéritifs*.

Why had the fellow risked his neck, or at any rate a broken limb, jumping out of the train? And why had he fired at Maigret?

One thing was certain: the man knew the line. He had opened the door just before the brakes went on. He wasn't travelling without a ticket, and if he couldn't face the station it would be for fear of being recognized. So he was known in Bergerac . . .

Not that that proved him a murderer . . . Maigret recalled his restlessness as he tossed about in the upper *couchette*, his deep sighs, and the time he tried so desperately to keep still.

'Duhourceau must be home by now. He'll be in his study

perhaps, reading the Paris papers. Or he may have brought some work to finish off at home . . . The surgeon will be going his evening rounds, followed by a sister . . . The police inspector . . .'

His musings drawled on lazily. He was in no hurry. As a rule, at the beginning of a case, he was all on edge with impatience, but as soon as he had something to go on, as soon as he had decided on his line of action, he was as cool and calm as could be.

But this time he had next to nothing to go on and no line of action at all, and yet he was thoroughly enjoying himself. He liked this drifting and paddling about, just keeping his mind afloat in a stream of stray impressions.

Perhaps it was because he was ill. He'd have to stay in bed for a fortnight anyhow – wasn't that what the doctor had said? So there was no use being in a hurry. He had plenty of time. Masses of time. Long days with nothing else to do but to make mental pictures of Bergerac and its surroundings and get all the characters into their proper places.

Leduc had brought him a handful of books on mental aberrations, but he had no more than dipped into them. He had found them stodgy, and gazing out of the window had seemed to him both more useful and more amusing.

It was time to switch the light on, but he didn't bother. He was too lazy. By the time Madame Maigret returned, it was quite dark. The window was wide open and a cold breeze blew in. The street lamps made a garland of light round the market-place below.

'Do you want to catch pneumonia?' said Madame Maigret, making straight for the window. 'If so, you're going the right way about it. Why didn't you ring and ask them to shut it?'

'Well?'

'Well what? I've seen a couple of houses, but I don't know what good that's going to do us.'

'Come on! Tell me what they're like.'

'Monsieur Duhourceau lives over on the other side of the Palais de Justice, in a square as big as the Place du Marché. A massive three-storey house. The first floor has a stone balcony. The room behind it was lit up: I suppose it would be his study. Downstairs there was a manservant closing the shutters.'

'Does it look a bright place?'

'Bright? What do you mean? . . . A big house like any other. A sombre place, if anything, though the crimson velvet curtains must have cost two thousand francs a window. Soft, silky stuff, but very heavy, falling in big folds . . .'

Maigret chuckled. It was exactly what he wanted. With a few touches he corrected the picture he had already formed in his mind.

'And the servant?'

'The manservant? Yes?'

'Was he wearing a striped waistcoat?'

'He was.'

Maigret could have clapped. He could see the place perfectly. A solid, dignified house, richly curtained, a carved stone balcony. Indoors, old furniture and a manservant with a striped waistcoat. The prosecutor himself in a morning coat and grey trousers, patent-leather boots, white hair standing up *en brosse* . . .

'That's right, isn't it? He does wear patent-leather boots?'

'Yes. Button boots. I noticed them when he called.'

Patent-leather boots! Like the man in the train! But weren't his lace-up boots? Of course. Maigret could remember the trembling hands that fumbled with the knots.

'And now the doctor's house.'

'It's almost on the edge of the town. A villa like those you see by the seaside.'

'English cottage style?'

'That kind of thing. A low roof, lawns, flower-beds, gravel paths. A beautiful garage. The shutters are painted green, and there's a wrought-iron lantern hanging over the front door ... The shutters were still open, and I could see his wife in the drawing-room with some needlework.'

'It wasn't her sister?'

'No. She's a good deal younger – in fact, she's very young. Very pretty too, and very well dressed. She drove up with the doctor as I was coming away. Nothing provincial about her. I'd bet anything her clothes come from Paris ...'

Interesting. But what had all this to do with a madman who attacked women at night in lonely places, first strangling them, then sticking a needle through their hearts?

Maigret made no attempt to answer that question. He was simply learning all he could, regardless of whether it was relevant or not.

'Did you meet anybody?'

'Nobody I knew. The people here don't seem to go out much in the evenings.'

'Is there a cinema?'

'I caught sight of one in a side street. They were showing a film I saw in Paris three years ago.'

*

Ten o'clock in the morning. Leduc drove up and parked his car below. A moment or two later he knocked at Maigret's door. The latter was smacking his lips over a bowl of beef tea that his wife had made herself.

'How are you getting on?'

'Sit down. No. Not on that chair – you'd block the view.'

Since leaving the *Police Judiciaire*, Leduc had grown stouter. He had also changed in manner, being gentler and more timid than he used to be.

'What's your cook giving you for lunch today?'

'Lamb cutlets. I have to avoid heavy food.'

'Tell me – have you been to Paris recently?'

Madame Maigret looked up sharply, surprised at the

bluntness of the question. As for Leduc, his face clouded and he looked at his friend reproachfully.

'What do you mean? . . . You know very well that . . .'

'Of course!'

Maigret knew very well that . . . But he studied Leduc's profile with its little reddish moustache. Then he looked down at his feet, shod in heavy shooting-boots.

'Between ourselves, what facilities are there in this part of the world for enjoying the charms of the fair sex?'

'Really!' protested Madame Maigret. 'You're letting your tongue run away with you.'

'Not at all. It's a most important question. In the country they don't have all the amenities of the town . . . How old is your cook?'

'Sixty-five! So you see . . .'

'No young blood about the place?'

What made it so awkward was the seriousness with which Maigret put the questions, for they were the kind of questions that are usually proffered in a playful, bantering tone.

'No little shepherdess, for instance?'

'There's only the cook's niece who comes from time to time to lend her a hand.'

'Sixteen? . . . Eighteen?'

'Nineteen. But really . . . !'

'I see!'

Leduc fidgeted, while Madame Maigret, even more embarrassed than he, withdrew to the darkest corner of the room.

'You're being abominably tactless,' she said.

'So that's that!' said Maigret doggedly. For a moment the cross-examination appeared to be over, but after a short silence he grunted:

'Duhourceau's a bachelor, I understand. How does he manage?'

'There's no mistaking you come from Paris. You speak of these things as if they were the most ordinary matters.

Do you think the prosecutor relates his peccadilloes to everyone he meets?'

'No. But as everything gets round sooner or later, you're bound to have heard.'

'I only know what people say.'

'There you are!'

'They say he goes once or twice a week to Bordeaux, where he ...'

Maigret had not once taken his eyes off his friend's face, and a queer smile floated on his lips. He had known another Leduc, and a much more outspoken one. None of these hesitations and country-town embarrassments.

'Do you know what you ought to do? After all, as you've been in the police yourself, they'd give you plenty of rope ... Start a little investigation, and see if you can find out who was away from Bergerac last Tuesday. But wait a moment – the people I'm most interested in are Dr Rivaud, the prosecutor, the police inspector, and ...'

Leduc jumped up from his seat. He looked at his straw hat like a man who is thinking of cramming it on his head and walking out of the room.

'A joke's all very well,' he said, 'but this one's gone far enough. I really don't know what's come over you. Since you've been wounded you ... you haven't been yourself at all ... Are you seriously suggesting that, in a little place like this where the least thing will set tongues wagging ... that I should take it upon myself to start nosing into the doings of the local inspector, to say nothing of the *procureur de la République*? I haven't the smallest right to do so ... As for your insinuations about myself ...'

'Sit down, Leduc.'

'I haven't much time.'

'Sit down, I tell you. Just listen to me and you'll understand. Here in Bergerac is a man who in ordinary life seems perfectly normal and probably exercises some profession, a man who now and again in a fit of madness ...'

'And you don't hesitate to put me down on the list of

possibles! Don't think I didn't see the point of your questions just now. You wanted to know if I had a mistress. Why? Because a man who's unsatisfied is more likely than another to . . .'

He was really angry. He had turned quite red and his eyes were glowing.

'The local police have taken the case in hand. It's nothing whatever to do with me. And if you want to get mixed up in . . .'

'. . . in something which is no business of mine! . . . Perhaps you're right, but just imagine that, in two or three days, or four, or five, that little nineteen-year-old of yours is found dead with a needle through her heart.'

But Leduc had had enough. This time he really did cram the straw hat on to his head. And he strutted out of the room, shutting the door a bit too violently behind him.

The moment he had gone, Madame Maigret came up to the bedside. She looked worried, even anxious.

'What on earth has he done to you that you should treat him like that? I've rarely seen you so disagreeable. One might almost think you really suspected him.'

'Don't you worry. He'll soon be back – you'll see – and he'll be tumbling over himself trying to make it up . . . And now be an angel and fill me a pipe. And these pillows are slipping down again . . .'

Half an hour later, when the doctor came to see him, Maigret smiled benignly.

'What did he say to you?'

'Who?'

'My friend Leduc. He's rather bothered about me, and I wouldn't mind betting he asked you to keep me under observation. You know, Doctor, I'm not at all mad, but . . .'

He got no farther, however, as a thermometer was thrust into his mouth. While his temperature was being taken, Dr Rivaud removed the dressing. The wound was slow in healing.

'You move about too much. There you are! Over a hundred and two. I don't need to ask you if you've been smoking. The air's thick with it.'

'You ought to forbid it altogether,' said Madame Maigret.

But her husband interrupted her:

'Can you tell me at what intervals our madman's crimes were committed?'

'Let me see ... The first was a month ago. The second a week later. While the one that miscarried was a week later still, and ...'

'Do you know what I think, Doctor? ... That there's a good chance another body will be found in the next day or two. If not, it means the chap feels he's being watched. But if there is another ...'

'Well?'

'It might enable us to eliminate some people. Suppose, for instance, you were in this room at the moment the crime was committed. That would put you out of the running straight away. Suppose the prosecutor was at Bordeaux, the police inspector in Paris, the landlord downstairs in his kitchen, and Leduc anywhere you like ...'

The surgeon stared at his patient.

'You seem to have restricted the range of possibilities already.'

'Probabilities.'

'It's all the same. You confine the suspects to the handful of people you've come in contact with.'

'Not even as many as that. I've left out the examining magistrate and his clerk and the police pathologist ... My list is, in fact, restricted to the people who've been to see me here in the hotel and who could inadvertently have dropped a railway ticket. As a matter of fact, where were you last Tuesday?'

'Last Tuesday?'

Taken aback, the doctor groped in his memory. He was still quite a young man, active and ambitious. His movements were decisive. Altogether he cut a very good figure.

'I think . . . wait a moment . . . Yes, I drove over to La Rochelle for . . .'

He broke off, bridling at the sight of the amused expression on Maigret's face.

'Am I to consider myself under examination? In that case I warn you . . .'

'Take it easy, Doctor. Don't forget that I've nothing to do the whole day long. And I'm used to living in a whirl of activity. So I've invented a little game to keep my mind busy. It's called *Madman* . . . And you'll admit that there's nothing to prevent a doctor being a madman, or a madman a doctor. It's even said that all mental specialists are their own patients. Nor is there anything to prevent a public prosecutor . . . ?'

He heard the doctor whisper to Madame Maigret:

'He hasn't been drinking, has he?'

As soon as they were alone together, she came over to her husband's bedside, her brow heavy with reproaches.

'Don't you see what you're doing? . . . I simply can't make you out. You're carrying on exactly as if you wanted everybody to believe you were the madman yourself . . . The doctor didn't say anything – he's too polite – but I could see . . . And now what are you smiling about?'

'Nothing. The sunshine. Those red and green stripes on the wall-paper. The women chattering in the market-place. That little lemon-yellow car that looks like some huge insect . . . and then the smell of *foie gras* . . . Only, of course – somewhere or other – there's a madman . . . There! Look at that girl. Little pear-shaped breasts and calves as stout as any mountaineer's. Why shouldn't the madman choose her next?'

Madame Maigret looked into his eyes and she could see he was not joking any longer. He wasn't playing *Madman* now to while the time away. On the contrary, he was speaking with intense seriousness. There was even a note of real trouble in his voice. He took hold of her hand before going on:

'You see, I don't think it's over. We've no right to assume it is. And I don't want . . . I don't want that fine young girl to pass under my window next time in a hearse, followed by a lot of people in black . . . Yes, there's a madman about. A man who laughs and talks, who comes and goes . . .'

Maigret's eyes were half-closed now. In a coaxing voice he murmured:

'Give me a pipe all the same.'

CHAPTER IV

Maigret's Reception

MAIGRET had chosen nine o'clock in the morning because it was his favourite time of the day. He loved the quality of morning sunshine, loved the sounds which made the start of a day's activity – doors opening and shutting, the early traffic in the street, the footfalls on the pavements – sounds which would steadily increase in volume to their midday climax.

Through his window he could see on a plane tree one of the notices he had had posted up in various parts of the town:

At 9 a.m. on Thursday morning, at the *Hôtel d'Angleterre*, Inspector Maigret will give 100 francs reward to anyone giving information concerning the murders that have recently been committed in the neighbourhood of Bergerac, apparently by some demented person.

'Shall I stay?' asked Madame Maigret, who, even in a hotel, found almost as much to keep her busy as she did in her own house.

'Yes, you can stay.'

'I'm not particularly anxious to. But in any case I don't expect anyone will come.'

Maigret smiled. Half past eight had struck only a moment before, yet, as he lit his pipe, he muttered:

'Here's one already.'

It was the noise of a car that he had at once recognized as Leduc's Ford. Madame Maigret had recognized it too.

'So he's come back again!'

'Didn't I tell you he would? We don't see eye to eye about the Madman of Bergerac, but that won't prevent his being here in a moment.'

'Who? The madman?'

'Perhaps. Even the madman. Or possibly several madmen. In fact there's every chance. A notice like the one I've had put up exerts a fatal attraction on every unbalanced or over-imaginative person ... Come in, Leduc.'

The latter hadn't even had time to knock. There was a somewhat contrite look on his face.

'You couldn't come yesterday?'

'Sorry. I couldn't manage it ... Good morning, Madame Maigret ... A pipe burst and I had to fetch a plumber ... Feeling better?'

'Fine, thanks, except for my back, which is stiff as a poker. Have you seen my notice?'

'What notice?'

He was lying, and Maigret was on the point of chaffing him about it. In the end, however, he decided to be merciful.

'Give my wife your hat, and come and sit down. I'm holding a reception here shortly, and I've even invited the madman himself.'

There was a knock at the door, though no steps had been heard entering the hotel. It was the landlord.

'Excuse me. I didn't know you had a visitor ... It's about that notice.'

'You've something to tell me?'

'Me? Certainly not. If I'd had anything to tell you I wouldn't have waited till you offered a reward. What I wanted to ask was whether we were to show up everybody who came.'

'By all means.'

Maigret looked at the man with half-closed eyes. Screwing his eyes up was becoming quite a habit with him. Or was it merely that the sun was in his eyes?

'Yes. Show them all up.' And when the landlord had gone he turned to Leduc and went on:

'He's a queer chap too. Strong as a bull and red as raw beef. One of those florid people who look as though they might burst at any moment.'

'Started life as a farm labourer somewhere round here. Then he married his employer, a woman of forty-five. He was no more than twenty.'

'And since then?'

'This is his third marriage. His wives seem wedded to a short life!'

'He'll be back again presently.'

'Why?'

'Hanged if I know. But he'll come all right – when everybody's here. He'll find some pretext or other. At what time does the prosecutor go to work?'

'Nine, I suppose.'

'I shouldn't be surprised if he looked in on us on his way. As for the doctor, you can take it from me he's dashing round the wards as fast as his legs will carry him. He won't linger over his cases this morning.'

Maigret had hardly finished his sentence when Monsieur Duhourceau emerged from a side street and toddled across the Place du Marché.

'If the police inspector turns up, it will complete the list.'

'What list?'

'The prosecutor, the inspector, the doctor, the proprietor of the hotel . . . and you.'

'Still on that tack? Look here, Maigret!...'

'Hush! Open the door to Monsieur Duhourceau. He can't make up his mind to knock.'

'I'll be back in an hour or two,' said Madame Maigret, who had put on her hat.

The prosecutor bowed ceremoniously to her as she crossed him at the doorway, then came forward to shake Maigret's hand – without, however, looking him in the face.

'I heard about your notice and I thought I'd better see you first. Of course it's understood that you're acting in a private capacity. Even so, I should like to have been consulted considering this is a case that is being investigated officially.'

'Sit down, won't you? Leduc, take *Monsieur le procureur*'s hat and stick. I'm holding a little reception, *Monsieur le procureur*, and I was just telling Leduc that the madman's been invited ... Ah! Here comes the inspector looking at his watch and wondering whether he'll have a drink downstairs before coming up.'

It was the truth. They saw him enter the hotel, but it was not till ten minutes later that he knocked at the bedroom door. He was disconcerted to find the prosecutor there, and felt called upon to explain his presence ...

'I thought it my duty to ...'

'Naturally,' broke in Maigret cheerily. 'We'll be wanting another chair, Leduc. Perhaps you'll find one on the landing ... I think I can see some of our customers gathering below. Only, no one wants to be the first.'

There were indeed three or four people wandering about in the Place du Marché, throwing frequent glances in the direction of the hotel. In fact, they looked exactly as if they were summoning up their courage. All of them stared at the doctor's car as it drew up at the entrance.

In spite of the buoyant sunshine, there were threads of nervousness in the air. The surgeon, like the others, was disconcerted not to find Maigret alone.

'Quite a council of war!' he said, with none too pleasant a smile.

Maigret noticed that he was badly shaved, and his tie suggested hasty dressing.

'Do you think we might expect the examining magistrate?' asked Maigret.

'He's away for the day,' answered the inspector, 'conducting an inquiry at Saintes.'

'Has he taken his clerk with him?'

'No. I saw him going out a moment ago. He lives over the way in that house with the blue shutters.'

There were steps in the passage. Two or three people were approaching. Then the steps ceased and there were loud whisperings.

'Open the door, Leduc.'

The woman who entered was not one of the people who had been gathering in the Place du Marché. She was one of the chambermaids of the hotel, the one who had had such a narrow escape from the madman's hands. Following her was a shy, awkward young man with fair hair.

'Can Albert come in too? He works in the garage and we're engaged to be married . . . He didn't like the idea of my coming here alone as he says my tongue might run away with me.'

'Come right in, and your fiancé . . . And you too if you like.'

The last words were addressed to the landlord, who was standing in the passage, his chef's cap in his hand.

'I just came up with Rosalie . . .'

'Certainly, certainly! Come in, do! . . . So your name's Rosalie?'

'Yes, monsieur . . . Only I don't know whether I'd be entitled to the reward, seeing as I've told the police everything already.'

The fiancé stared angrily in front of him and muttered:

'Providing it's true . . .'

'Of course it's true. Do you think I'd have invented it?'

'I suppose it's true that a rich gentleman proposed to you! And that your mother was brought up by the gypsies!'

The girl was furious, but she wasn't going to give in. A buxom peasant girl with firm flesh and brawny limbs.

'I won't take back a word of it . . . He came up behind me. I suddenly felt a hand slipping round under my chin, and over I went. But I caught hold of it and bit it for all I was worth. Wait a moment – there was a gold ring on one of the fingers . . .'

'You didn't see him?'

'Not properly. He dashed off into the trees, so I only saw his back view. And I'd hardly had time to pick myself up and get my breath back.'

'You wouldn't be able to recognize him, then? I think you said so to the police.'

Rosalie did not answer. There was an obstinate, hostile look on her face.

'Would you recognize the ring?'

And Maigret's eyes wandered round the room, resting for a moment on one after the other of his guests' hands: Leduc's podgy ones with their heavy signet ring; the long graceful hands of Dr Rivaud with only a wedding ring; Duhourceau's, with white parched skin, that were fidgeting with a handkerchief he had just taken from his pocket.

'A gold ring,' she repeated sullenly.

'And you've no idea who it was that assaulted you?'

'Can I say something, monsieur?' pleaded the fiancé, his forehead beaded with sweat.

'Fire away.'

'I don't want Rosalie to get into trouble. She's a good girl, and I say it to her face. But she has dreams every night. Sometimes she tells me them. And sometimes she'll tell me the same thing again a few days later just as if it had really happened. It's the same when she reads a story.'

'Fill me a pipe, Leduc, will you?'

Through the window, Maigret could see a group of at least ten people talking in undertones in front of the hotel.

Had they come to give evidence, or merely to see what was going on? He turned and looked at the maid.

'You've no idea, Rosalie?... I think you have.'

The girl said nothing. But her eyes rested for a second on the public prosecutor, whose patent-leather boots caught Maigret's eye once more. Only these were button boots ...

'Give her a hundred francs, Leduc. You don't mind acting as my secretary, do you?... Are you satisfied with her?' he asked the landlord.

'She's a good maid. I can't say she isn't.'

'Right! Send in the next.'

The examining magistrate's clerk had meanwhile worked his way into the room and was standing against the wall.

'Oh! So you've come? Find yourself a chair if you can.'

'I'm afraid I haven't much time,' said the doctor, looking at his watch.

'Go on! Time enough!'

And Maigret lit his pipe with his eyes on the door, which opened to admit a young man. He had oozing eyes and a mop of tow-coloured hair, and was dressed in rags.

'I trust you're not going to ...' muttered the prosecutor.

'Come in, my boy. When did you have your last fit?'

'He left the hospital a week ago,' said the doctor.

An obvious epileptic, the type of creature who, in the country, is inevitably regarded as the village idiot.

'What have you got to tell me?'

'Me?'

'Yes, you. Spit it out.'

But instead of speaking, the wretch burst into tears. After a moment his sobs became so convulsive that he seemed on the verge of another attack. At last, between them, he managed to stammer:

'They're always down on me ... I've done nothing ... I swear I haven't ... So why shouldn't I have a hundred francs like the others ... to buy myself a suit with.'

'A hundred francs,' said Maigret to Leduc. 'Next, please.'

The prosecutor was visibly losing patience, while the police inspector pretended to be bored.

'If *we* dealt out money like that,' he murmured, 'we'd have the Council down on us in no time.'

Rosalie and her young man, who were still in the room, were fighting it out in angry whispers in a corner. Two newcomers had been ushered in by the landlord, who then listened by the half-open door for any others who might be coming.

'Are you really expecting to find something out?' sighed Monsieur Duhourceau.

'Oh, dear, no . . . Nothing at all.'

'In that case . . .'

'I told you the madman might be coming, if not several madmen. Do you think I was mistaken?'

The next witness was a road-worker who three days previously had seen a shadow flitting between the trees.

'Did the shadow do anything?'

'No. The chap made off quick enough when I came up.'

'And you couldn't recognize him, of course . . . Fifty francs for the shadow, Leduc. That's quite enough.'

Maigret was the only one to keep his good humour. There were now two or three dozen people below, gathered in little groups, throwing curious glances up at the windows of the hotel.

'And you?'

It was an old peasant, dressed in mourning, who had been waiting with a dull scowl on his face.

'I'm the father of the first one. Yes, it was my lass that was the first to be killed. And I've come to tell you that if ever I set hands on the fellow, I'll . . .'

His eyes too rested for a moment on the public prosecutor.

'You've no idea, I suppose?'

'Well, I wouldn't call it an idea. But I'm not afraid to speak my mind. They wouldn't dare touch a man as had lost his daughter . . . And what I say is, why don't they look in the right quarter? Why don't they look where there's been trouble before? . . . You're a stranger to the place. You don't know . . . But anybody could tell you there's been things going on, though they may not know just what they might be . . .'

Dr Rivaud had risen to his feet and was shifting restlessly about. The police inspector looked aside and pretended not to be listening. As for the prosecutor, he seemed turned to stone.

'Many thanks, old man.'

'And I'll tell you this, that I don't want any of your hundred francs or your fifty francs either . . . But if you should ever pass my way . . . Anybody'll tell you where my place is . . .'

He didn't ask if he might go. Without so much as a nod of farewell he slouched away, and his rounded shoulders disappeared through the doorway.

His departure was followed by a long silence, during which Maigret was apparently preoccupied with his pipe, pressing down the half-burnt tobacco with his one serviceable hand.

'Strike me a match, Leduc.'

A silence that had something pathetic in it, and which appeared to have also taken hold of the people standing in the Place du Marché, who seemed fixed in an unnatural stillness.

No sound but the steps of the old peasant crunching the gravel below, and then:

'For God's sake hold your tongue . . .'

It was Rosalie's Albert who spoke, and who was surprised himself to find he had spoken the words out loud. Rosalie stared straight in front of her with pursed lips, perhaps obediently, or perhaps only biding her time.

'Well, gentlemen,' sighed Maigret at last, 'that's not so bad for a start, is it?'

'We've been through all this already,' said the police inspector, picking up his hat and rising.

Maigret ignored the reproof. He looked at nobody. Gazing at his counterpane, he said:

'Do you think, Doctor, that after an attack has passed, the madman would remember what he's done?'

'It's practically certain.'

The landlord was standing in the middle of the room now, feeling very conspicuous in his white clothes.

'Have a look outside the door, Leduc. See if there's anybody else.'

'You must excuse me,' said Dr Rivaud, 'but I really must be going. I've an appointment at eleven, and it too is a question of life and death.'

'I'll come down with you,' said the police inspector.

'And what about you, *Monsieur le procureur*?'

'Hum!... Yes... I think I...'

Somehow Maigret seemed dissatisfied. Had something gone wrong? His eye moved restlessly from one to the other and out of the window. Everyone was standing, and on the point of going.

But Maigret, raising himself slightly in the bed, said quietly:

'At last... A moment, gentlemen... I don't think we're finished yet.'

He pointed to a woman who was crossing the Place du Marché at a run. The surgeon turned to look and promptly exclaimed:

'Françoise!'

'You know her?'

'She's my sister-in-law... She must be coming to fetch me. An urgent call. Some accident, I suppose.'

There were voices below and hurried steps on the stairs. Then the door opened and Françoise burst breathless into the room, staring wild-eyed around her.

'Jacques!... Inspector!... *Monsieur le procureur!*...'

She was young, hardly past twenty, slim, pretty, and impetuous.

But her dress was covered with earth, and even torn in

one place. Instinctively she kept putting her hands to her neck.

'I ... I've seen him ... He tried to ...'

She could hardly get the words out. Everyone stood still, staring at her. Then she went up to her brother-in-law.

'Look!'

She showed him her neck. There were marks on it.

'It was over in the Moulin-Neuf wood ... I was walking along when ...'

'I thought we'd find out something,' said Maigret, who had quite recovered his placidity. Leduc, who really knew him very well, looked at him, puzzled.

'You saw him, I suppose?'

'Not very well. I don't know how I managed to shake him off. I think he must have tripped over a root. Anyhow, he loosed his grip for a second and I broke free ... I hit him ...'

'Describe him.'

'I hardly know how to. Some sort of a tramp. Dressed like any peasant. His ears stuck out ... One thing I'm sure of – it was no one I'd ever seen before.'

'He ran away?'

'I heard a car passing along the road. He must have heard it too ... And he knew I was going to shout ... In a second he disappeared into a thicket.'

She was getting her breath back, though she still panted, with one hand on her breast, the other at her neck.

'My God, I had a fright ... If it hadn't been for that car ... I didn't stop running all the way here.'

'But wouldn't it have been shorter to go home?'

'I knew there was nobody there except my sister.'

'Were you to the left of the farm?' asked the local inspector.

'A little beyond the old quarry.'

'I'll have the wood searched at once. It's not too late.'

Dr Rivaud looked annoyed. With a frown on his face he studied the girl, who was now leaning on the table, breathing more normally. There was a spark of mockery in Leduc's eye as he caught Maigret's. And he couldn't help saying:

'This proves one thing anyhow, and that is that the madman didn't accept your invitation after all.'

The inspector went downstairs and hurried across to the police station in the Town Hall. The prosecutor stood slowly brushing his bowler with his sleeve. Then he turned to Françoise.

'As soon as the examining magistrate returns, I must ask you to go and see him. He'll take a statement from you, which you'll have to sign.'

He held his dry hand out to Maigret.

'I suppose you don't want us any more?'

'It was good of you to come. I had no right to expect it.'

At a sign from Maigret, Leduc cleared the room. Rosalie and her young man were still sparring as they left. Returning to the bedside with a smile on his lips, he was surprised to see an anxious expression on his friend's face.

'Well?'

'Nothing.'

'It didn't work, did it?'

'On the contrary. It overworked! Fill me another pipe, will you, before my wife comes back?'

'But I thought you were expecting the madman here?'

'Perhaps I was. But don't let's talk about it now . . . You know, it would be dreadful if there was to be another murder. Because this time . . .'

'What?'

'Never mind. Don't try to understand. Here's my wife crossing the market-place. She'll say I've been smoking too much and take away the tobacco. Take a bit out of the pouch and stuff it under the pillow.'

He was hot. No doubt his temperature was up again.

'Leave me now, if you don't mind . . . Just put the telephone there where I can reach it.'

'I'm having lunch here today. It's always good on Thursdays. *Confit d'oie* . . . I'll look in again before I go.'

'Do . . . By the way, about that girl – you know, the one you spoke to me about – is it long since you saw her?'

Leduc bristled. Staring hard into Maigret's eyes, he snapped:

'We've had enough of that.'

And he went downstairs, leaving his straw hat on the table.

CHAPTER V

A Disconcerting Find

'OUI, *Madame* . . . *À l'Hôtel d'Angleterre* . . . But please understand that you are perfectly free not to come . . .'

Leduc had left. Madame Maigret was climbing the stairs. Dr Rivaud was standing by his car in front of the hotel, with his sister-in-law and the prosecutor.

It was to Madame Rivaud that Maigret was telephoning. Françoise had said she was alone in the house. He asked her to come and see him. It did not surprise him in the least to find that the voice at the other end of the line was an anxious one.

Madame Maigret listened to the end of the conversation as she took off her hat.

'Is it true what they say – that there's been another assault? I met some people who were hurrying off to the wood.'

Maigret was too absorbed in his own thoughts to answer. The aspect of the town seemed to change under his eyes as the news spread rapidly. More and more people were hurrying down a street which branched off on the left of the Place du Marché.

'Isn't there a crossing along there?'

'Yes, it's a long street that changes gradually into a

country road. Moulin-Neuf is after the second turning. In
spite of its name, there's no mill there now, only a large
white-washed farm. When I passed, they were harnessing
some oxen to a cart. The farmyard was full of poultry,
including some fine young turkeys.'

Maigret listened like a blind man to whom a landscape is
being described.

'Is it a big farm?'

'I don't know. They've queer measures of land in these
parts. Do you know what a *journal* is? Two hundred *journ-
aux*, they told me – but it means nothing to me. The wood
begins just beyond the house. Farther on you come to the
main road to Perigueux.'

Doubtless the country *gendarmes* were out there by
now. Maigret could imagine them slowly combing the
wood.

'I think you'd better go back. I'd like you to be on the
spot.'

Without a murmur she put her hat on again. Downstairs in the hall, she crossed a young woman who was
coming in. She turned to look at her critically, perhaps not
altogether benevolently.

It was Madame Rivaud.

*

'Do sit down . . . I hope you'll forgive my having bothered
you, particularly for so little. For I'm not even sure I've
any questions to ask you. It's such a complicated business . . .'

He kept his eyes riveted on her, and she sat before him
as though hypnotized. Maigret was puzzled by her, but not
altogether astonished. He had somehow guessed that he
would find her interesting, but she was a more curious
specimen than he had dared to expect.

He had not seen her sister Françoise in the most favour-
able light, but he could only imagine her cutting an elegant
and even dashing figure. Certainly there was nothing
provincial about her.

Madame Rivaud was not nearly so good-looking. In fact, she could not have been called beautiful at all. She was between twenty-five and thirty, neither tall nor short, but definitely on the stout side. Her clothes must have been made by a pretty humble dressmaker; if not, she didn't know how to wear them.

But what excited Maigret's interest were her eyes. Sad eyes. Anxious eyes. Yet for all their anxiety, there was resignation in them, too.

She looked at Maigret. She was obviously frightened, yet fear seemed only to paralyse her. With a little exaggeration one could say that she sat as though expecting to be hit.

It was impossible to imagine her as anything but a model of country-town respectability. She was fidgeting with her handkerchief. No doubt she would be dabbing her eyes with it on the first suitable occasion.

'How long have you been married, madame?'

She didn't answer at once. The question frightened her. Everything frightened her.

'Five years,' she said at last in a dull voice.

'Were you already living in Bergerac?'

Again she looked at Maigret for a considerable time before answering:

'I was living in Algiers with my mother and sister.'

Maigret found it quite difficult to go on. The least word seemed to scare her.

'And Dr Rivaud was living there too?'

'He spent two years at the hospital there.'

Maigret was studying her hands. Somehow they didn't seem the right hands for a doctor's wife. Surely those hands had known rough work. How could he manoeuvre the conversation tactfully on to that subject?

'Your mother . . .' he began.

But he didn't finish the sentence. Madame Rivaud was sitting with her face to the window. And all at once she jumped from her chair, looking more frightened than ever. The door of a car slammed below.

It was Dr Rivaud, who dashed into the hotel and up the stairs, gave one knock on the door, and burst straight in.

'What are you doing here?'

He spoke to his wife in a hard, dry voice without a glance at Maigret. It was only after a moment that he turned to him to say:

'What's the meaning of this? If you wanted to see my wife, why couldn't you speak to me about it?'

She hung her head, while Maigret assumed an expression of innocent astonishment.

'Really, Doctor! ... What is there to be so angry about? I felt I'd like to make Madame Rivaud's acquaintance. As I'm tied to my bed, I asked her here.'

'Have you finished cross-examining her?'

'There's been no cross-examination, Doctor. Merely a little friendly chat. When you arrived we had just got on to the subject of Algiers. Did you like it out there?'

Maigret spoke in a leisurely, off-hand way, but his casualness was only on the surface. In reality he was mustering all the energy he possessed, determined to let nothing escape him as he studied the two people before him. Madame Rivaud seemed on the verge of tears, while her husband's eye roved over the room as though looking for some clue to the conversation that had been taking place.

Of one thing Maigret was sure. There was a secret.

What could it be? He was unable to guess. All he knew was that Rivaud was hiding something from him. So was the public prosecutor, for that matter. Whatever it was, it was probably something very complicated and obscure.

'Tell me, Doctor – was Madame Rivaud your patient? Is that how you came to know her?'

The surgeon shot a swift glance at his wife.

'I may as well tell you at once that that is of no importance whatever. And now, if you don't mind, I'll drive my wife home, and ...'

'Of course. Of course ...'

'Of course what?'

'Nothing . . . I beg your pardon . . . I hardly realized I was speaking out loud.' And then Maigret went on: 'This is a strange business, Doctor. Very strange. And alarming. The deeper I get into it the more alarming I find it . . . Your sister-in-law must have had a nasty scare. It was marvellous how she managed to pull herself together so quickly. She's plucky.'

Rivaud stood there uneasily, waiting for Maigret to go on, the latter watching him narrowly. Wasn't he thinking that the detective knew a good deal more than he pretended?

At last Maigret actually felt he was making headway. But in a moment all the theories he had so laboriously constructed were dashed to the ground.

It began with a *gendarme* cycling across the Place du Marché towards the public prosecutor's office, into the entrance of which he plunged. An instant later the telephone rang. Maigret took it.

'Hallo! . . . This is the hospital . . . Is Dr Rivaud there? . . .'

The doctor snatched the receiver impatiently from Maigret's hand. He listened, thunderstruck, then slowly replaced it, staring vacantly before him.

'They've found him,' he said at last.

'Who?'

'The man . . . the madman. Or rather his corpse . . . In the Moulin-Neuf Wood.'

Madame Rivaud's glance flitted from one to the other of the two men.

'They're asking me to do the post-mortem. But . . .'

An idea seemed to strike him. It was now his turn to look suspiciously at Maigret.

'When you were shot the other night . . . you fired back . . . naturally?'

'I didn't have time to.'

But now another idea struck the doctor. He passed his hand in bewilderment across his forehead.

'They think the man's been dead several days. In that case ... this morning ... how could Françoise ... ?'

Then, turning to his wife, he said:

'Come on.'

She followed him dutifully, and a minute later their car drove off. Monsieur Duhourceau must have telephoned for a taxi, for an empty one drew up and waited at his door. The *gendarme* who had brought him the news reappeared and cycled back the way he'd come. The aspect of the town had changed once more. A fever of excitement and curiosity was mounting every moment.

It was quite a stream of people that poured into the street leading to Moulin-Neuf, including the landlord of the *Hôtel d' Angleterre*.

But there was Maigret glued to his bed, with a back that was stiff from being always in the same position, staring ponderously out on to the sun-bathed market-place.

*

'What's the matter?'

'Nothing.'

As Madame Maigret came in, she could only see her husband's profile, but that was enough. She knew very well he was out of humour. Nor was she long to guess the cause of it. She came to the bed, and without another word picked up his pipe and began filling it.

'That's better, isn't it?' she said when it was lit. 'Now, listen to me and I'll try and tell you all about it. I was there when they found the body, and the *gendarmes* let me come quite close.'

Maigret still stared out of the window. It wasn't the Place du Marché, however, that he really saw, but the wood that lay beyond the Moulin-Neuf Farm.

'It's all pine trees there except for the oaks or plane trees bordering the road. People were arriving all the time, some by car, some on foot. They'd called out the *gendarmes* from all the villages around, so as to have the wood completely surrounded. I could see a line of them beating slowly down towards the road . . . It's quite hilly there . . . Some people had joined in the chase – the old farmer for instance whose daughter was killed. He was holding a Service revolver and was obviously ready to shoot at anything or anybody, but the *gendarmes* didn't dare say a word . . .'

Maigret had never seen the wood by daylight, but he could picture it well enough – the earth covered with pine needles and mottled with patches of light and shade, the *gendarmes*' uniforms showing between the trees.

'Then we heard a shout, and there was a boy standing, pointing to something at the foot of a tree.'

'Patent-leather boots?'

'Yes. And thick grey socks, hand-knitted. I looked specially, as I thought of what you'd told me.'

'How old?'

'Middle-aged or elderly, but I really couldn't say. He was lying face downwards . . . And when they raised the head I simply couldn't help looking away. You understand. He'd been lying there for a good week – at least that's what they were saying . . . Those that looked couldn't recognize him, so he appears to be a stranger.'

'Was he wounded?'

'A huge hole in the side of his head.'

'What are they doing now?'

'They're chiefly busy keeping back the crowd, which is getting thicker every moment. They've sent for the prosecutor and Dr Rivaud. After they've seen the body on the spot, they'll move it to the hospital for the post-mortem.'

The Place du Marché was emptier than Maigret had ever seen it. The only creature who seemed quite happy to be there was a little coffee-coloured dog that basked in the sun, unconcerned.

Twelve struck with slow strokes. A crowd of working men and women streamed out of a printing-works in one of the side streets, most of them on bicycles. With one accord they turned towards Moulin-Neuf.

'How was he dressed?'

'In black. At least the overcoat was. But I really can't say very much. It wasn't a pleasant sight to stare at.'

She felt sick at the thought of it. But that didn't prevent her saying:

'Would you like me to go back?'

*

Once more Maigret was alone. He saw the landlord crossing the market-place. From the pavement the latter called out to him:

'You've heard the news, I suppose?... And to think I've got to come back and see to the lunch!'

For a long time there was nothing for Maigret to look at. Only the clear, empty sky above, the empty-looking houses all around, and the silent sunny market-place.

It was not till an hour had passed that the sound of an approaching crowd was audible. The body was being taken to the hospital, escorted by half the population of Bergerac. The Place du Marché was soon swarming. The hotel filled up, and the clink of glasses rose from the ground floor.

A timid knock on Maigret's door. Leduc put his head in, hesitated, smiled a little awkwardly.

'May I come in?'

He sat down by the bed and lit his meerschaum pipe in silence. Then at last he sighed:

'Well, well!... So there we are!'

He was disconcerted, when Maigret turned towards him, to see the broad grin on his face. Still more when the latter said:

'Pleased?'

'But...'

'Come, come? You all are. You, the doctor, the prosecutor, the police inspector – all of you delighted at the way I've been made a fool of. That troublesome detective from Paris! Thought he'd chuck his weight about, did he? Thought himself very clever! Worse still, other people began to think he might be. And some people began to be quite nervous about it . . . But that's all over now. He's merely made an ass of himself. And serve him right!'

'You admit . . . ?'

'That I was mistaken?'

'Well, they've found the man, haven't they? And he corresponds to your description of the man in the train. I saw the body myself. A middle-aged sort of man. Rather badly dressed, though respectably. There's a bullet-hole in the side of the head, and it seems to have been fired at close quarters.'

'Yes . . .'

'So close that Monsieur Duhourceau and the police agree that everything points to suicide. They think it was quite a week ago, perhaps immediately after he shot you.'

'They found a gun beside him, then?'

'No. That's the only snag. There was a revolver in his pocket, and with only one cartridge fired.'

'The one that so nearly did for me.'

'That's what they want to find out . . . Certainly, if it's suicide, it goes a long way to clearing up the case. Realizing someone was after him, he felt the game was up, and . . .'

'And if it's not suicide?'

'There are other possible explanations. He may have assaulted someone who was armed, someone who killed him quite properly in self-defence, but was nevertheless too frightened to say anything about it . . . It would be just like these country people.'

'And Françoise. What about her little adventure of this morning?'

'We hadn't forgotten that. We think it might have been no more than a spiteful practical joke.'

'I see,' said Maigret, blowing a ring of smoke towards the ceiling. 'What everyone wants is to get the case over and done with as speedily as possible.'

'It's not that . . . But you must see that there's really no point in dragging things on . . . now that . . .'

Maigret laughed out loud at his friend's embarrassment.

'There's still that second-class ticket I told you about. Somebody'll have to find an explanation for that. How did it jump out of a dead man's pocket into a passage of the *Hôtel d'Angleterre*?'

Leduc stared stonily at the crimson carpet. After a long pause he said:

'Do you want some good advice?'

'To let the whole thing drop! That's it, isn't it? To set my mind on getting well and clear out of Bergerac as soon as I'm fit to travel...'

'And come and spend a few days with me at La Ribaudière, as you were intending to do in the first place. I've spoken to Dr Rivaud about it, and he says that, with proper precautions, there's no reason why you shouldn't be moved now.'

'What does the prosecutor say?'

'I don't understand...'

'Oh, I'm sure he had something to say about it. Didn't he say that I had no right whatever to poke my nose into the case?'

Poor Leduc! He was trying so hard to put it nicely. He wanted to smooth down everybody. But Maigret was being as pig-headed as could be.

Heroically Leduc struggled on:

'You must realize that according to the regulations...' Then, suddenly plucking up his courage, he burst out:

'Listen to me, old chap. I may as well put it plainly. With that little comedy of yours this morning, you've succeeded in putting everybody's back up. Once a week the prosecutor has dinner with the prefect, and he says he'll speak about you, so that you have your knuckles rapped by your superiors in Paris. What irritated them more than anything was the way you chucked those hundred-franc notes about. They say...'

'That I'm encouraging the dregs of the population to wag their tongues.'

'How do you know?'

'That I'm inciting them to sling mud at respectable people.'

Leduc relapsed into silence. Yes, that was exactly what they said, and what's more, he couldn't help agreeing with them. It was some time before he began again timidly:

'If only you had some real idea to work on, I'd feel differently about it, but ...'

'But I haven't . . . Or rather I've four or five. Two of them looked very promising this morning. Then all of a sudden they went up in smoke.'

'You see! ... And there's another thing. What possessed you to telephone to Madame Rivaud? You couldn't have made a greater blunder. You've made Rivaud an enemy for life ... He's so jealous of her that few people can boast of having exchanged a word with her. He hardly lets her out of the house.'

'Yet Françoise is his mistress. Why should he be jealous of one but not of the other?'

'I don't know. I can't explain it. It's true she goes about freely enough. Even drives about all alone in the car. Perhaps he makes a distinction between mistresses and wives. You never know ... Anyhow, I heard him say to the prosecutor that your asking her here was gross bad manners, and that he was itching to teach you a lesson.'

'That's a happy thought!'

'What is?'

'That he has every opportunity. He dresses my wound twice a day.'

Maigret laughed a little too heartily for it to seem altogether on the right side of his face. He laughed like a man who knows he's got himself in a mess, but who knows also that it's too late to withdraw, and that the only thing left him is to put as good a face on it as possible.

'Aren't you going to have lunch? I thought you said something about *confit d'oie.*'

He laughed again, and this time there was unmistakably a rueful note in it. There was Leduc who could come and go as he pleased, wander through the woods and round the Moulin-Neuf Farm, nose around the doctor's house and the public prosecutor's . . . And then finish up with *confit d'oie* and *truffes en serviette* . . .

There was a fascinating hand to be played . . . But Maigret was forced to lie there, tied to his bed, with the same little scene in front of him the whole livelong day . . . And every time he made an incautious movement, he almost yelled with the pain. And he even had to have his pipes filled for him, and his wife took advantage of it to cut his smoking down . . .

'Well? What do you think about it? Will you come to my place?'

'I'd love to . . . But not till it's all over.'

'But now that our madman's dead . . .'

'Who knows? Run along and have your lunch, and if they ask you what I intend to do, say you don't know . . . And now to work!'

He said it exactly as if he had some heavy manual job to perform, like kneading dough or digging over a potato patch.

As a matter of fact, he had a lot of digging to do, but it was a rather different sort of excavation. It wasn't spadefuls of earth that he had to turn over, but mental images, faces. Faces more than anything.

There was the prosecutor's face with its mixture of fierceness and cold disdain. The doctor's – keen, intelligent, but worried. And the rather insipid features of his wife's. Timid as a hare, she was . . . What would he have been treating her for in the hospital at Algiers? . . . Françoise, slight, pretty, and eager. Victim of a silly practical joke. Or that's what they were trying to make out . . .

And Rosalie dreaming all night – to her young man's despair. How far had those two gone in their relations? . . . That look of hers at Monsieur Duhourceau – and the old peasant had looked at him in much the same way. What did those glances mean? Was there something that had been hushed up?... And the man who had jumped from the train, shot Maigret, and then been shot in turn. Or shot himself?... Leduc and his housekeeper's niece – it can easily land you in a mess, that sort of thing... The landlord of the *Hôtel d'Angleterre* had already buried two wives and looked hefty enough to kill twenty...

Why did Françoise – or rather why was Dr Rivaud jealous of his wife but not of her? Why was Leduc always beating about the bush? Did he know more than he pretended?... Why?... Why?... Why?...

And now they wanted to ship Maigret off to La Ribaudière as quickly as possible. No need to ask why this time! He was making a nuisance of himself.

He laughed once again, a fat contented laugh, and when Madame Maigret came into the room a quarter of an hour later, she found him blissfully asleep.

CHAPTER VI

The Seal

MAIGRET was in the throes of a harassing dream. The heat was terrible and the low tide had laid bare an immense stretch of sand the colour of ripe red corn. There was more sand than sea; in fact, there was hardly any sea at all. It must be out there somewhere, far away in the distance, but all that could be seen were little pools scattered here and there in the otherwise unbroken stretch of sand.

Was Maigret a seal? Perhaps not quite – but neither was he a whale. Probably something between the two. Some large animal, anyhow – a large round shiny lump lying on the sand.

He was all alone in that endless hot expanse. And it was

absolutely necessary that he should by some means or other reach the sea, where at last he would be free.

Only he couldn't move. He had flippers like a seal, but he didn't know how to use them. Besides, his whole body was stiff and heavy. If he did manage to raise himself a little, it was only to sink down again on to the burning sand.

Worse still, the sand was soft, and with every movement he sank in a little deeper.

At all costs he must reach the sea. Why was it he was so stiff and heavy? He had a vague idea some man had shot him. But he couldn't remember clearly. Nothing was clear — at least only one thing. He was a big, black, sweating, helpless lump struggling to reach the sea.

*

When he opened his eyes he saw a bright rectangle of sunshine. It made him blink. Then he saw his wife having breakfast, at the same time keeping a watchful eye on him.

And from the look in her eye, he knew at once that something was amiss. He knew that look well: a grave, maternal, slightly worried look.

'Are you feeling bad?' she asked.

The next thing that struck him was that his head was very heavy.

'Why do you ask?'

'Why indeed? You've been heaving and groaning all night long.'

She came over to the bed to kiss him good-morning.

'You're looking rotten,' she went on. 'I suppose you've been having nightmares.'

The word at once reminded him of the seal. What a funny dream! But it made him feel uncomfortable even now, and though he was on the point of laughing, he didn't. It wasn't so funny as all that, and the look in Madame Maigret's eye didn't make it any funnier. Sitting on the edge of his bed, she began talking gently, as though afraid of rubbing him up the wrong way.

'We really must come to a decision . . .'

'What decision?'

'Leduc and I were talking things over yesterday. There's no doubt about it: you'd be much better off at his place. In restful surroundings you'd soon pull up.'

She didn't dare look him in the face, and it didn't take him a second to see what she was driving at.

'So you think so too!' he muttered.

'What do you mean?'

'You think I'm out of my depth. You think I'll only make a hash of things and get into trouble over it.'

He spoke somewhat heatedly, and the effort brought sweat to his forehead and upper lip.

'Now, now! Keep calm. The doctor will be here in a minute.'

He hadn't appeared the previous evening, so Maigret had not seen him since he'd come to collect his wife. The prospect of seeing him again banished for the moment all other preoccupations.

'You'll leave me alone with him.'

'And we'll go to Leduc's, shan't we?'

'No, we won't . . . There's his car now. Put your hat on.'

As a rule, Rivaud took the stairs three at a time and strode into his patient's bedroom. Today he mounted step by step and came in rather stiffly, though he bowed quite graciously to Madame Maigret as she left the room. Coming over towards Maigret, he put his dispatch-case down on the bedside table without so much as a word.

The routine in the morning was always the same. He would put the thermometer under Maigret's tongue and then start undoing the bandages.

That was the situation this morning when the conversation started.

'As a matter of course,' began the doctor, 'nothing

could affect my attitude to a patient. I'll give you exactly the same attention as before. Only, from now on, I should like our relations to end there. And, considering you're merely acting unofficially, I've a right to forbid your worrying my family in any way.'

It wasn't difficult to guess that the speech had been prepared beforehand. Maigret's features betrayed nothing while the thermometer was taken out of his mouth. He heard the doctor mutter:

'A hundred point two.'

It was a lot. He knew it. Rivaud frowned and, without looking at his patient, went on:

'If it hadn't been for yesterday, I should have no hesitation in telling you to go and finish your cure in some quiet country place. But if I tell you so now, it's liable to be misconstrued . . . Am I hurting you?'

He was probing the wound as he spoke.

'No. Go on.'

But Rivaud had nothing more to say, and not another word was spoken. He bandaged Maigret up again, put his things away, and washed his hands. At the door, however, he turned and looked the detective in the face.

A difficult look to interpret. Difficult even to say what side of the man was uppermost. Was it the surgeon, the husband of the enigmatic Madame Rivaud, or the brother-in-law of Françoise?

Only one thing was certain. It was a worried look. For a moment he seemed on the point of saying something, but he thought better of it and went out into the passage, where a whispered conversation took place between him and Madame Maigret.

The trouble was that Maigret could now remember his dream perfectly. Was it an evil omen? There certainly were others. When his wound was dressed, for instance, it had hurt much more than on the last two days, though he hadn't admitted it. Another bad sign was that persistent temperature.

He reached for his pipe, which Madame Maigret had filled before leaving, but then changed his mind. Really, he didn't feel inclined for it. And that was a bad sign too!

His wife came in heaving a sigh.

'What did he say?'

'He didn't want to say anything. But I plied him with questions, and he finally told me he had advised you to have a complete rest.'

'Quite so. And now tell me how the case is proceeding.'

Madame Maigret sat down with an air of resignation, though every line of her body expressed disapproval and misgiving. She couldn't help herself. She deplored his obstinacy and doubted his judgement.

'The post-mortem?'

'As near as they can tell the man must have died soon after shooting you.'

'They haven't found another revolver?'

'No . . . They've no clue to his identity. There's a photograph of the corpse in the morning papers.'

'Let's see.'

She handed him the paper, and it was with a rather queer sensation that he looked at the picture. For, unreasonable though it was, he had the feeling that he was the one person in the world who had known the man.

It's true he'd never seen him properly; but they'd spent a night together. He recalled his companion's troubled sleep – that is, if he'd slept at all – his deep sighs, and those sounds that Maigret had taken for sobs . . .

And the two legs hanging down from the upper *couchette*, the patent-leather boots, the thick grey socks . . .

The photograph was horrible, like all police photographs of corpses, touched up as they are to make them look more like a living person and thus facilitate identification.

A dull face. Glassy eyes. And Maigret was not surprised to see a grey beard. Why had he always thought of him with a beard? Even in the railway carriage he had never pictured him otherwise.

Anyhow, he had been right. Scraggy and shapeless though it was, this was a beard. The hairs were an inch or more long and about the same length all over.

'All the same, this case is no business of yours. You can't get over that . . .'

Madame Maigret was at him again, though she spoke very gently and apologetically. She was genuinely concerned about his condition. By the way she looked at him, you'd have thought he was seriously ill.

'At dinner last night I was listening to what the people were saying. One and all, they're against you. You could question them till you're black in the face, you wouldn't get a thing out of them. And if that's the case, surely . . .'

'Get a pencil and paper, will you?'

He dictated a telegram to a friend of his who was now in the Algiers police:

Urgent please send information Dr Rivaud at Algiers hospital five years ago greetings thanks.

Madame Maigret's pursed lips were eloquent. She did whatever he asked, but she had no faith in this investigation. She couldn't take it seriously. She was only humouring him.

He was conscious of the fact and it infuriated him. Scepticism in other people did not offend him, but in her it was intolerable.

'I'm not asking your advice,' he said bitingly as the blood mounted to his cheeks. 'All I ask you to do is to send off this telegram and bring me any information you hear. You can leave the rest to me.'

She threw him a contrite look, but he was too angry to respond.

'From now on, you can keep your thoughts to yourself. In other words, you needn't go shaking your head over me when you talk to Leduc or the doctor or any other of those precious fools.'

He turned over on to his side, but so clumsily that once

more his mind went back to the seal floundering in the sand.

*

He was using his left hand, which made his writing heavier and clumsier than usual. He breathed uneasily, being in an uncomfortable position. Two boys were playing marbles under his window, and half a dozen times he nearly shouted out to them to shut up.

1st Crime: Léontine Moreau of Moulin-Neuf strangled on the high road. Long needle driven through heart.

Maigret sighed and added:

(Time? Exact spot? How strong was the victim?)

And he sighed again to think how quickly, in the ordinary way, he'd have had such questions answered. Running a case from a sick-bed was indeed a laborious business. But he plodded on.

2nd Crime: Station-master's daughter found in same condition. (Same questions.)

3rd Crime (abortive): Rosalie attacked. Aggressor routed. Fiancé says she dreams and reads novels.

4th Crime: Man jumps out of train as it starts slowing down before the station. Shoots me when I follow.

Maigret often did this sort of thing. Pretty useless in itself. But it filled up moments of forced inaction, and he generally felt better after it.

5th Crime: Same man (no room for doubt on that point) shot through the brain, probably soon after Crime No. 4.

6th Crime (doubtful): Françoise assaulted in Moulin-Neuf Wood. Man makes off as car passes along the road. (How near the road was she? Did she see the car? If so, why didn't she stop it?)

Note: All six take place in Moulin-Neuf Wood.

He crumpled up the sheet of paper, and with a shrug

of his good shoulder threw it into a corner. Then he took another and began again.

> Possibly mad:
> Duhourceau?
> Rivaud?
> Françoise?
> Madame Rivaud?
> Rosalie?
> Inspector?
> Landlord?
> Leduc?
> Man in the train?

But why was there any need for a lunatic in the story? Maigret frowned suddenly. Funny he hadn't thought of that! Who was it who had spoken of a madman?

Everybody. It seemed to be universally accepted. Perhaps it was the doctor who had been most definite on the subject. And the prosecutor had been only too glad to take it for granted.

Suppose one dropped the madman out of the picture? Or suppose there was somebody pretending to be mad?

That needle, for instance. Couldn't it have been introduced for no other purpose than to make people think it was a madman or a sadist, at any rate somebody with an unbalanced mind?

Maigret took another sheet, and in capital letters wrote: QUESTIONS. Even though he was using his left hand he tried to ornament the letters with fancy squiggles, like a schoolboy dawdling over his work.

1. Was Rosalie really assaulted or did she only imagine it?
2. Was Françoise really assaulted?
3. If they were, was it by the same man who murdered the first two?
4. Is the man in the train the murderer?
5. Did he commit suicide?
6. If not, who is the murderer's murderer?

Madame Maigret returned as he was slowly wading

through the last words. She merely glanced at the bed, took off her coat and hat, and sat down beside him.

'Here! I can do that for you,' she said, calmly taking the pencil and paper from his hands.

He was at a loss to know how to interpret the gesture. Was she returning to the charge? Or, on the contrary, was she trying to make it up? He couldn't make up his mind whether to flare up again or to melt.

He turned his head away awkwardly, while she glanced through what he had written.

'Have you any idea?' she asked gently.

'Not the ghost of one!'

He spoke the words savagely. And they were no more than the truth. He hadn't the ghost of an idea. In fact, he would really have liked to do just what they all wanted him to do – chuck the thing up altogether and go and have a real holiday at Leduc's, where, among the clucking of hens and other nice country noises, he could forget all about being a detective . . .

But he wasn't going to walk back. He wasn't going to take advice from anybody . . .

Did she understand at last? Was she really going to help him instead of urging him to throw up the sponge? . . . Those were the questions that his troubled eyes were asking.

And she answered with a word she rarely used:

'My poor Maigret!'

For she only called him Maigret on rather special occasions. It implied recognition of his superiority as the man, the master-mind, and head of the house. Her tone this time was not one of great conviction, perhaps. But he wasn't out to cavil. He was simply dying for a few crumbs of consolation and encouragement.

'Shove another pillow under my back, will you?'

There! It was all over!

'And now the pipe, please.'

The two boys below were quarrelling now, and one of

them got his face slapped. There was a long silence before the howl came, but when it did it was a good one, and the wretched kid walked slowly off to tell his mother.

'I met Leduc in the street.'

'Did he speak to you?'

'Of course,' she answered, smiling. 'He once more begged me to use all my influence to induce you to go to La Ribaudière. He had just left the prosecutor's.'

'Oh!'

'He rattled on rather volubly, like a man trying to cover his embarrassment.'

'Did you go to the mortuary to have another look at the body?'

'There's no mortuary here. It's lying at the police station. There was a queue of at least fifty people lined up to see it. I had to wait my turn.'

'No one's identified it, I suppose?'

'Not yet.'

'You noticed the socks?'

'They're of good wool and certainly hand-knitted.'

'Which goes to show the man had some sort of domestic background. Unless he was a tramp. They often get hand-knitted socks from charities, knitted by young ladies of good family.'

'Only tramps don't travel second class – if they go by train at all.'

'For that matter, there aren't so many people who do go second class. A second-class *couchette* suggests a man of some means. Or someone who travels a lot, like a commercial traveller. What about the boots?'

'The police looked for a trade-mark. They found the name of a firm that has branches all over the country.'

'And the suit?'

'Of very good black cloth, but it was worn almost threadbare in places. I should think he'd had it quite three years. The overcoat too.'

'A hat?'

'They didn't find one, though they looked along the railway line, thinking he might have lost it there.'

Maigret tried to remember whether he had seen the man in a hat. He couldn't be sure.

'Did you notice anything else?'

'The police told me the shirt was mended at the neck and both cuffs. Neatly done, they said.'

'The domestic background again . . . And now, what did they find in his pockets?'

'Absolutely nothing except a short ivory cigarette-holder.'

They were talking it over like two partners, as naturally as could be. Both were relieved that hostilities were over. Maigret puffed away contentedly at his pipe.

'Here's Leduc.'

They watched him cross the Place du Marché. His hat was tipped slightly backwards and he walked with almost a slouch. When he came into the room, he was too pre-occupied even to say good-morning.

'I've been seeing the prosecutor.'

'I know.'

'Yes, of course . . . We met in the street . . . Then I went to the police station to make sure it was true – what he told me . . . It's simply bewildering . . . ?'

'Let's hear it.'

Leduc mopped his forehead and drank half the glass of lemonade that had been prepared for Maigret.

'You don't mind, do you? . . . I've never been so flabber-gasted in my life . . . They sent the finger-prints to Paris, as a matter of course . . . Well, the answer's just come.'

'Go on.'

'The man whom you jumped out of the train after died years ago.'

'What are you talking about?'

'I say that officially this corpse that's lying at the police station has been a corpse for years. He was a man called Meyer – though known by the name of Samuel – who was condemned to death at Algiers, and . . .'

Maigret was leaning forward in the bed.

'And executed?'

'No. He died in hospital a few days before.'

Madame Maigret couldn't help smiling maternally as she watched the glow of happiness that spread over her husband's face. He noticed it and nearly smiled back, but dignity got the upper hand and he kept a grave face.

'And what had he done, this Samuel?'

'We don't know. It was only a short telegram in code, but it said further particulars would follow. We ought to hear by this evening . . . Of course they may be making a mistake. And there's always the chance of two men's finger-prints being alike. One in two hundred thousand – isn't that what Bertillon says? A negligible chance you may say, but I suppose it must happen sometimes.'

'And how is Duhourceau taking the blow?'

'He's annoyed, naturally. Thinks he may have to call in outside help. But he's afraid they might send chaps who'd take their orders from you. That's what he wanted to see me about. Wanted to know whether you had a lot of influence at headquarters.'

'Fill me another pipe,' said Maigret to his wife.

'That's the third.'

'Never mind. I'll bet anything you like I'm right down to normal . . . Samuel. Meyer. Sounds Jewish to me. The family counts a lot with the Jews, so we needn't be surprised he wore hand-knitted socks. They're thrifty too, which can explain why a man who could afford a second-class sleeper should wear a suit threadbare . . .'

Maigret was loquacious, almost jocular. Leduc, however, was worried and not very responsive.

'Don't mind me,' his friend went on. 'You've no idea what I've been through in the last few hours. You've no idea what it feels like, when you're a seal, to stew on

burning-hot sand with the sea ever so far away . . . But the
tide's come in at last and we're afloat . . . You can't think
how good it feels . . .'

He burst out laughing at the look of pained bewilderment on Leduc's face.

CHAPTER VII

Samuel

THE same evening brought news from two sources. The
time for the doctor's visit was approaching when a telegram arrived from Algiers.

Doctor Rivaud unknown all hospitals here greetings Martin.

Maigret had hardly glanced at it when Leduc appeared.
The telegram caught his eye at once, but he asked no
questions. Maigret, however, held it out to him.

'Have a look at this.'

Leduc read it through.

'What can you expect?'

He shrugged his shoulders, and though he said no more,
his whole attitude expressed what he was thinking:

'It's no use hoping to understand anything in this case.
Every day brings further complications, and if you had a
grain of sense you'd let me take you off to La Ribaudière.'

Madame Maigret was out. In spite of the gathering
twilight, Maigret did not think of switching on the light.
The street lamps were lit, and he liked to look out at the
ring of lights that encircled the Place du Marché, and the
windows of the houses as they lit up one by one. The first
was always the same, a window in the second house to the
left of the garage; and, by the lamp inside, the same dressmaker was always sitting in the same position, bending
over her work.

'The police have had news too,' grunted Leduc.

He said it reluctantly. He didn't want Maigret to think he was ready to help him. Or perhaps the police had asked him not to pass on any information to the enemy.

'News of Samuel?'

'Yes. The particulars came by the afternoon post. And then Lucas telephoned from Paris. He'd had his eye on the man at one time, though it's several years ago now.'

'What do they say?'

'They don't know exactly where he came from. Somewhere in Eastern Europe, possibly Jugoslavia. An uncommunicative man who never talked about himself. He had a business in Algiers. Guess what.'

'Something very dull, I should imagine.'

'Postage-stamps.'

Maigret was delighted. Dealing in stamps seemed to him somehow just right for the man in the train.

'A business which naturally was only cover for another. But it was so well done that, though the police were watching them, they didn't find out anything till Samuel was put on trial for murder. Then it all came to light. His real business was supplying forged passports, immigration papers, and labour permits. He had a whole network of agents in Vienna, Bucharest, Warsaw, and all over the shop.'

The sky outside was a deep dark blue, the tops of the houses barely visible against it.

'Strange,' muttered Maigret.

What he found strange was not Samuel's profession, but to run up against it in a place like Bergerac. This had started as a thoroughly provincial case – the local maniac of a small country town – and now it was being invaded by the cosmopolitan underworld with ramifications extending from Warsaw to Algiers.

People like this Samuel – he had dealt with hundreds in his time. And he had always studied them with a curiosity that was mixed with some other feeling. Repulsion was too strong a word. A sort of slightly embarrassed wonderment. It wasn't a question of race – they were of all races – but as though they belonged to a different species altogether from the one we call human.

You'd find them as barmen in Scandinavia, as gangsters in America, head-waiters in Germany, or wholesalers in North Africa. You'd find them running theatres, night clubs, or clandestine gambling saloons.

And now they were cropping up again in this peaceful little town of Bergerac, which you would have taken for the most remote place imaginable from all the terror, sordidness, and tragedy that their doings involved.

Strange indeed.

Between Budapest and Odessa, between Tallinn and Constantinople, there were large tracts of country where the population was too dense. In particular, there were hundreds of thousands of hungry Jews whose only ambition was to seek a better existence in some other land. With children in their arms, and dragging their old folk behind them, they'd board some midnight express or stow themselves away in the steerage of a ship, while on their tragic faces resignation had not yet been supplanted by hope.

All the year round, by tens, by hundreds, and by thousands, Poles, Jews, Rumanians, Italians were streaming outwards to the four corners of the globe. France alone had absorbed train-loads and train-loads. In every town in the country there were people who at every birth, death, or marriage had to spell their outlandish names letter by letter at the Town Hall . . .

But before any family could set out, documents were needed. Passports, permits, visas. All had to wait their turn. Some would be refused. Others would despair before their applications were answered.

That's where Samuel came in, Samuel and his like. Men who spoke ten languages, who knew every frontier in

Europe, the rubber stamp of every consulate, and even the signatures of the officials. They could see to everything!

Their real activity would be concealed behind the façade of some other business, preferably international.

Postage-stamps. What could be better?

To Mr A. Levy, Bucharest.
Sir,
    I am this day dispatching two hundred rare stamps of Jugoslavia, Rumania, and other countries. I hope shortly to secure specimens of the Greek ones you were inquiring about...

And nobody need know they weren't postage-stamps at all.

There was another traffic, too, which no doubt interested Samuel, as it did most of his kind.

In the *maisons spéciales* of South America it was French girls who formed the quality. Their purveyors worked in Paris on the Grands Boulevards. But the smaller fry, the rank and file, came from the East of Europe. Country girls who left home at fifteen or sixteen, returning – if ever they did – at twenty, with their dowries in their pockets.

How well Maigret knew it all! At the Quai des Orfèvres it was his daily bread. In the ordinary way he would have thought nothing of it, but here in Bergerac it rather disturbed the picture. In spite of the mention of Algiers, he had regarded it as a local drama played by local people, while now ...

But Leduc was speaking.

'I never heard of a show of that kind run from Algiers, but they say he did a lot of business with the Arabs, and even with the Negroes inland.'

'There was a murder, you said?'

'A double one. Two of his own race who were found lying dead on a bit of waste ground. Both had come from Berlin. There was a lot of nosing around. Samuel's activities were disclosed and those of his two agents – for that's what the two men were. The idea was that they'd come to complain of something. No doubt he was doing them out of their commission. Perhaps they threatened him.'

'So he did away with them.'

'It took a long time to get sufficient evidence against him, but in the end they did and he was condemned to death.

'He fell ill, however, so seriously that he was moved from the prison infirmary to the town hospital, where he died a few days later.

'That's all I know.'

                        *

The doctor was astonished to find the two men in the dark. With a curt movement he switched on the light. Then he put his dispatch-case down on the table, nodded a good-evening, slipped off his light overcoat, and started washing his hands in the basin.

'I'll leave you now,' said Leduc. 'See you again to-morrow.'

He hadn't realized the doctor would be coming, and was none too pleased at being found there. It was all very well for Maigret, but Leduc lived in the district. He didn't want to rub people up the wrong way.

'*Au revoir, Docteur*,' he said, slinking out.

Rivaud merely grunted as he soaped his hands.

'How's the temperature?'

'Behaving very nicely.'

Maigret was in the same buoyant good humour now as he had been during the first few days, when it had felt so good to be alive.

'Does it still hurt?'

'Oh, that's nothing. I'm used to it by now.'

Once more the doctor went through the accustomed gestures, unbandaging, dressing, rebandaging. His face was within a foot or two of Maigret's. And suddenly the latter blurted out:

'One would hardly take you for a Jew.'

No response. Not a flicker. Not the faintest variation in the surgeon's regular breathing. Only after the job was finished did he say:

'No doubt about it now! You can move whenever you like.'

'What do you mean?'

'You can move whenever you like. Wasn't there a question of your spending a few days with Leduc?'

A man of prodigious self-control, if ever there was one! For a good quarter of an hour Maigret had been fixing him with a steady stare, and he hadn't turned a hair. His careful capable hands had never trembled, never faltered.

'I'll only be coming every other day now. The other days I'll send my assistant. You can have every confidence in him.'

'As much as in you?'

There were moments – though they could hardly be called frequent – when Maigret could not repress a pert remark like that. But what really gave them their flavour was the artless way in which they were said.

'Good evening!'

That was all he got for an answer. The doctor was gone, leaving Maigret to resume his mental puppet-show. The man in the train, from being a vague figure in the background, had now stepped forward to play the principal part.

His character was now well defined, assuming he ran true to type. His only unorthodoxy so far was that of having died twice.

Was he the man who went about strangling women? Was he the man who had a mania for sticking needles through hearts?

If he was, there were several questions that were hard to answer, two in particular.

First of all, why should he choose the neighbourhood of Bergerac for the scene of his activities? Not only were people of his sort invariably townsfolk, but the big towns were so much safer and more convenient for such exploits . . .

And apparently he had no connexion with Bergerac at all. At least, nobody had been able to identify him. Moreover, with those patent-leather boots, he hardly seemed cast for the part of wild man of the woods.

If he didn't live in the woods, where did he hang out? Did he come and go by train each time he felt the urge to do some strangling? . . .

Or was somebody hiding him? Who could it be? The doctor perhaps. They had at least Algiers in common. Or could it be Duhourceau?

Secondly, the recent crimes had nothing in common with those he had been condemned to death for. Those had been essentially reasonable murders. To get rid of two dangerous accomplices – whatever else it was, you couldn't call it mad.

The Bergerac murders, on the other hand, were committed by a madman, a sadist, or a sexual pervert. Unless the needle was merely a blind . . .

Though, of course, if Samuel had been sane in Algiers, that wouldn't stop him going mad afterwards . . .

'I wonder if Duhourceau's ever been to Algiers . . . !' muttered Maigret to himself.

His wife returned. She was tired out. Throwing her hat on to the table, she sank into the easy-chair.

'What a trade! I'm sorry for you. To have to prowl around like that from one year's end to the other!'

'Any news?'

'Nothing interesting. Nobody's yet been able to identify the dead man. It seems they've had some information from Paris, but they won't give it out.'

'I know it.'

'Leduc told you? That's nice of him. One couldn't blame him if he washed his hands of you. Everybody's up against you.'

'What do they think about the case now?'

'They don't know what to think. Some say that Samuel has nothing to do with it at all. A man who wanted to kill himself. First he tries throwing himself out of a train, but his nerve fails him – he hangs on and the train isn't going fast enough. In the end, however, he succeeds with a revolver . . . That's the way many people look at it . . . And naturally they're expecting the murders to go on.'

'Have you been past the doctor's house again?'

'Yes, but there was nothing to see. On the other hand, I was told something, though it may be of no importance at all. Two or three times a woman has visited the house, and she's thought to be Dr Rivaud's mother-in-law. A middle-aged woman, they say, and decidedly common. Nobody knows anything about her or where she lives, and she hasn't been seen for quite two years . . .'

'What would her name be? . . . What's Françoise called? Mademoiselle . . . ?'

'Mademoiselle Françoise. I've never heard her called anything but that. I've no idea what her surname is.'

'Hand me the telephone.'

He rang up the police station.

'Is that the inspector's secretary? . . . No. No need to bother him . . . I only want to know the surname of Mademoiselle Françoise, Madame Rivaud's sister. No objection, have you? . . . Beausoleil? . . . Many thanks.'

Maigret grinned.

'He'd have liked not to tell me. They hate the idea of helping me even that much! . . . Beausoleil. That's a gorgeous name!

'And now there's a very boring job for you to do. I want you to go downstairs and ask for the telephone directory – not the local one, but the big one for the whole of France. Look up the numbers of every medical school in the country and then telephone to each in turn. Ask for the registrar's office, and inquire whether anyone of the name of Jacques Rivaud is on their list of qualified men . . . Where's the telephone downstairs?'

'There's a box in the lounge, but it doesn't stop people hearing every word you say.'

'Splendid.'

'But you don't mean to say . . .! That Rivaud isn't . . .! Good heavens! . . .'

'Run along, or you'll be too late.'

'And I've got to ring up every university in France?'

'Yes. Go on.'

Left alone, he felt rather penitent. It was rather a lot to ask. And she had come in dead-tired . . . If only it hadn't been in France! In many countries they had medical directories which would tell you in two winks whether a doctor was real or bogus. While in France . . .

He'd heard of more cases than one. Men who'd been practising for fifteen or twenty years, respected in their districts, adored by their patients . . . And then one fine day, for some trivial reason, the truth would leak out – they hadn't the vestige of a qualification.

Maigret had forgotten to ask his wife to fill him a pipe before going, but with considerable labour he managed to do it for himself. Meanwhile his thoughts returned to Bergerac.

He had always loved the atmosphere of a house, and it fascinated him to speculate on that of the doctor's and the prosecutor's. There was certainly something haunting about the doctor's.

Not on the surface. In fact, quite the opposite. A gay little villa with clean, simple lines, well-lit rooms, and bright-coloured curtains.

'They must be a happy household . . .'

That's what the passers-by must say as they peeped into the little garden and saw the brightly polished brass knocker, the car purring in front of the garage . . . And that supple, graceful girl, Françoise, jumping in and driving off . . . Or it might be Rivaud, who, with his forceful, capable look, cut as good a figure as she did . . .

But behind that . . .

What would they say to each other in the evenings, those three?

Was Madame Rivaud aware of what was going on between her husband and her sister?

She wasn't pretty. And certainly she knew it. Nothing romantic or exciting about her. More like the resigned, long-suffering mother of a family . . .

Two sisters could hardly be more unlike. For Françoise was simply overflowing with life . . . Yes, it was an interesting question – whether Madame Rivaud knew. Would she meekly accept it? It often happened. Maigret had come across such situations time and again, even in the most respectable families . . .

Or were there, on the contrary, a lot of lies and false pretences? Secret meetings . . . Kisses behind doors . . .

What sort of people were these Beausoleils? And how had they fetched up in Algiers? . . . Common. That's what was said of the mother. And even Madame Rivaud – there were little things which, if you looked closely, hinted at a humbler origin. She had never quite been able to pick up the step. Françoise was more intelligent, more adaptable . . . And, of course, she'd started younger. She could pass herself off anywhere.

Were they jealous of each other? Did they hate each other? Or would they have long heart-to-heart talks?

And their mother . . . Maigret couldn't help picturing her as a stout busybody, delighted at having got her daughters settled, and lecturing them on how nice they ought to be to so rich and important a gentleman as Dr Rivaud.

Perhaps the rich gentleman paid her a small annuity.

But there was a limit after all to what could be imagined. If only he had been able to drop in and have a look! Even for five minutes. To see the rooms, the ornaments, the things left lying about, which told of the daily occupations of those who lived in them . . .

Duhourceau's house too. He would have given a good deal for five minutes there. Certainly there was some connexion between Duhourceau and the doctor. You could tell it by their attitudes. There was some sort of an alliance ...

Abruptly Maigret reached for the telephone and asked the landlord to come up. As soon as the man appeared, he asked him bluntly:

'Do you know if Monsieur Duhourceau often dines at the Rivauds'?'

'Every Monday. I know very well because it's my nephew who drives him in his taxi. You see ...'

'Thank you.'

'Is that all?'

'That's all.'

The landlord went off, puzzled, while Maigret, returning to the doctor's villa, spread a clean white cloth and laid the table for four ... The *procureur de la République* would sit on Madame Rivaud's right ...

'Monday night! ... And it was the following night I travelled down from Paris with Samuel. The following night – or rather early Wednesday morning – that Samuel was killed.'

An idea suddenly flashed into his mind. With the feeling that he was making a huge stride forward, he grabbed the receiver again.

'Hallo! ... Is that the exchange? ... *Police Judiciaire* ...'

He spoke almost roughly, but he was inwardly wondering whether it would go down.

'I want to know if Dr Rivaud received a call from Paris last Tuesday week.'

'Hold on, will you? I'll find out.'

It didn't take a minute.

'Yes. At two in the afternoon. A call from Paris. The number calling was *Archives* 14–67.'

'Have you a numeral list of Paris subscribers? If you have, I'd like to know who *Archives* 14–67 is.'

'I think I've seen one. Hold on again.'

A nice girl. Pretty too, by the sound of her voice. And gay. Maigret smiled unconsciously.

'Hallo! ... I've found it. It's the *Restaurant des Quatres Sergents*, Place de la Bastille.'

'Was it a three-minute call?'

'Three periods. Nine minutes altogether.'

A nine-minute call at two o'clock. The train left at five-forty. Maigret fumed with impatience. It was all he could do not to jump out of bed. He felt he was getting on the trail at last. It was no longer the time for leisurely musings. He mustn't make a mistake now.

The truth was not far off. Very likely he had all the data he needed. It might be simply a question of seeing it clearly in its right perspective. But it was precisely at such moments as this that there was the greatest risk of dashing off on a wild-goose chase.

Back to the doctor's villa again. A Monday night. A table laid for four. Monsieur Duhourceau sitting down on the hostess's right ... Monsieur Duhourceau – why was it Rosalie had looked at him like that? Had he a bad name in the town? Was there a side of his life that ill accorded with his age and the dignity of his position? In a country town it was easy enough to get a bad name. You only had to pat a girl on the cheek to set tongues wagging ...

And Françoise? ... Was she the type that set elderly men thinking of things they shouldn't? ... Monday night – and twenty-four hours later Maigret and Samuel were in the train. Was Samuel afraid? Wasn't that the most obvious explanation of his restlessness, his trembling hands trying to tie his bootlaces?

Maigret was sweating. From downstairs came the clatter of plates. It would soon be dinner-time.

'*Did he jump out of the train to escape from somebody or to meet somebody?*'

That was perhaps the most crucial question of all. In fact, Maigret felt pretty sure it was. If he could answer that, it would take him a long way. Once more he repeated:

'*Was it to escape from somebody or to meet somebody?*' Which did the telephone call suggest?

His wife entered, so flustered herself that she did not notice the state of excitement to which Maigret had worked himself up.

'We must call in another doctor at once. A real one . . . It's simply monstrous. It's a crime . . . And to think . . .'

She looked at her husband as though to make sure he was safe and sound.

'No one's ever qualified under the name of Jacques Rivaud. He simply isn't a doctor! . . . Every register has been searched . . . And now we're getting to the bottom of it – that temperature of yours that wouldn't go down. Of course the wound wouldn't heal! . . .'

'I know,' said Maigret to himself triumphantly. 'I'm sure of it. *It was to meet somebody.*'

The telephone rang. The landlord's voice saying:

'Monsieur Duhourceau asks if he can come up.'

CHAPTER VIII

A Collector of Books

THE minute which elapsed before the prosecutor appeared saw a complete change in Maigret's features. His face became dull and resigned, like that of any other invalid who is sick to death of lying in bed.

This change in his expression seemed even to affect the room. It too looked dull. A commonplace and dreary hotel bedroom, devoid of personality. It wasn't even tidy. The bed had not been made since the morning, the bedside table was cluttered with medicine, glasses, and spoons, and Madame Maigret's hat was still lying where she had thrown it down on the table.

The latter had just lit the spirit-lamp to make an infusion, and that didn't add to the dignity of the room. One could hardly say it looked sordid: yet it was not far off.

Two or three rigid little knocks on the door. Madame Maigret opened it, and once again the prosecutor unthinkingly handed her his hat and stick.

'Good evening, Inspector,' he said, coming towards the bed.

He didn't seem embarrassed. On the contrary, his manner was more like that of a man who has pulled himself thoroughly together to accomplish some task.

'Good evening, *Monsieur le procureur*. Won't you sit down?'

For the first time, Maigret noticed a smile on the prosecutor's forbidding face. Just a little one at the corners of the mouth. It had, of course, been put there on purpose.

'I must confess I've been feeling a bit guilty about you ... That surprises you, does it? ... I couldn't help reproaching myself for having been rather curt with you ... Though you must admit that your own manner is sometimes rather – disconcerting ...'

Sitting with both hands spread out on his knees, he leant forward towards Maigret, who stared back at him with bovine eyes, devoid of thought.

'So I thought I'd look in to let you know how we were getting on ...'

Certainly Maigret was listening, but he would have been hard put to it to repeat a single word of what was said to him. What he was really concentrating on was the face in front of him, which he studied detail by detail.

A very fair complexion, almost too fair, set off by the grey hair ... Monsieur Duhourceau was certainly not troubled by his liver. Nor was he either gouty or apoplectic ...

What would be the weak spot in his constitution? For after all you didn't reach the age of sixty-five without having a weak spot.

'Arterio-sclerosis,' answered Maigret to himself.

And he glanced at the thin fingers, the hands with their

silky skin, the veins standing out and looking as hard as glass . . .

A small man, dry, highly strung, intelligent, and irascible. 'And morally ? Isn't there a weak spot there too ?'

Of course there was. For in spite of all the prosecutor's dignity and arrogance, there was something vague, evasive, and shamefaced about him.

Meanwhile he was talking:

'In two or three days at the outside we'll have the case finished and filed. The facts speak for themselves . . . We must keep to the point. How Samuel dodged execution and had somebody else buried in his place – that's for the Algiers people to go into. That is, if they think it worth while . . . I don't for a moment suppose they will . . .'

There were moments when his voice wavered ever so slightly. They were when he looked into Maigret's eyes for some response, only to come up against that empty, bovine stare. He didn't know quite how to take it. Was the inspector listening ? Was he being ironical ?

Clearing his voice, he went on:

'Anyhow, this Samuel, who may have been none too sane in Africa, escapes and comes to France, where he definitely becomes insane. There are plenty of indications. It's a type of case that's frequently met with, as Dr Rivaud will tell you. In the course of his fits of mania he commits the two murders. In the train he thinks you are after him, and when you jump out too he's certain of it. He fires at you and brings you down, but, finally losing his nerve, he shoots himself . . .'

With an airy sweep of the hand, he added:

'The fact that no revolver was found by his side doesn't bother me in the least. There are dozens of cases on record in which the same thing's happened. Somebody has passed and picked it up – a vagrant perhaps, or a child – and never said a word about it. Too scared to come forward. Sometimes it's ten or twenty years afterwards that the whole story comes to light . . . The important thing in this case was to make sure the gun was fired close to the head. The post-mortem leaves no doubt on that point. There, in a few words, you have . . .'

Maigret for his part was asking himself:

'What is his vice?'

Not drink. Not gambling. And strangely enough, Maigret was tempted to add: not women.

Avarice? That seemed much nearer the mark. It needed no effort at all to picture Monsieur Duhourceau, having locked every door, opening the safe and laying its contents out on the table – bundles of notes, bags of gold coins, bonds . . .

All in all, he gave the impression of a solitary person. Gambling is a sociable vice, women too. So is drink, nearly always . . .

'Have you ever been in Algiers, Monsieur Duhourceau?'

'Me?'

When a man says 'me' like that, you can bet your boots he's trying to gain time.

'Why do you ask me that? Do I look like a colonial? No, I've never set foot in Algiers. In fact, I've never crossed the Mediterranean. My longest journey was a trip to the Norwegian fjords. That was in 1923 . . .'

'Of course . . . I really don't know what made me ask the question. Stupid of me. Perhaps it's this wound of mine. You've no idea how much it's run me down . . .'

It was an old trick of Maigret's to rattle along unconcernedly, jumping abruptly from one subject to another. His listener would suspect a trap, and, making a great effort not to give anything away, would end by getting all hot and bothered and losing the thread of his own ideas.

'It's left me pretty weak. That's what I was saying to the doctor. By the way, who does the cooking at their place?'

'The cooking?'

'Do they have a cook? If it's one of the two sisters, it's certainly not Françoise. It's easier to see her driving a high-powered car than standing over the kitchen range stirring a soup ... Would you mind passing me that glass of water?'

Maigret stretched out his hand for it, but so clumsily that, instead of taking it, he knocked it out of the prosecutor's hand, spilling the contents over the latter's legs.

'I'm so sorry. I really don't know what's the matter with me. Fortunately it won't leave a mark.' And turning to his wife: 'Bring a cloth, will you?'

Monsieur Duhourceau was furious. The water had gone right through his trousers and must be trickling down his calf.

'Don't bother, madame,' he said, pulling out his hand-kerchief. 'As your husband says, it won't leave a mark. So it doesn't matter in the least.'

The words were charged with sarcasm.

This little incident, coming on top of Maigret's none too tactful ramblings, had put the prosecutor thoroughly out of countenance. The engaging manner he had adopted at the start had completely evaporated.

He was standing now, but he did not go, as he had not yet said all he had come to say. With an effort he regained his self-possession, but there was precious little cordiality in his voice as he asked:

'For your part, Inspector, what are your intentions?'

'The same as ever.'

'You mean ... ?'

'To arrest the murderer, of course. And after that ... Well, if there's any time left, I'll have a peep at that La Ribaudière, where I ought to have been spending this last week or more.'

Monsieur Duhourceau went white with rage. What? He had taken the trouble to pay this friendly call, to explain things patiently. He had been treating Maigret almost deferentially.

And the latter had first poured a glass of water down his legs – and what's more, done it on purpose (the prosecutor felt sure of that) – and then had the cheek to say:

'I'll arrest the murderer.'

Yes, that's what he'd said to him, to him, *procureur de la République*, who had taken infinite pains to explain that there was no longer anybody to arrest. It wasn't only cheek: it sounded almost like a threat. The only thing to do now was to walk out and slam the door.

But Monsieur Duhourceau didn't. In fact, he even mustered some sort of a smile.

'You're very obstinate, Inspector.'

'Oh, you know ... When you're lying in bed all day with nothing to do ... By the way, I wonder if you'd have any books to lend me?'

Still jumping from subject to subject. Still putting out feelers. And this time he thought he saw a flicker of anxiety trouble the prosecutor's eye.

'I'll send you some.'

'Amusing ones. Nothing too serious.'

'I must be going now.'

'My wife will give you your hat and stick. Are you dining at home?'

Maigret held out his hand, and the prosecutor had to shake it. The door shut, while Maigret lay back against his pillows, looking thoughtfully at the ceiling.

'Do you really think ... ?' began his wife.

'Is Rosalie still working in the hotel?'

'So far as I know. In fact, I think it was her I saw on the stairs just now.'

'Fetch her.'

'People will say ...'

'Never mind if they do.'

While waiting for the maid, Maigret thought to himself:

'Duhourceau's afraid. He's been afraid all along. Afraid I'll discover the criminal. Afraid I'll delve into his private life. Rivaud's afraid too. So's his wife.'

What did they fear? And what had they to do with Samuel, the dealer in forged papers, and wretched girls from Eastern Europe?

The Rivauds had at least something in common with him. They'd come from Algiers, and Rivaud could quite well be a Jew, though it was by no means certain. There was no question of Duhourceau's being one, and there was no reason to disbelieve his statement that he had never been in Africa.

The door opened, and Rosalie, wiping her big red hands on her coarse linen apron, was led into the room by Madame Maigret.

'You wanted to see me?'

'Yes. Come in and sit down.'

'We're not allowed to sit down in the visitors' rooms.'

The way in which she said it warned Maigret of a change. She was no longer the familiar chatterbox. They'd been getting at her, telling her to mind her p's and q's.

'I only wanted to ask you a simple question. Have you ever worked at Monsieur Duhourceau's?'

'I was two years with him.'

'I thought you might have been. As cook or housemaid?'

'Housemaid.'

'You went all over the house, polishing the floors, and dusting . . . ?'

'I did the rooms . . .'

'Exactly. You did the rooms. And in doing the rooms you must have found out a thing or two. How long ago was it?'

'It's a year last month that I left the place.'

'So you were the same pretty girl you are now. Yes, yes, it's no use pretending you're not.'

Maigret wasn't laughing. He had an art all of his own of saying things like that quite gravely, in the most convincing manner. As a matter of fact, it wasn't far from the truth, for Rosalie was a pleasant-looking girl. Her buxom figure had certainly attracted many an inquisitive hand.

'Did the prosecutor sometimes watch you at work?'

'What an idea! Perhaps you think I got him to carry my pails for me!'

Rosalie was very scornful, but she softened at once as her eye lit on Madame Maigret, who was pottering about the room, tidying and brushing up the crumbs. She kept her eyes fixed on her, and at last she couldn't help saying:

'I'll bring you a little hand-brush in the morning. There's a spare one downstairs. That broom's such a clumsy thing.'

'Did he often have women visitors?'

'I don't know.'

'Yes, you do. Come on! Speak out. There's nothing to be frightened of. Don't forget I was on your side yesterday when the others wouldn't believe you.'

'It wouldn't do anybody any good.'

'What wouldn't?'

'If I did speak out. You see, there's Albert. It would spoil his chances. He's trying to get a government job, and if the prosecutor was against him . . . You see what I mean . . . Besides, they might shut me up in a madhouse – because I dream seven nights out of seven.'

She was working herself up and only needed a little egging on.

'So there was a lady visitor now and again?'

'No, there wasn't.'

'Then, perhaps on his trips to Bordeaux.'

'I don't care two pins about his trips to Bordeaux.'

'Come on, now! There's a little bit of scandal somewhere, isn't there?'

'And everybody knows about it . . . You can't keep things dark for ever. They've a way of coming out by themselves . . . It was a good two years ago . . . A parcel came from Paris, but when they came to look at it, the label was more than half gone and they couldn't tell who it was for. And there was no sender's name on it either . . .

'They waited a week, thinking someone might turn up to claim it. And then they opened it . . . You'd never guess what they found . . .

'Photographs. But not ordinary ones . . . I hardly know

how to say it. Women with no clothes on . . . And not alone either . . . You see what I mean ? . . .

'As you can imagine, everybody was guessing who had pictures of that sort sent them from Paris. I think they even called the police in.

'And then, one day, another parcel came, just the same as the first one. Same paper, same string, same label as the bit that had been left before . . . Guess who it was addressed to ! . . . Monsieur Duhourceau, if you please.'

Maigret was not in the least surprised. Hadn't he already decided that the prosecutor was a solitary man ?

'Monsieur Duhourceau was away at the time, or I suppose he'd have stopped the second parcel coming . . .'

So it wasn't to count out his money that the prosecutor would lock his study door at night. In the fine but sombre room on the first floor – the one with the carved stone balcony outside – he would sit poring over naughty photographs and forbidden books.

'Listen, Rosalie ! Not a word you say here will ever be repeated. And now confess that when you heard what you've just told me, you went and had a look at the books in his study.'

'Who told you so ? . . . Well, since you know it already, I admit I did . . . A lot of the bookcases have doors to them with a sort of wire netting, and they're always kept locked. Only, I once found one where the key had been left in the lock . . .'

'What did you find ?'

'You know very well what I found. It was so awful that I had nightmares for a week and I couldn't endure Albert coming anywhere near me.'

Oho ! Her relations with the fair young man were no longer a mystery.

'Big books, weren't they ? Handsome books ?'

'Yes . . . But they were all sorts . . . Terrible ones. Things you'd never think of . . .'

Was that the sum total of Monsieur Duhourceau's

iniquity? If so, it was rather pitiful. A lonely old bachelor who occupied a high position and didn't dare smile at a girl for fear of raising the devil.

And the only consolation he could find was to become a collector in this murky backwater of art, filling his locked bookcases with licentious engravings, erotic photographs, and those books which the catalogues amiably describe as 'works for connoisseurs'.

No wonder he was afraid.

Only it wasn't easy to see what relation that could have with the two murders – still less with Samuel ... Unless the latter had had still another string to his bow, and had dealt in naughty pictures. It could have fitted in very well with stamps.

Maigret wondered. Certainly it couldn't be ruled out ...

Meanwhile Rosalie stood awkwardly, shifting from one foot to the other, astonished herself at having said so much.

'If your wife hadn't been here I should never have dreamt of talking about such things.'

'Did Dr Rivaud often come to the house?'

'Hardly ever. He used to telephone.'

'Nor anyone of his family?'

'No. Except, of course, for Mademoiselle Françoise the time she was acting as his secretary.'

'Whose? The prosecutor's?'

'Yes. She brought her typewriter with her – a funny little thing that shut up in a box.'

'What did she see to – his professional work?'

'Oh, I wouldn't know anything about that. All I can tell you is that she'd work on one side and he on the other.'

'On the other side of what?'

'Of the big curtain that ran right across one end of the library.'

'And?'

'And nothing! Don't you go putting words into my mouth. All the time she was there I never saw a thing you could take exception to.'

'How long did it last?'

'Barely six months. After that she went off to her mother's in Paris or Bordeaux, I'm not sure which, and it was ever so long before we saw her in the town again . . .'

'And Monsieur Duhourceau never overstepped the mark in his dealings with you?'

'He'd have caught it, if he had!'

'Well, Rosalie, thank you for what you've told me. Don't be frightened. You won't get into any trouble over it, and Albert will never know you came.'

After shutting the door behind Rosalie, Madame Maigret sighed.

'Oh, dear, oh, dear! To think an educated, intelligent man – and in such a position too . . .'

Madame Maigret was always astonished when she ran into anything that was ugly. It was impossible for her to imagine any more noxious instincts than those of a good wife whose only regret was to have had no children.

'Don't you think that girl exaggerates? If you ask me, she's out to make herself interesting. She'd say anything for the sake of being listened to. And I wouldn't mind betting she was never attacked at all . . .'

'Nor would I.'

'And the same goes for Françoise. She's not strong. A powerful man would get her down with one hand – and yet she says she drove him off.'

'You're quite right.'

'I'll go farther. If this sort of thing goes on another week, we'll have such a jumble of truth and lies being told that we shan't know whether to believe anybody. These stories work on people's minds, and from thinking things they come to believe they're true . . . There's Monsieur Duhourceau being painted in the most lurid colours. It'll be the police inspector's turn next . . . And as for you, heaven knows what they're saying about you already. It won't be long before I have to stick my marriage lines up on the wall if I'm not to pass for your mistress . . .'

An affectionate smile spread over Maigret's face as he looked at her. She was quite incensed. All these complications were rather upsetting.

'And to crown it all, a doctor who isn't a doctor! . . .'

'Who knows?'

'What do you mean "who knows"? Haven't I telephoned to every university in France?'

'Your water's boiling away. Aren't you making an infusion?'

'That's one thing that won't do you any harm! It's my prescription, not that impostor's.'

As he drank, he kept her hand in his.

'If all goes well we'll be out of the wood in two or three days.'

'And as soon as you are – I know you – you'll only be plunging into another.'

CHAPTER IX

The Kidnapping of an Old-time Artiste

It tickled Maigret to see the sulky look which came into Leduc's face.

'What do you want me to do?' grumbled the latter. 'What do you mean by a delicate mission?'

'A mission which only you can fulfil. Come on! There's no need to look so glum about it. I'm not going to ask you to burgle the prosecutor's house, nor even Dr Rivaud's.'

Maigret held out a Bordeaux newspaper, pointing to a small advertisement:

A certain Madame Beausoleil, formerly of Algiers, now believed in Bordeaux, is urgently requested to present herself at once at the following address, where she will learn of something to her advantage. Maigret, Notary, *Hôtel d'Angleterre*, Bergerac.

Leduc did not smile. The sulky expression only deepened.

'And you want me to play the notary?'

His voice expressed such intense distaste that Madame Maigret, at the other end of the room, burst out laughing.

'Oh, no. I'm the notary. The notice is appearing this morning in a dozen papers of the Bordeaux district as well as in the chief Paris dailies.'

'Why Bordeaux?'

'Never mind that. How many trains arrive from Bordeaux in the course of the morning?'

'Three or four, I think. Perhaps more.'

'Well, look here! It's a nice bright day. Not too hot. Not too cold. Your mission is to go and meet each train as it comes in, until Madame Beausoleil appears.'

'I don't know her.'

'Nor do I. I couldn't even tell you whether she's tall or short. But I fancy you will be able to spot her all right. She'll be anything from forty-five to sixty, vulgar, and probably showy. The chances are she's stout.'

'The advertisement tells her to come to the hotel. So I don't see why I . . .'

'Quite so. Quite so. Only I have an idea there'll be somebody else at the station who'll try to stop the good lady coming. See? Understand the mission? Bring her all the same. Use your winning ways.'

Maigret had never seen the station, but lying in front of him was a picture postcard of it. The platform was in a blaze of sun, but even in the shadow you could make out the station-master's office and the lamp-room.

It tickled Maigret to think of poor Leduc in his straw hat, pacing up and down that sunny platform waiting for the train, then rushing up to elderly ladies to ask them if their name was Beausoleil.

'I'm counting on you.'

'Very well . . . Since it's all arranged . . .'

He walked off sorrowfully. Even the car was taking it badly and had to be cranked repeatedly before she'd start.

A little later Dr Rivaud's assistant arrived, bowing profusely to Madame Maigret and then to her husband. A ginger-headed young man, shy and bony, who tripped over every piece of furniture and apologized with a running fire of beg-your-pardons and excuse-me's.

'Excuse me! Might I have a little hot water?'

And as he nearly bowled over the bedside table:

'I'm so sorry . . . I beg your pardon . . .'

As he dressed the wound he kept on saying:

'You'll tell me if I'm hurting you . . . Just a moment. Excuse me . . . Could you lift yourself a little higher in the bed? . . . Thank you. Thank you. That's splendid.'

Meanwhile Maigret smiled to think of Leduc parking the old Ford outside the station.

'Is Dr Rivaud very busy?'

'Very busy, yes. He always is.'

'A very active man, I dare say.'

'Extremely so. In fact he's extraordinary . . . Am I hurting you? . . . Thank you . . . He begins at seven in the morning with the free consultations. Then there's his private clinic. And then the hospital . . . He never leaves anything important to me. Always wants to see to it himself.'

'I suppose it's never crossed your mind that he might not be qualified?'

The young man nearly choked, then decided that Maigret was only pulling his leg.

'You're joking . . . My chief is not merely a doctor, he's a great doctor. If he set up in Paris he'd be famous in no time.'

The young man was absolutely sincere. His words rang with an admiration that made no reserves.

'Do you know where he qualified?'

'Montpellier, I think. In fact, I'm practically sure. I've heard him speak of the professors there. After that he was in Paris, where he was assistant to Dr Martel.'

'You're sure of that?'

'There's a picture hanging in his consulting-room – a photograph of Dr Martel surrounded by his pupils.'

'That's odd.'

'I beg your pardon, but did you really think he wasn't qualified?'

'Not particularly.'

'You can take it from me: he's a great man. I've only one reproach to make, and that is that he works too hard. At the rate he's going he'll wear himself out. Sometimes you can see it's telling on him.'

'How?'

'His nerves seem on edge.'

'Lately?'

'From time to time ... But now you mention it, yes – these last few days too ... If only he'd stop now and again. But you see how it was with you. Yours wasn't a very serious case even at the start, but it's practically over before he hands it over to me. Most surgeons would have passed it on to their assistants on the second day ...'

'Is he very much liked by his colleagues?'

'They all admire him.'

'I asked if they liked him.'

'Yes ... I think so ... There's no reason why they shouldn't.'

All the same, the tone had changed. Admiration was not the same thing as affection, and the assistant's voice showed it.

'Have you often been to his house?'

'Never. But I see him every day in the hospital.'

'So you don't know his family? ...'

The wound had been examined and the bandages were being replaced. The blinds were down, shutting out the sun, but every sound that was made in the Place du Marché floated into the room.

'He has a beautiful sister-in-law.'

The young medico went on bandaging, pretending not to have heard.

'He goes to Bordeaux now and again, I suppose?'

'He's called there sometimes. If he liked, he'd be called much farther afield than that. To Nice, Paris, and even abroad.'

'Really? But he is still quite young.'

'In a surgeon that's an asset. A lot of people don't like to have the older men operating on them.'

That was all. The job was finished. The assistant washed his hands, and after a final 'excuse me', he was gone.

Here were some fresh features to be added to Dr Rivaud's portrait. Amongst his colleagues he appeared to pass for a really remarkable surgeon. A man of boundless energy.

Was he ambitious? In the ordinary way one would have taken it for granted. Yet, if he was, why did he bury himself in a place like Bergerac?

'I can't make head or tail of it: can you?' said Madame Maigret as soon as they were alone.

'Put up the blind, will you? . . . One thing's certain anyhow. With a reputation like that, the man can't be altogether a quack. It's not so difficult to impose upon patients, but he works in a hospital with colleagues and assistants . . .'

'But if the universities say he isn't qualified . . . ?'

'One thing at a time . . . For the moment I'm thinking of Leduc, and wondering how he's going to tackle Madame Beausoleil. She may prove rather a handful . . . Didn't you hear a train just now? If it's from Bordeaux, there's a chance of their showing up at any moment.'

'What do you expect Madame Beausoleil to tell you?'

'You'll see . . . Throw me the matches, will you?'

He was very much better. His temperature was rarely over ninety-nine and the stiffness in his right arm had practically disappeared. The most encouraging sign of all was his inability to keep still in bed. Every minute he was fidgeting, stretching, turning over, or rearranging his pillows.

'I think you ought to ring up a few people.'

'Who?'

'I want to know the whereabouts of the chief people I'm

interested in. Come and sit on the bed so that I can hear what they say at the other end.'

'Who shall I begin with?'

'The prosecutor. And as soon as you hear his voice, ring off.'

It was done. Madame Maigret did the talking while he stared out on to the Place du Marché, puffing away at his pipe.

'He's at home.'

'Now the hospital. Ask for Rivaud.'

They heard his voice answering: so that disposed of him.

'And now for his house. Do you think you'd recognize his sister-in-law's voice?'

'I think I would.'

'Well, if she answers, ask for Madame Rivaud. And if Madame Rivaud answers, ask for Françoise.'

It was the elder sister who answered. She said Françoise was out, but could she take a message?

Maigret made a sign which meant:

'Ring off.'

So there were three people who'd spend half the morning wondering who had rung them up.

Five minutes later the hotel omnibus came from the station, depositing three travellers and their luggage at the entrance below. Then a postman passed on a bicycle with the mail-bag over his shoulder.

And finally the hooting of the well-known horn, followed by the Ford. Maigret could see there was somebody beside Leduc, and he thought there was a third person sitting behind.

He wasn't wrong. Leduc emerged first, looking anxiously round him, poor man: as though afraid he was making a fool of himself. Then he helped out his front-seat passenger, a stout lady who almost fell into his arms.

Meanwhile a girl had already leapt out from the back. Instinctively she looked up, to throw a venomous look in the direction of Maigret's window.

It was Françoise, dressed in a smartly tailored suit of tender green.

*

'Would you rather I went?' asked Madame Maigret.

'Why should you?... Open the door for them. Here they are.'

A noise – one might almost say a row – approaching from the staircase. Heavy breathing from the stout lady, who came into the room mopping her brow.

'Where's this notary who isn't a notary?'

The voice was certainly vulgar. And not only the voice. She might have been hardly more than forty-five. In any case, she had not yet renounced her claims to beauty, for she was made up like any actress.

A fair woman, abundant in bosom – and elsewhere. Her lips were full and lacking in firmness.

Looking at her, Maigret's first impression was that he had already seen her. Of course he had – over and over again! For she was the very embodiment of a type he knew well, a type that was now becoming rare – the old-time *chanteuse de café-concert*. A heart-shaped mouth. A narrow waist. A saucy, challenging eye. And those milk-white shoulders, disclosed to the maximum. That little swing and swagger in the walk, and that way of looking at you as though across the foot-lights.

'Madame Beausoleil?' asked Maigret gallantly. 'Please take a chair... And you too, mademoiselle...'

Françoise did not accept the invitation. Her nerves were as taut as a harp string.

'I warn you I shall complain,' she said. 'It's unheard of...'

Leduc remained by the door, standing so piteously that it was easy to see things hadn't gone any too smoothly.

'Calm yourself, mademoiselle. And forgive me for having wanted to see your mother.'

'Who said she was my mother?'

Madame Beausoleil was quite out of her depth. Bewildered, she looked from Françoise, tense with fury, to the placid-faced invalid in bed.

'I took it for granted,' said the latter. 'The fact that you went to see her at the station . . .'

'Mademoiselle wanted to stop her mother coming,' sighed Leduc, staring at the carpet.

'Oh! And what did you do?'

It was Françoise who answered:

'He threatened us. He even said something about a warrant. If he's got a warrant, let him show it. Otherwise . . .'

Her hand was stretched towards the telephone. There was not much doubt about it: Leduc had somewhat overstepped his rights. And he wasn't proud of it at all.

'I had to say something,' he muttered. 'They were on the point of making a scene.'

'One moment, mademoiselle,' asked Maigret. 'Who are you going to ring up?'

'The prosecutor.'

'Sit down . . . Mind you, you're quite free to telephone if you want to, but perhaps it would be better for everybody if you weren't in too much of a hurry.'

'*Maman*, I forbid you to answer.'

'I can't understand a word of this. What I'd like to know is: are you a notary or a policeman?'

'A policeman.'

She smiled, as much as to say:

'In that case . . .'

It wasn't hard to guess she'd had dealings with the police before, and that she preserved a respect, or at least a fear, of that institution.

'But I can't see why . . . why I . . .'

'You have nothing to fear, madame. You'll understand in a moment. I've merely a few questions to ask you.'

'Then there's no legacy?'

'I don't know that yet.'

'It's disgusting,' snarled Françoise. 'Don't answer, *Maman.*'

She couldn't keep still. She had sat down after all, but was now on her feet again. With her finger-nails she was fraying the edge of her handkerchief, throwing a baneful glance at Leduc from time to time.

'I take it that you're an *artiste lyrique* by profession?'

He knew very well that those two little words would go straight to her heart.

'Yes, monsieur. I sang at the *Olympia* at the time of...'

'I seem to remember your name ... Beausoleil ... Yvonne, isn't it?'

'Joséphine Beausoleil ... But the doctors recommended a warmer climate, and I went on tour in Italy, Turkey, Syria, and Egypt...'

At the time of the *cafés-chantants*. He could easily picture her on one of the little stages they had in those resorts that had been so fashionable in Paris and elsewhere, frequented by the officers and other bright sparks of the day ... And after singing her song she would come down from the stage, and go round the tables carrying a tray, finally joining the company at one of them and drinking champagne...

'You fetched up in Algiers?'

'Yes. I'd had my first daughter in Cairo.'

Françoise looked as though at any moment she might go into a fit of hysterics or throw herself at Maigret and scratch his eyes out.

'Of unknown father?'

'Nothing of the kind! I knew him very well. An English officer attached to the...'

'While your second girl, Françoise, was perhaps born in Algiers?'

'Yes. And that was the end of my theatrical career ... I was ill for quite a long time, and though I got over it, I never recovered my voice.'

'So then?'

'Her father looked after me, right up to the day he was recalled to France ... You see, he was in the Customs ...'

It was all just what Maigret had imagined. Madame Beausoleil had knocked about the world. Then, still good-looking, and with two children on her hands, she had managed to put her relationships on to a semi-permanent footing ... The two girls growing up in Algiers ... Wouldn't they naturally follow their mother's career?

'I wanted them to be dancers. That's a much less thankless job than singing. Particularly abroad. Germaine had begun to take lessons with an old friend of mine who had settled out there ...'

'But she fell ill?'

'Did she tell you that? ... As a matter of fact, she'd never been very strong. That's what comes of travelling so much when you're tiny. At least I always put it down to that. You see, I'd never leave her with anybody else. I had a little hammock for her, and I used to sling it between the luggage racks ...'

A good soul, obviously. She was quite at her ease now, and she couldn't understand why Françoise should have made such a fuss. Why shouldn't she come and see Maigret? A very nicely spoken man, he was. He came straight to the point, in a language she could understand. And he didn't hurt her feelings.

She was an artiste. *Artiste lyrique.* She'd travelled. She'd had affairs. She'd had two children ... But wasn't that all in the natural order of things?

'Was it chest trouble?'

'No. In her head. She was always complaining of headaches ... And then one day she caught meningitis and had to be rushed off to the hospital.'

A pause. So far it had just gushed out of its own accord, but Joséphine Beausoleil had now come to the critical point. She seemed to know she was on dangerous ground, for she looked inquiringly at Françoise, wondering what she ought to say next.

'The inspector has no right to question you, *Maman*. Don't answer another word.'

That was easy to say. But she, Joséphine Beausoleil, knew very well that it was a risky business rubbing the police up the wrong way. She didn't want to offend anybody.

Leduc had quite recovered his self-respect and was now throwing looks at Maigret which said:

'We're making headway.'

'Listen, madame! . . . You're quite at liberty to speak or not – just as you think fit. You've every right to refuse. But it doesn't alter the fact that you can be made to speak sooner or later . . . somewhere or other . . . in the Assize Court, for instance . . .'

'But I haven't done anything.'

'Exactly. And that's why, in my opinion, the wisest course would be to be perfectly frank . . . As for you, Mademoiselle Françoise . . .'

But Françoise wasn't listening. She had picked up the telephone receiver and was speaking breathlessly. Her voice was anxious, feverish, and she kept on glancing furtively at Leduc as though she expected him to snatch the instrument out of her hand.

'Hallo! . . . He's going round the wards? . . . Never mind. Tell him he must come at once. There's not a minute to lose. To the *Hôtel d'Angleterre* . . . Say it's from Mademoiselle Françoise . . . Yes. He'll understand . . .'

She listened a moment longer, then put the receiver down and turned a look of defiance on Maigret.

'He's coming . . . Don't say anything, *Maman*.'

She was trembling. Beads of sweat rolled down her forehead and wetted her chestnut hair at the temples.

'You see, Inspector . . .' began Madame Beausoleil. 'What can I do?'

Without answering her, Maigret turned to the daughter.

'Mademoiselle Françoise, please take note of the fact that I made no attempt to stop you telephoning. And I shan't ask your mother any more questions. But let me give you a word of advice. Since you've asked Dr Rivaud to come, ask the prosecutor too. You'll find him at his house.'

She tried to guess his thoughts. She hesitated. But in the end she snatched up the receiver again.

'Hallo! ... 167, please.'

'Here! Leduc!'

And Maigret whispered a few words into his ear.

Leduc seemed surprised and embarrassed.

'Do you think ...?' he began. But he broke off, and half a minute later they could hear him cranking the Ford.

'Hallo! ... It's Françoise speaking ... Yes ... I'm speaking from the *Hôtel d'Angleterre* – the inspector's room. My mother's here ... Yes, the inspector wants you to come ... No ... No! ... No, I assure you ...'

This torrent of 'no's' burst out of her in a flood of anguish.

'NO! ... I tell you ...'

She stood by the bedside table, tense, panting.

Maigret smiled at her as he lit his pipe, while Madame Beausoleil repowdered her face.

CHAPTER X

A Flight Frustrated

THE silence seemed to have lasted an age when all at once Françoise frowned. She was looking out of the window with acute anxiety on her face. Then suddenly she turned her head away.

It was Madame Rivaud crossing the Place du Marché, coming towards the hotel. Was it an optical illusion? Or was it that the gravity of the moment made everything seem dramatic? Even at that distance she seemed like a person in a play. She walked as though she was being driven on by some invisible force that had completely taken hold of her.

As she came closer it could be seen that her face was pale and her hair dishevelled. Her overcoat was unbuttoned.

'Here's Germaine,' said Madame Beausoleil at last. 'Someone must have told her I was here.'

Madame Maigret went instinctively to open the door. When Madame Rivaud entered, it was written all over her that she was living through a tragic moment.

She made, nevertheless, a great effort to control herself. She even managed to smile. But there was a wild, lost look in her eyes, and from time to time her features twitched involuntarily.

'Excuse me, Inspector ... But I heard my mother and sister were here ...'

'Who told you?'

'Who ...?' she repeated, trembling.

What a contrast they presented – those two sisters. Germaine was obviously the one who had to make the sacrifices, who had to take a back seat. She had never quite outgrown her plebeian origin, and so was entitled to less consideration than Françoise. Even her mother looked critically at her.

'What! Do you mean you don't know?'

'It was someone I met.'

'You haven't seen your husband?'

'No ... Really ... I swear I haven't.'

Maigret, puzzled, looked in turn at the three women, than out on to the Place du Marché, where there was no sign of either Rivaud or Leduc. What did that mean? Leduc had been dispatched to keep an eye on the doctor in case the latter made off instead of coming to the hotel. He looked at Madame Rivaud. She was out of breath from running. Then he studied her sister's drawn features. He had forgotten his wife's presence, but suddenly she bent over him, saying:

'Give me that pipe. You've had quite enough.'

He was about to protest, but as he opened his mouth he noticed a little piece of paper which she had dropped on the bed. On it was scribbled:

Madame R. has just passed a note to Françoise, who is holding it in her left hand.

*

The sunshine outside. All the noises of the town blending into a chant which Maigret knew by heart. Madame Beausoleil waited, sitting bolt upright in her chair, like a woman who at any rate knows how to hold herself properly. Madame Rivaud, on the other hand, had quite lost countenance. She had no more dignity than a guilty schoolgirl.

'Mademoiselle Françoise . . .' began Maigret.

She shook from head to foot. For a second she looked straight into Maigret's eyes. A hard, intelligent look. For all her nervousness she was not one to lose her head.

'Mademoiselle Françoise, would you mind coming over here?'

Good old Madame Maigret! Did she guess what was coming! Anyhow she made a movement towards the door. But she was not quick enough. Françoise made a dash for it, rushed out, along the passage, and down the stairs.

'What's the matter with her?' asked Joséphine Beausoleil, quite concerned.

Maigret did not move. He couldn't. Nor could he very well send his wife off in pursuit. He merely turned to Madame Rivaud and asked:

'When did your husband give you that note?'

'What note?'

Maigret took pity on her. Besides, what was the good of insisting? He turned to his wife.

'Is there a window on the landing looking out on to the back?'

'Yes.'

'Have a look. See if anything's happening.'

The prosecutor chose that moment to make his entry. He came in stiffly. And, to cover his uneasiness no doubt, his expression was severe and even threatening.

'I received a telephone message asking me to . . .'

'Sit down, Monsieur Duhourceau.'

'But . . . the person who telephoned . . .'

'Françoise has just escaped. Perhaps she'll be caught. But, on the other hand, perhaps not . . . Do sit down, please. You know Madame Beausoleil, I think . . .'

'I? . . . Nothing of the sort!'

He tried to fathom Maigret's look. For the latter seemed to be talking for the sake of talking, while really thinking of other things; or rather he seemed with his mind's eye to be watching some scene that was hidden from the rest of them. He looked out of the window, listened, then stared at Madame Rivaud.

Suddenly there were noises. Perhaps a shot had been fired but anyhow there was a general hustle and scurry. Running steps on the stairs. Doors slamming. People calling.

'What's up? . . . Who is it? . . .'

More shouts. Noise of something being broken. Steps rushing in pursuit on the floor above. Another door slammed, a glass one, and the glass crashed in splinters.

Madame Maigret burst into the room, locking the door behind her.

'I think Leduc's got them,' she panted.

'Leduc?' asked the prosecutor suspiciously.

'The doctor's car was in the lane behind. He was sitting in it, waiting for somebody. Françoise ran up to it and was just getting in when Leduc drove up in the Ford. I almost shouted to him to be quick, for he simply sat there and looked at them. But he had his own idea. He quietly pulled out a revolver and punctured one of the tyres . . .

'The other two didn't know what to do. The doctor looked wildly round him, first this way, then that . . . But when he saw Leduc coming towards him, still holding his revolver, he jumped out, caught Françoise by the arm, and dashed into the hotel, dragging her after him . . .

'Leduc's on their heels . . . They're upstairs.'

*

'I should be grateful for some explanation,' snapped the prosecutor, though he was pale as death.

'It's quite simple,' answered Maigret. 'By means of a little advertisement I got Madame Beausoleil to come and see me. But she wasn't the only one to see it in the paper, and Dr Rivaud, who didn't wish the interview to take place, sent Françoise to the station to intercept her . . .

'However, I had foreseen that manoeuvre and posted Leduc at the station too. Françoise tried to stop her mother, but he swept the pair of them into his car and brought them here willy-nilly.

'You'll see how it all links up . . . Françoise, seeing things were going from bad to worse, rang up Rivaud and told him to come at once.

'I sent Leduc to keep track of Rivaud, but he must have arrived at the hospital too late. Rivaud had gone. Where to? . . . That I can only guess, but it's not very difficult . . .

'He drove home, wrote a note for Françoise and told Madame Rivaud to give it to her. I expect he brought his wife part of the way here. She wasn't long in coming. Then he drove round to the lane at the back . . . Do you see? . . . That's where Françoise was to join him . . .

'A minute more and they might have made it. But in the meantime Leduc was careering round in the old Ford, looking everywhere for the doctor's car. He's no fool. An excellent idea that – snooping round to the back . . . And when he saw the two of them – well, you know as much as I do about that.'

The shindy on the floor above was louder than ever. Then suddenly it ceased. Dead silence. A silence so impressive that in the room below no one moved an eyelid.

Leduc's voice now. Giving orders. But it was impossible

to make out what he said . . . Then more noise: bangs, bat-
terings and wrenchings – until, abruptly, a door gave way.

*

Silence again, and this time it was positively painful.
What did it mean? Why was no one moving, upstairs?

At last there were steps on the floor above. A man's
steps, slow and ponderous.

Madame Rivaud stood riveted where she was, wide-eyed,
breathless. Joséphine Beausoleil was on the verge of tears.

'They must be dead,' said Maigret gravely, looking at
the ceiling.

'What? . . . What do you mean? . . .'

Madame Rivaud was jolted out of her stillness. She
darted forward towards the bed, her panic-stricken eyes
staring into Maigret's.

'It's not true . . . It can't be . . . Say it isn't true . . .'

The steps came down the stairs and approached the
bedroom door. The handle was tried, and it was a moment
before anyone remembered that Madame Maigret had
locked it. She hastily turned the key.

It was Leduc who entered. His tie was askew, and a
lock of hair had fallen over his forehead.

'Dead?'

'Both of them.'

He raised an arm to bar the door as Madame Rivaud ran
towards it.

'Not yet.'

'It isn't true. I know it isn't . . . Let me see them,' she
panted.

Madame Beausoleil was trying desperately to take it in.
Monsieur Duhourceau fixed his eyes on the carpet. Perhaps
at bottom he was the most astonished and upset of any of
them.

'How? . . . Both of them? . . .' he at last managed to
stammer, looking up at Leduc.

'We dashed upstairs after them, but they had time to slip

into one of the rooms and lock the door behind them. They had to fetch an axe to break it down; meanwhile I watched through the keyhole.'

Madame Rivaud listened avidly. She seemed almost out of her mind. So much so that Leduc shot an inquiring look at Maigret to know if he ought to go on.

Why not? Just as well get it over. It would all come out before long. Maigret nodded.

'They were in each other's arms. She was holding on to him frantically. I could hear her say:

'"I won't . . . No. It's impossible . . . I'd rather . . ."

'And it was she who dragged the revolver out of his pocket.

'"Both of us . . ." she said. "Shoot . . . Shoot as you kiss me! . . ."

'I couldn't see any more, as we started to hack the door down.'

He wiped his forehead. You could see his knees were shaking.

'It took us half a minute to get it down, and of course we were too late. Did you hear the shots? . . . Perhaps not, with all that banging going on . . .

'Rivaud was already dead when I bent over him. The girl's eyes seemed to be looking at me, but I thought it was the same with her . . . I thought it was all over. And then suddenly, when I least expected it . . .'

'What was it?' asked the prosecutor, with something like a sob in his voice.

'She smiled . . . She smiled at me . . . I had the door put across the doorway and gave orders nobody was to go in. They're telephoning to the hospital and the police.'

For all her efforts, Madame Beausoleil was unable to take it in. She stared vacantly at Leduc. Then, turning to Maigret, she asked in a dreamy voice:

'What's he saying?'

The door opened and the landlord came in. His face was redder than ever, and as he spoke he breathed a gust of alcohol into the air. He had been downstairs and, to pull himself together, had swilled down a stiff drink at the bar. The shoulder of his white coat was dirty and a seam had burst.

'A doctor's arrived. Shall I show him up?'

'I'll go,' said Leduc reluctantly.

'*Monsieur le procureur?*' went on the landlord. 'I didn't know you were here. I suppose you've heard? . . . It's a sight I shall never forget. Enough to make your heart bleed. Such a fine-looking couple . . . To see them lying there holding each other . . .'

'That'll do,' said Maigret. 'Leave us.'

'Ought I to shut the hotel? The crowd's gathering thick and fast. When I rang up the police, the inspector wasn't there, but they're sending some men round . . .'

As soon as he had gone, Maigret looked round for Germaine Rivaud. He found her stretched full-length on Madame Maigret's bed, with her head buried in the pillow. There were no tears, no sobs. Nothing but long, painful groans, as might have come from a wounded animal.

Madame Beausoleil, who had at last grasped the situation, dried her eyes and in a firm decisive voice asked:

'May I go and see them?'

'Presently. The doctor's there now.'

Madame Maigret hovered round Germaine. But what help or consolation could she offer? The prosecutor mumbled:

'I told you . . .'

Through the window came the half-subdued murmur of an expectant crowd. Two policemen had arrived and were elbowing their way through, while the onlookers complained resentfully of their roughness.

Maigret filled himself a pipe. He could use both hands now. At the same time he looked thoughtfully out of the window at the little grocer's shop over the way, all of whose customers he now knew by sight . . . But his mind was elsewhere.

'You left the child at Bordeaux, Madame Beausoleil?'

'Yes ... I ...'

She looked inquiringly at the prosecutor, but she got no help from him.

'About three years old, I suppose?'

'Two.'

'A boy?'

'A little girl ... But ...'

'Her mother was Françoise, wasn't she?'

But Monsieur Duhourceau intervened. Rising from his chair, he began:

'Really, Inspector ... I must ask you ...'

'You're quite right. Perhaps you'd like to call on me another time. Or rather, the first day I'm allowed out, I'll pay you a visit myself.'

The prosecutor was obviously relieved.

'By that time,' went on Maigret, 'it will all be cleared up ... It is now, for that matter, or practically so. And no doubt your place is upstairs, seeing to the official side of things.'

Monsieur Duhourceau made off precipitately, without thinking of saying good-bye. He fled, in fact, like a schoolboy who has suddenly been let off a punishment.

With his departure the atmosphere of the room became at once more intimate. The four of them were left together, Germaine still groaning, while Madame Maigret vainly tried to soothe her by putting cold compresses on her forehead. But Germaine pushed them away, letting the water trickle down on to the pillow.

Madame Beausoleil sat down again with a sigh.

'Who ever would have thought ... ?'

A good woman at heart. In her way a thoroughly moral one. That is, if morality is living according to your lights. Was it her fault if her lights were not so steady as some people's?

Big round tears began to well up from her lined middle-aged eyes and run down her cheeks, washing away the make-up.

'She was your favourite, wasn't she?'

Germaine's presence didn't worry her at all, though it's only fair to add that the latter wasn't listening.

'Of course. She had the looks. And such style too. Far more intelligent than her sister. Oh, it wasn't Germaine's fault. You can't blame her, as she was ill such a lot, and couldn't help being backward . . . When the doctor married her, Françoise was too young – barely thirteen. But, believe me or not, I had an idea even then that there'd be trouble later . . . And you see what's happened . . .'

'What was Rivaud's name in Algiers?'

'Dr Meyer . . . I suppose there's no use trying to hide it any longer. Considering what you've found out already, you're bound to know it all in the end.'

'This man Samuel was his father?'

'Yes.'

'And he arranged his father's escape from the hospital in Algiers?'

'That's right. In fact, that's how things started with Germaine. There were only three of them in that wing of the hospital: Germaine, Samuel, as he was called, and another. One night Rivaud set the place on fire, and it was this third person who was left in the flames and afterwards given out to be Samuel. It sounds terrible, but the doctor always swore the man was dead already. I think he was telling the truth. After all, he wasn't a bad man. You could tell that from the way he treated his father. He could have washed his hands of him after the way he'd behaved . . .'

'So that's how it was done . . . The man was burnt beyond all recognition and reported as Samuel . . . And it was after that . . . ?'

'That Jacques married Germaine.'

'And he brought the three of you to France?'

'Not at once. We were quite a time in Spain waiting for his papers. For it was then that he changed his name to Rivaud.'

'And Samuel?'

'He was shipped off to America and told never to come back. The trial seemed to have unhinged him. He was already a bit queer. Then as soon as the papers came in the name of Rivaud we all came to France.'

'To Bergerac?'

'Jacques and the two girls.'

'And you?'

'He gave me an allowance and set me up in Bordeaux . . . I should have preferred Marseilles or Nice – particularly Nice – but he wanted to keep an eye on me . . . Goodness! How he worked! Whatever they say about him, nobody can deny he was a good doctor. And I feel sure he wouldn't have done *that* to a patient, not even for his own father . . .'

To shut out the hubbub of the crowd, Maigret had had the windows shut. The room was getting hot and stuffy and full of pipe-smoke.

Germaine was still wailing like a child.

'She's been worse than before,' her mother explained, 'since the operation on her head. And she was always rather gloomy . . . You see, having spent so much of her life in bed . . . But, as I said, she was worse afterwards. She would cry for nothing at all. And scared of the least thing . . .'

Bergerac had accepted the newcomers without a suspicion. A quiet little town where a dangerous, hectic past could gradually be forgotten.

Nobody guessed a thing. They gossiped about 'the doctor's house', 'the doctor's car', 'the doctor's wife', 'the doctor's sister-in-law'. And all they saw was a cosy little villa in English cottage style: a handsome, stylish car; a dashing lively young sister.

The gossip might not always be kindly. A little scandal perhaps . . . The doctor and Françoise . . . But what was that compared to the things that no one guessed?

Meanwhile, in a little flat in Bordeaux, Joséphine Beausoleil was peacefully winding up her restless life. She who had known so much care for the morrow, who had been dependent on the whims of so many men, could at last adopt the ways and habits of a woman of private, even if modest, means.

No doubt she was respected in her district. She could lead a regular life and pay her bills regularly. And when, from time to time, her daughters came to see her, there was always the same satisfaction in seeing them drive up in that handsome, stylish car.

She was crying again now, and blowing her nose into an inadequate handkerchief that was almost all lace.

'If only you'd known Françoise . . . For instance, when she came to have the baby . . . Oh, there's no harm in speaking in front of Germaine. She knows all about it . . .'

Madame Maigret listened, horrified by this unbelievable world that was being unfolded before her.

Cars had arrived outside. They brought the police pathologist and the examining magistrate and his clerk. The local inspector too, who had been run to earth in the market-place of a neighbouring village where he was busy buying some rabbits.

There was a knock on the door and Leduc cautiously looked in, throwing an inquiring glance at Maigret to know if he was intruding.

'Later on, old chap . . . If you don't mind . . .'

Maigret did not want anything to disturb an atmosphere that encouraged Madame Beausoleil to be so confiding. Leduc nevertheless came up to the bed to whisper:

'If they want to see the bodies before they're moved . . .'

'No. There's no point in it.'

Indeed, what good could it do? Even Madame Beausoleil, who had wanted to see them before, was now only waiting for Leduc's departure to resume her confidences. She felt at ease with the big man who was lying in bed and who looked at her good-naturedly, comprehendingly.

Yes, he understood. He never looked surprised. Never asked stupid questions.

'You were talking of Françoise . . .'

'Oh, yes . . . Well, when the child was born . . . But perhaps you don't know . . .'

'I know.'

'Who told you?'

'Monsieur Duhourceau was there, wasn't he?'

'Yes. And I've never seen a man so jumpy and so miserable. He said it was a crime to bring children into the world, as there was no knowing if it wouldn't kill the mother . . . He could hear her groaning from the other room . . . Though I did what I could for him – I kept on filling up his glass . . .'

'You've quite a big flat?'

'Three rooms.'

'You had a midwife?'

'Yes . . . Rivaud said he couldn't manage all alone.'

'You live near the harbour?'

'Near the bridge, in a little street where . . .'

Again a scene that Maigret could picture almost as well as if it had been from memory. But at the same time there was another – the one that was being enacted at that very moment overhead.

Rivaud and Françoise. The doctor and the undertakers dragging the couple apart. The prosecutor was no doubt whiter than those printed forms that the examining magistrate's clerk would be filling up with a shaking hand . . .

And the police inspector who an hour before had been thinking of nothing but rabbits . . .

'When Monsieur Duhourceau heard he'd got a daughter he actually cried. Yes, he did, as true as I'm here, and he put his head on my shoulder . . . I thought he was going to be taken really bad . . . I didn't want to let him go into the room, because . . . After all . . .'

She stopped, suddenly on her guard, and shot a mistrustful glance at Maigret.

'I'm only a poor woman that's done the best I could . . . It's a shame to take advantage of it to make me say more than I . . .'

Germaine Rivaud had stopped moaning. Sitting on the edge of the bed, she stared with wide eyes straight in front of her.

The worst moment of all had come. They were carrying

the bodies down on stretchers ... treading heavily, carefully on the stairs ... step by step ...

And someone calling out:

'Steady now! Look out!'

A little later someone knocked on the door. It was Leduc, and he too had had a drink to stiffen himself up.

'It's all over.'

Below, the ambulance drove off ...

CHAPTER XI

The Putative Father

'WHAT name shall I say?'

'Inspector Maigret.'

The latter smiled at nothing in particular – merely because it felt so good to be on his feet again and walking about like anybody else. He was even rather proud of it, like a child enjoying its first unaided steps.

All the same, he was none too steady on his legs, and when the manservant had gone to announce him he rather hastily dragged a chair towards him and sank into it, for he was conscious of a sweat breaking out on his forehead.

It was the manservant with the striped waistcoat. A man of extremely rustic features whose head was a trifle turned by the high position to which he had risen!

'Will you come this way, sir?' he said, reappearing. *'Monsieur le procureur* will see you in a moment.'

The manservant had probably no idea what a labour it could be to climb a flight of stairs! Maigret knew all about it before he reached the first floor. He was hot all over. He leant on to the banisters, counting the steps.

Eight more ...

But at last he was at the top.

'This way, please. If you wouldn't mind waiting a moment . . .'

The house was just as Maigret had imagined it. And there he was, in the study with the tall windows that his mind had so often dwelt on.

The white ceiling was divided by heavy, varnished oak beams. An immense fireplace. And all those bookcases. They almost covered the walls.

There was no one there. No steps could be heard in the house, as all the floors were thickly carpeted. Maigret was longing to sit down. Instead of doing so, however, he walked over to one of the bookcases, the lower half of which was enclosed by metal-grilled doors behind which hung green curtains, hiding the shelves from view.

It was with some difficulty that he thrust one of his thick fingers through the lattice-work to draw aside one of the curtains. When he did so, all he discovered was empty shelves.

Turning round, he found Monsieur Duhourceau watching him.

'I've been expecting you for the last two days . . . I must confess . . .'

He looked as if he had lost ten pounds, if not twenty. His cheeks sagged, and the lines at the corners of his mouth were twice as deep as they had been.

'Won't you sit down, Inspector?'

The prosecutor was ill at ease. He couldn't look Maigret in the face. He sat down in his usual place in front of a desk laden with files and documents.

More than once he had treated Maigret with scant civility. More than once he had been openly hostile. He had, however, had plenty of time to regret it, and it seemed to Maigret most charitable to finish off quickly.

An ageing man of sixty-five, all alone in that large house, practically alone in that town of Bergerac in which he was the highest officer of the law . . . In fact, all alone in life . . .

'I see you've burnt your books.'

No answer from Monsieur Duhourceau. Only a faint flush mounting to his haggard cheeks.

'And now let's get this case wound up. It's clear enough. I don't think there's room for any two opinions about it . . .

'To begin with, there's a certain Meyer, a commercial adventurer who's ready to put his hand to anything profitable, not excluding those branches of trade that are forbidden by law. He trades under the name of Samuel.

'At the same time he has social ambitions – not for himself but for his son. The latter studies medicine under the real family name, and this young Dr Meyer becomes assistant to the great Dr Martel. A brilliant future seems assured . . .

'Then the trouble begins.

'First act: Two of Samuel's accomplices come to Algiers and threaten him. He dispatches them into the next world.

'Second act: Samuel is condemned to death. But his son, Dr Meyer (not known as his son, of course), intervenes. Diagnoses meningitis or something of the kind. Has the old man removed to his own hospital and saves him with the help of a fire.

'Another man is buried in Samuel's place. Madame Beausoleil says he was dead already. It may be true; it may not. But there's nobody to contradict her.

'Dr Meyer doesn't seem to have been suspected. But he nevertheless thought it wiser to marry the other patient who was in the wing of the hospital he burnt down. Perhaps she knew something. Perhaps he was vaguely in love with her . . .

'To make things surer still, he left the country with her and the two Beausoleils, to begin another life under a fresh name.

'He's Dr Rivaud now. A man of remarkable intelligence and boundless ambition. It can't have taken him very long to find out that his wife was rather colourless.'

The prosecutor sat still. This part of the story was of no great interest, but he was listening for the sequel with keen apprehension.

'The second act finishes with Samuel in America and Madame Beausoleil in Bordeaux, while Dr Rivaud with his wife and sister-in-law have settled down in Bergerac . . .

'Why is Françoise with her sister rather than with her mother? Is Rivaud already attached to her? . . . However that may be, it happens in the end, as it was bound to happen. He falls for her . . .

'And now for the third act. By some means or other – I have no idea how – the public prosecutor of Bergerac begins to find out something of Rivaud's past . . . Is that correct?'

'Absolutely correct.'

'Then his mouth must be kept shut . . . Rivaud knows what others know – that the prosecutor has a relatively harmless failing, that he collects "books for connoisseurs". He knows that's a pastime of lonely bachelors who find stamp-collecting rather tame, and he's shrewd enough to see that such a man will be easy game for Françoise . . . Forgive me speaking bluntly, *Monsieur le procureur*.

'So her help is enlisted. She is introduced into your house to do some secretarial work. She plays her cards adroitly and, before very long, what was planned takes place.

'But that's not enough. Rivaud doesn't want to start wandering again. He's getting on splendidly. His name's beginning to be known, and he's determined not to change it.

'A temporary affair with Françoise is not enough. He must have a stronger hold over you than that. She is going to have a baby. She must convince you that the baby will be yours.

'Again she succeeds. And now they hold you in a vice. For you too have a secret that must not come to light – a secret birth in Joséphine Beausoleil's flat in Bordeaux, and secret visits thenceforward, when you go to see the child you take to be yours.'

Maigret had the delicacy not to look at Monsieur Duhourceau as he spoke.

'You see, Rivaud was, above all, ambitious. He knew himself to be abler than other men, and nothing was going to stop him getting to the top. He was ready to go to any lengths to keep his buried past underground. He really loved Françoise, he loved her dearly – but not so much as he loved his career. For that, he was ready to push her, once at any rate, into your arms ... Might I ask you one question? Was it once?'

'Only once.'

'Then she edged away?'

'On various pretexts ... She thought it shameful ...'

'No, no! She loved Rivaud – as much as he did her. Perhaps more. And it was only to save him ...'

Maigret still kept his eyes turned away from the man who sat listening at his desk. He stared into the open fireplace, where in spite of the sunshine three logs were blazing.

'Everything went just as they intended it. They had you just where they wanted you. And that finishes the third act.

'The fourth brings us back to the old Meyer, alias Samuel, of Jugoslavia and Algiers, and now of America. Madame Beausoleil told me his trial had affected his reason. Now his mind went altogether. I asked the *P.J.* to cable to America for information. They tell me he attacked two women somewhere near Chicago. In each case, after strangling them, he stuck a needle through the heart.

'He wasn't caught, and fleeing the country, he came to France, finally turning up in Bergerac practically penniless. Rivaud gave him money and told him to clear out. He did so, but in another fit of madness he left a corpse behind him.

'Exactly the same. First strangulation, then the needle. It was in the woods by Moulin-Neuf. He was on his way to the station ... I don't know whether you suspected the truth.'

'No, I can swear to that ... Not then.'

'He came back, and the same thing happened ... He

came a third time – that is, if Rosalie didn't dream it – but she beat him off. Each time Rivaud bribed him to go away. What else could he do? He couldn't put him in an asylum, still less have him arrested.'

'Then I began to suspect something,' said the prosecutor with a painful effort. 'I didn't know everything, but I felt sure Rivaud had something to do with it. I didn't have it out with him. But – one day when we were talking – I said, *We've got to stop these murders. They can't go on* . . . I could see he understood . . . that I . . . that there were limits . . .'

'Ah! So that's what brought matters to a head . . . And when was it you told him that?'

'The last time I dined in his house . . .'

'On the Monday night?'

'Yes . . . The Monday night.'

For a moment neither spoke. Then very quietly Maigret went on:

'The following afternoon Samuel rang up from Paris. A nine-minute call. Heaven knows what they said. Perhaps there was an argument. Perhaps Rivaud tried to persuade his father not to come. In the end, however, he must have told him he'd be arrested if he appeared at the station. He must have told him to jump out before. He must have arranged to meet him in the wood . . .'

The prosecutor was pale as death. He couldn't have uttered a word to save his life.

'And that's all. Rivaud killed him and emptied his pockets of everything that could help to identify him. Including his second-class railway ticket. Funny that such a thorough person should then have dropped it outside my door.

'Yes. Rivaud killed him . . .

'Nothing was to stand between him and his ambitions. Certainly not a criminal lunatic of a father . . . Not even his wife. She would always have been a drag. I may be wrong, but I can't help thinking that one day or other he'd have shoved her off too into a better world. Then he could have married Françoise – the girl he loved and who had given him a daughter, the girl who was ready to do anything for him ... Yes, absolutely anything. To simulate that faked attack in the wood in order to clear him of suspicion ... And even to ...'

But the prosecutor just managed to utter:

'Enough!'

And Maigret got up simply, as though this had been any other sort of visit.

'That's all, *Monsieur le procureur.*'

'But ...'

'They were a pair – those two. The one as spirited as the other. Not the sort to knuckle under ...'

He was talking to a poor sunken old man. All the official arrogance had withered to nothing.

'And now they're dead. Those who are left will give no trouble: Madame Rivaud is neither brilliant nor dangerous – nor is she guilty of anything. She'll have enough to live on. She'll join her mother in Bordeaux or elsewhere, and together they'll bring up the child ... They won't talk.'

Maigret picked up his hat from a chair.

'As for me, I must be getting back to Paris. I've been away long enough.'

He walked up to the desk.

'Good-bye, *Monsieur le procureur.*'

The latter pounced upon the outstretched hand with such gratitude that Maigret feared a flood of thanks. To stave them off he hastily added:

'No hard feelings!'

A few moments later the manservant with the striped waistcoat was showing him out. He slowly crossed the sunlit market-place and dragged himself rather laboriously back to the *Hôtel d'Angleterre*, where he said to the proprietor:

'We'll have *truffes en serviette* and *foie gras* for lunch, if you please. And you can serve the bill with it. We're off.'